The Price of Love

Brenda smiled at the exchange between Gil and his grandfather. Taking a cup of coffee, she walked over to the fireplace to look at the array of family pictures proudly displayed on the mantle.

Gil came up behind her. "Mama's monster museum," he quipped.

"Shame on you, MaGil Jackson. I'll have you know that all my children are good looking, including you," his mother replied.

"I have been duly chastened. This is my sister, Carol," he pointed to a picture of his twin. "And her husband, Wayne, and their three boys, Mike, Curt and Stevie." He moved on to the next picture. "These are my brothers, Richard and Dylan." Gil smiled broadly at the next picture. "And this is my son, David."

Brenda's heart stopped when she got a good look at the little boy. The blood drained from her face, and she felt a trembling begin deep inside her body. Her mouth went dry. She nearly choked on her coffee.

She had to be wrong. It just couldn't be! Pain lanced through her brain.

Those eyes! That face, so like—

Surely fate couldn't be so cruel!

The Price of Love

Beverly Clark

Indigo Sensuous Love Stories

Indigo Romances are published by
Genesis Press, Inc.
315 Third Avenue North
Columbus, Mississippi 39701

The Price of Love

ISBN 1-885478-61-5

Printed in the United States of America

FIRST EDITION

Book Design by Mary Beth Vickers

Dedication

To Wil Colom, the charming gentleman who inspired me in the writing of my hero, Gil Jackson.

To my family for providing the inspiration I needed to create the other wonderful characters in this book.

To Doris Smith for helping me get through the revision period with my sanity in tact.

Chapter One

Brenda Davis had just stooped down behind the counter to search for a quilt catalog when she heard the jangle of the shop bell. She straightened, easing her lips into a customer-welcoming smile. When she saw that it was Shirley Edwards, she smiled in fond recognition because she and the elderly woman had become friendly since Brenda started working at the Quilt Lodge six weeks earlier.

As Mrs. Edwards descended the steps, Brenda's gaze collided with that of the man who followed her inside. A fluttering sensation began in the pit of her stomach making her feel as though she were in an elevator that had suddenly lurched downward.

Shirley Edward's voice broke the spell. "Brenda, dear, I'd like you to meet my nephew, MaGil Jackson."

He stepped forward and said, "You can call me Gil. Everyone else does."

"Brenda is—" his aunt began.

"I know. The lady you can't say enough good things about." His lips spread into a lazy smile, and his eyes raked boldy over her. "Now I understand why."

Brenda's insides melted under the heated rays of that gaze.

MaGil Jackson had to be, if not the most handsome, the most arresting male she'd ever seen. He was a tall man of African-American descent, six two or three. And even though he was wearing an overcoat, she could tell that he was magnificently made by the way the heavy cloth shaped his body.

His near-black eyes sparkling like shiny pools of pitch were deeply set above high cheekbones. His Native American

1

heritage was obvious in the thrust of his nose and the copper tinge to his brown skin.

Although his coal black hair was nearly straight, it gave the impression of having a strong tendency to curl given the short style he chose to wear it. He had a full, sensual mouth that made her feel desperate to know how his lips would feel on hers.

He removed his glove and extended his hand. Her breath caught in her throat. The contact was pure high voltage, but then she knew it would be. Brenda had never felt for any man what she instantly felt for this one, and it scared the hell out of her. Clearing her throat, she smiled politely at him before quickly returning her attention to his aunt.

"What may I help you with this morning, Mrs. Edwards?"

"Has that order of purple velour quilt squares come in yet?"

"Yes, it sure has." Brenda turned to lift the box from the shelf behind her and brought it over to the counter. "I had intended to call you today to let you know, but now I don't have to because you're here."

"My car is being repaired," Shirley Edwards explained, then shifting her gaze, looked up at Gil and smiling proudly said, "So I got my handsome nephew to bring me here." The older woman's eyes twinkled as she gazed at the box of quilt squares before her. "There are so many to choose from!" she exclaimed.

"If you need help in making your selections, I'd be more than happy to—"

Mrs. Edwards patted Brenda's hand. "Oh, no, dear. I'll take these over to a table and look through them. You and Gil can get to know each other." With that she headed for a table by the windows.

Brenda wanted desperately to call her back and beg her not to leave her alone with this man.

"Where are you from, Ms. Davis?" Gil asked.

"St. Paul," she managed to utter. The low, seductive quality in his voice made Brenda's stomach flutter in the same odd way it had when she first set eyes on him. When she heard the shop bell jangle, a relieved sigh left her lips. "If you'll excuse me, Mr. Jackson. I have customers."

Brenda quickly moved away to greet the scourge to all shopkeepers in Long Rapids: Geneva and Mary Perkins. As she offered to help the two elderly sisters, she could feel Gil Jackson's eyes on her back and it made her uncomfortable. She hoped that his aunt made up her mind quickly about those quilt squares, but she knew there wasn't a chance of that happening because Shirley Edwards was a perfectionist and always took her time.

From the corner of her eye, Brenda saw Gil Jackson viewing the memorabilia rack on the wall. Although he appeared to be soulfully concentrating on the ancient trapping tools before him, Brenda had a feeling they weren't his primary focus. She couldn't help wishing that he would encourage his aunt to hurry. Most men had little patience when it came to waiting for females to finish their shopping. But it was just her luck that Gil Jackson happened not to be one of them. He seemed to have the patience of Job.

As soon as the Perkins sisters spotted the stack of sale items on the sale table, they quickly deserted Brenda to scramble over there to rummage.

Brenda saw Gil's triumphant smile at finally getting her alone. She knew he wouldn't hesitate to seize the opportunity to speak to her. She wasn't disappointed.

"Now that you're free for the moment, I'd like to ask you out to dinner, Ms Davis—Brenda."

"I'm sorry, I can't." And she moved to walk away.

His fingers circled her wrist.

"Mr. Jackson!" she said in a low voice, then glanced around her to see if anyone noticed. No one had. She tried to pull free of his hold, but he wouldn't to let her go.

He eased his sensually full mouth into a soul-robbing smile. "The name is Gil, Brenda."

Brenda could feel the sexual magnetism that made him so self-confident. "If you would please excuse me, *Gil*."

3

"No."

"I beg your pardon!"

"You don't have to *beg* me for anything, sweetheart."

"Mr. Jackson, I—"

"Gil. If not tonight, then what evening will you be free?"

"I really don't have time to talk with you, okay? Another customer just signaled for my help. Now, if you will excuse me?"

Conceding defeat, he released her wrist and she walked away.

As she waited on the customer, she knew Gil was watching her and it made her feel like shouting at him to look elsewhere.

Gradually the Lodge emptied of people until Shirley Edwards and her nephew were the only ones remaining. Brenda wiped sweat-dampened palms down the sides of her gray wool skirt. What was the matter with her? She'd never reacted to a man the way she was reacting to this one.

"I have enough squares to finish my quilt, Brenda." Mrs. Edwards clapped her hands, her face wearing a satisfied smile. "Did you and Gil have a nice talk? It would please me if my two favorite people joined me for dinner this evening."

"I'm sorry, Mrs. Edwards, but I can't."

"Tomorrow then?"

"No, I really don't think so."

"Maybe another time, Aunt Shirley," Gil smoothly inserted.

Refusing to take no for answer, his aunt said, "Well, maybe next week would be better for you, Brenda."

Brenda longed to tell her that no week would be any better if her nephew was included in the invitation. And that the last thing she wanted was to be in his disturbing presence. When she glanced at him, she could tell from the amused expression on his face that he'd guessed her thoughts.

"There will be other times, Brenda Davis," he said softly.

She wanted to say not in this lifetime, but didn't want to be deliberately rude to him with his aunt standing there. And he knew it. Damn him!

4

His black, shiny mesmerizing eyes beckoned to her the way reflecting pools of tar had drawn animals to their fate long ago. She shuddered at the realization of her own vulnerability.

"It's been interesting talking to you, Brenda, and I'm looking forward to our next meeting."

He made it sound as though it was a foregone conclusion that they would meet again, and it irked Brenda. It irked her even more because she knew that if his aunt had her way that would be exactly what would happen.

Shirley Edwards shifted her gaze from Brenda to her nephew, then back again. "I'll call you at the beginning of next week about dinner, dear. I'm going to bake Gil's favorite sock-it-to-me cake for dessert." She gazed meaningfully at Gil, then innocently at Brenda. "You did say that you'd never tasted one before when I mentioned it the last time I was here. Well, now you'll get your chance."

"You're in for a real treat, Brenda," Gil said huskily.

Brenda absorbed the double meaning in his words, feeling as though he had intimately whispered them in her ear. She gulped. "I—I'm sure it will be."

The look in his eyes said that he intended to make it his business to see that she enjoyed more than just the dessert.

"Later, Brenda Davis," Gil said, that rich, seductive voice of his drizzling over her senses like warm syrup over hot biscuits.

The nerve of the man, Brenda thought as she stood watching him and his aunt leave the Lodge.

"Brenda?"

She jerked around. "Laura! I didn't hear you come downstairs."

Laura frowned. "Are you all right?"

Brenda offered what she hoped was a reassuring smile. "Yes, I'm fine. Really."

"I'm glad." Laura sighed wearily. "I've been feeling so tired lately. Do you mind closing up for me this evening?"

"No, of course not." Brenda noticed that Laura's usually

5

alive brown eyes were dull, and there was a slight slump to her slender shoulders.

Yawning and stretching Laura said, "I'm going to go back upstairs and lie down while Jon-Marc is still sleeping."

"You do look all in. It's no trouble for me to close the shop, you know that."

"Thanks, Brenda. I've come to depend on you. If you left, I don't know what I'd do."

"Don't worry that you'll have to find out anytime in the near future because I'm not going anywhere. I love working here at the Lodge." Brenda walked over to the door to lock it and turn the closed sign around.

"You know if there's anything I can help you with, I'd be more than happy to do it." Laura offered.

"Yes, I know you would." She and Laura Carson were friends, apart from their employer/employee relationship.

"Well, I'm going on up. See you in the morning."

"Good night, Laura."

Brenda did the paperwork, then locked the register and went through the store making sure the windows were secure. Thoughts of Gil Jackson assailed her. Of all the men in the world why did she have to meet this one particularly aggressive male. The feelings he aroused in her, though exciting, could prove to be more than she wanted to deal with.

She sensed that he could do irreparable damage to her emotional equilibrium, and she had no intentions of letting him or any man do that.

Chapter Two

"I saw the way you were gawking at Brenda, Gillie," Shirley Edwards said to her nephew once they were in his car heading for her house. Before he could answer, she quickly added, "And don't try to tell me you're not interested in her because I know you are. I think you two are perfect for each other."

"Now don't start, Aunt Shirley."

"Start what? In my opinion you already did that, Gillie."

His hands tightened on the steering wheel. "For God's sakes, Aunt Shirley, don't call me that."

She laughed. "You been Gillie to me since you was a little bitty boy."

"In case you hadn't noticed, I'm not that little bitty boy any more, Aunt Shirley. I've grown up."

"Indeed you have, into a fine man, if the truth be told. Brenda is a nice girl. You couldn't pick a better young woman to marry."

"Marry!" He put on the brakes hard. "Now, wait a minute, Aunt Shirley, I hardly know the woman, and already you have us practically engaged."

Ignoring his outburst, she went on. "It's about time you married again. Little David needs brothers and sisters."

Gil started to say something, but changed his mind. It wouldn't do any good. Once his aunt got an idea into her head there was no convincing her to the contrary. She was a born matchmaker and wouldn't listen to any protests on his part.

"Don't you try humoring me with your silence, Gillie."

"I wouldn't think of it, Aunt Shirley."

7

Glancing skeptically at him, she mumbled, "Tell me anything. I'm not so old I can't tell when two young people are attracted to one another. It was love at first sight for me and your Uncle John. It happens to some people that way. I think it's happened with you and Brenda."

"Aunt Shirley, I—never mind."

"Young people nowadays don't always know the right way to react in situations like this, but you don't have to worry. I'm here to help you, Gillie."

Gil knew he was in for it now. He wanted to approach Brenda Davis in his own way. He knew instinctively that they'd be good together. Those hazel eyes of hers had immediately captured his attention. Her light-brown-sugar skin made him fantasize how sweet she would taste. She had a figure that would put the goddess Venus to shame. Her long, silky red-brown hair begged a man to tangle his fingers in it.

Yes, she was his kind of woman all right, and he intended to let her know in no uncertain terms the next time they met how much he wanted her. Judging from the look in her eyes and her reaction when he touched her, he realized that he might have come on a little strong. His aunt's idea to have them both over for dinner at her house would help smooth things over.

There was no doubt about it; the woman intrigued him. He recognized the feminine armor she wore and was confident that in time he could dismantle it. He hadn't felt this alive since his wife's death two years ago. He would make Brenda Davis his new project. She was a challenge, and he always enjoyed taking up challenges. As for marriage, his aunt was over-projecting. He wasn't ready for that yet.

He wanted Brenda Davis and he intended to make her admit that she wanted him just as much.

"I'll call you when Brenda agrees on a day to come for dinner," his aunt said.

"Now Aunt Shirley."

"Don't you 'now Aunt Shirley' me. You don't have to tell me where your mind wondered off to just now. Not to worry, Gillie. I'll take care of everything."

"That's what I'm afraid of," he muttered under his breath. With a resigned sigh, he said, "Have it your way, Aunt Shirley. But please, don't call me Gillie, all right?"

That night after she'd bathed and was preparing for bed, Brenda's thoughts strayed to Gil Jackson. She couldn't seem to get him out of her mind.

Be careful, girlfriend. You remember what happened the last time you let yourself get too deeply involved with a man.

She shuddered at the recollection. As if she could forget. There was no way she was going to let Gil Jackson or any other man get close enough for that. She'd been there, done that, and paid a very high price, one she refused to ever pay again. She wouldn't allow herself to get involved with this man.

Deep inside she wondered if she had the strength or the weapons to ward him off if he chose to come after her. Would he come after her? she asked herself. That was a stupid question. The look in his eyes said he would, with all guns blazing.

Damn him! Why did he have to come into her life right now? After making that arduous transition from a past filled with pain and misery, she had finally reached the point where she felt confident about herself and her future. She wasn't about to let anyone rob her of this chance. Gil Jackson had better beware. The problem was that she was intensely attracted to the man. "Damn you for making me feel this way, MaGil Jackson."

"Quilt Lodge," Brenda answered cheerfully Monday morning.

"Brenda, this is Shirley Edwards."

"Yes, Mrs. Edwards."

"Is a week from this past Sunday a good day for you to

come to my house for dinner?"

"Mrs. Edwards, I really don't think—"

"It would mean so much to me, Brenda. Since my husband died I don't have many people over. Please say you'll come."

How could she refuse a plea like that? "All right, Mrs. Edwards."

"Please, call me Shirley. Would six o'clock be convenient?"

"That'll be fine. What can I bring?"

"If you'll just bring your own lovely self, that'll be enough. Let me give you my address." That done Shirley said, "See you on Sunday. Bye now."

Brenda tore off the sheet with the address from the store's notepad. She didn't have to ask whether Gil Jackson would be there. How was she going to deal with this? At least they wouldn't be alone together. That was something she guessed.

⊷⊰◈⊱⊶

A week had passed since Brenda had met Gil Jackson, and he hadn't contacted her or come into the Lodge. Maybe he had decided not to pursue her. No, she was sure that wasn't the case. He was just giving her plenty of time to think about him. And think about him she had.

Brenda heard Laura coming down the stairs with her grandson. She smiled at the boy. "How are you this morning, little man?"

He smiled back but didn't answer, just buried his face in Laura's shoulder.

"He's all right," Laura answered. "I'm taking him to the pediatrician, though I'm sure it's only a cold, but—"

"But because of his grandfather you're being extra cautious."

"You got it. Carl Wintercloud is looking for any excuse to take Jon-Marc away from me."

"I wish there was some way the two of you could resolve this."

"Me too. There just doesn't seem to be a solution. At least not one we can both agree on. If only Stephanie and Jason hadn't died in that plane crash."

Brenda sympathized with her friend. Laura had agreed to be a surrogate for her daughter because Stephanie had been unable to carry a baby to term. No sooner than the in vitro fertilization procedure was deemed successful, Laura's daughter and son-in-law were killed in a plane accident, leaving Laura pregnant and with the responsibility of raising their child alone.

Brenda knew that Laura loved her grandson but worried that he wouldn't have a balanced childhood without a father figure to guide him since Laura was a widow and had no intention of ever marrying again.

Jon-Marc's grandfather wanted custody, but considering that Carl Wintercloud hadn't exactly been the best of fathers where his own son was concerned, Laura wasn't sure he would be what the boy needed. And because Laura wouldn't consider giving him custody, he was threatening to take her to court. So that left them at odds. Laura was expecting a visit from his lawyer any day.

The word *lawyer* incensed Brenda. She hated them all with a passion. She knew from experience how devious and corrupt they could be when it came to winning their cases. She hoped that Laura didn't have to go through what she had four years ago. She wouldn't wish that kind of hell on her worst enemy.

"Are you going to be able to handle things by yourself, Brenda? You know that Mondays can be a real zoo. And it could turn into a disaster if the Perkins sisters decide to descend."

Brenda laughed wryly. "Oh, I think I can handle it."

"I'll try to get back as soon as I can to help you, but I have an appointment with my attorney after I leave the pediatrician's office."

"Don't worry about it, just do what you have to do."

It was late afternoon by the time Laura and Jon-Marc returned. Laura came back downstairs to help Brenda after putting her grandson down for his nap.

"How is Jon-Marc?" Brenda asked.

"He only has a cold, not to mention late teething pangs."

"What about your appointment with Ms. Rainey? How did that go?"

Laura frowned wearily. "That's a different story. Not so good. Carl Wintercloud intends to go the full nine yards with his suit. His lawyer is coming here to talk to me tomorrow."

"About what?"

"A compromise, I guess, from what Ella said. I wonder about that. Carl Wintercloud doesn't seem like the kind of man who compromises. He's half Chippewa Indian. You have no idea how intractable some Native American males can be when it comes to their heritage since the number of Indians is dwindling and their blood diluted by marriages into other races."

"How do you know all that?"

"One of my old friends from school, Betina Manning, was married to an Indian for twelve years."

"Carl Wintercloud is also black, isn't he?"

"Yes, but he's afraid that Jon-Marc won't know about the Indian side of his heritage if he isn't around full time to teach him. I told him I wouldn't stand in the way of that, but for some reason he doesn't trust me to keep my word."

"I'm sure this lawyer isn't helping him to see your side."

Laura gave Brenda a sidelong glance. "You really despise lawyers, don't you?"

"With a passion. If you'd been through what I have because of them, believe me, you'd feel the same way I do."

"You've never told me about that. You know you can talk to me about anything, Brenda."

"I know I can, Laura. The subject isn't one I feel comfortable discussing with anyone."

"If you should change your mind, I'm here."

"I won't forget."

—⋘⋙—

The rest of the workday proved hectic, and by closing time Brenda was exhausted and more than ready to go home. She groaned suddenly, remembering that she had no food at her place, which meant that she would have to go to the grocery store. She wasn't looking forward to the prospect, but she was tired of eating the same old take-out foods, and frozen dinners were a real appetite turn off.

Fifteen minutes later, in the market, turning her shopping cart in the direction of the produce department, Brenda collided with Gil Jackson's cart.

He grinned. "It seems that we had the same idea. I couldn't face the prospect of leftovers tonight. And I'm definitely burned out on fastfoods."

Brenda cleared her throat. "I'm really tired, Mr. Jackson. Now if you don't mind moving, I'd like to get on with my shopping."

"You're a prickly little thing, aren't you, Brenda Davis?"

"If you'll excuse me."

"What are you afraid of, Brenda?"

"Mr. Jackson—"

"Gil."

"*Gil*, would you please move out of my way!"

"You say *please* so sweetly, Brenda, but I intend to get more than in your way."

Brenda's face heated with temper. "Why me, Gil? I'm not interested in you."

"You're also a sweet liar, and I'm going to prove it to you."

Brenda pulled her shopping cart back.

"Oh, I'm not going to do it now, but in my own good time, warrior lady." Smiling, he turned his shopping cart away from hers and headed down another aisle.

Brenda stood there a moment before guiding her cart to the vegetable bins. She didn't like the look in Gil's eyes or the confident tone of his voice. She wasn't a liar and she wasn't afraid of him. She just didn't want to have anything to do with him, past being polite. She didn't need or want Gil Jackson in her life. Somehow she'd convince him of it.

Or are you trying to convince yourself?

———⋘◆⋙———

Brenda relaxed after eating a dinner of broiled chicken breast, soup, and hot cider. For some reason Gil Jackson crept into her thoughts again. How was she going to keep him from pursuing her? She didn't want the complications he would bring to her life, but what could she do to discourage him?

That night a familiar dream tormented her sleep...

"Mama, I can't believe you and Daddy did this to me!" she cried.

"It's for your own good, Sheila."

She glanced at her parents and then at Bailey Johnson, their attorney. How she hated that man.

"I despise you, Mr. Johnson. If not for you, I'd have my baby back with me."

"You have your whole life ahead of you, Sheila," her father inserted firmly. "There was no need for you to sacrifice your entire future to care for an out-of-wedlock mistake. We know of any number of young men who would marry you in a minute if you gave them some encouragement."

"Your choices, not mine. All I wanted was my baby. Why couldn't you understand that?"

"The child is in a good home, Sheila."

"That child happens to be your grandchild. I could have made a good home for him." She turned to Bailey Johnson. "You ruined my chances by supplying distorted information to the judge, casting doubts on my fitness as a mother. You have no idea how much I hate you and everything you stand for."

"Don't—"

"Don't what, Mama? I'm never going to forgive you or Daddy for this. Never. Never. Never."

Brenda woke up crying, her body drenched in sweat and trembling uncontrollaby. It had been two years since she'd had that particular dream. Why tonight? She clutched her pillow to her chest and sat in the middle of the bed rocking herself.

"Oh, God, how am I ever going to endure this."

Where was her son? She'd been unable to find out the name of the adoptive parents. The judge said the records were sealed to protect the child. All she could find out was that her son was in a good home, not where the adoptive couple lived or anything else about them. When the judge denied her appeal, ruling that she couldn't get her son back, she'd been devastated.

She could certainly identify with Laura's problems. Lawyers were not to be trusted. They could tear a person's life apart and merrily go on to the next case without a thought to the destruction they left in their wake.

She hated all lawyers and always would.

Brenda was in the pattern room of the Quilt Lodge straightening up when she heard the shop bell. Smoothing down her navy and winter-white plaid skirt and adjusting the collar of her long-sleeved blue blouse, she went out to greet the customer and offer assistance.

She stopped dead in her tracks when she saw who was standing there.

"How are you, Brenda?" Gil asked.

"Fine," she said in a stilted voice.

"You are definitely that, pretty woman."

"How can I help you, Mr. Jack—Gil."

"I've come to see Laura Carson."

"She's upstairs. I'll let her know you're here." Stepping over to the counter, Brenda picked up the receiver and buzzed Laura's com line. "A Mr. MaGil Jackson is here to see you, Laura."

"Good. He's the lawyer I've been expecting. Send him on up."

Sparing Gil a look of utter contempt, Brenda said, "You

can go on up, *Mr. Jackson*."

As she watched him climb the stairs, a feeling of rage began to build inside her. So Gil Jackson was a lawyer, the lawyer Carl Wintercloud had hired to help him take Jon-Marc away from Laura.

—⊰◈⊱—

"Would you like some coffee, Mr. Jackson?" Laura offered.

"No, thank you, Mrs. Carson. May I call you Laura?"

"If you want to. Let's get down to business. I know why you're here."

"I wonder if you really do."

"You want me to give custody of my grandson to your client."

"No, I don't. The reason I came here is to help both of you."

"I can't see how taking Jon-Marc away from me will accomplish that."

"It won't, so I'm not going to try to convince you that it will. You and Carl have to find a way to share this special little boy's life. He needs both of you."

"What do you suggest?"

"A meeting with Carl so the two of you can discuss it calmly and rationally."

"You know Carl Wintercloud, and you ask me to do something like that, Mr. Jackson?"

"Please, call me Gil. I can see that you're two very stubborn people. I also know that you both love that little boy very much. There has to be some common ground on which to work things out to the benefit of all concerned. If you would just meet with Carl."

Laura walked over to the window and looked out. A minute passed then she turned to face Gil. "All right. Have Carl get in touch with me."

"You won't be sorry, Laura."

"Something tells me I will be. You're a very persuasive

16

man, Gil. Have you ever considered going into politics?"

"I've been asked to do that. I'm considering it."

"The country needs honest, dedicated public officials. I've heard that you're an advocate for Indian rights as well as the rights of African-Americans."

"I'm a quarter Chippewa. Carl is in fact my cousin. But don't think because of that I'll deal unfairly with you. I want what's best for all concerned. Jon-Marc is the one to benefit most from a peace only the two of you can forge. You can accomplish that only if you work together.

"Being a father myself, I can understand what you must be going through. If someone were to try to take David..." He cleared his throat and smiled. "I'll get off my soapbox now. I can see myself out, Laura. I hope you and Carl can find a way to solve your problems."

"You really mean that, don't you?"

"Yes, I do. I'll tell Carl that you're willing to negotiate a peace treaty." He gave a short smile. "My cousin is a naturally wary individual, so don't take offense at some of the things he says. I'm sure if anyone can bring him around it'll be you. If you need any help, don't hesitate to call me." He took out a business card and wrote his home phone number on the back and handed it to her.

"Ella Rainey said you were a formidable man, Mr. Jackson."

"I'll bet she did. Ella and I go way back. I had a crush on her in law school. It broke my heart when she married Jack Rainey."

"She didn't tell me that."

"She wouldn't. Tell her as much as I admire her I don't want to have to lock horns with her in court over this case. I'd better be going. Hang in there. You and Carl will find a way."

"I hope you're right, Gil."

—❖—

Downstairs, curiosity and impatience were eating Brenda

alive. She was desperate to know what was going on above her. What was Gil Jackson discussing with Laura? Surely he wouldn't try to convince her to give up her grandson? Now that she knew he was a lawyer she didn't put anything past him. She had to warn Laura about that man.

Anger flared hot and heavy inside Brenda like kerosene thrown on a fire when she saw Gil descend the stairs.

"Brenda, Aunt Shirley told me you had accepted her invitation to have dinner on Sunday." He grinned. "And of course she insisted that I join the two of you." When he saw the belligerent look on Brenda's face, he frowned. "What's wrong, Brenda?"

"Nothing is wrong," she ground out.

"Then why are you looking at me as though you hate me?"

"I see you got the message. Now if you'll excuse me, I have work to do." She headed in the direction of the pattern room.

Gil put a hand on her arm. "What did I say to deserve this frigid treatment?"

"I don't like you, Mr. Jackson, or anyone like you. Is that honest enough for you?"

When he didn't say anything and just stood there, studying her, his eyes glittering and his jaw tensing, she felt a frisson of healthy fear skitter down her spine as she waited for him to speak.

He said finally, "I'll see you on Sunday, Brenda. I know you'll come because you wouldn't want to hurt Aunt Shirley's feelings." He added with soft menace, "I have to tell you that anyone who does will have me to deal with. Am I making myself clear?"

"Are you threatening me?"

"Just remember what I said."

"I'll be there. I wouldn't dream of hurting her. But in the future, I'll just have to convince your aunt not to include you in the same invitation."

"Good luck." He smiled. "Personally I've never been able to change her mind once she's made it up. See you Sunday.

Chapter Three

Brenda wished that the evening ahead was over and done with. Spending time in Gil Jackson's company wasn't high on the list of things she looked forward to doing. If it wouldn't have hurt Shirley Edwards feelings, she'd have begged off.

Brenda walked over to the closet and searched for something to wear. Her eyes stopped on the forest-green velvet dress she'd bought on sale at the beginning of summer. It fit her body as though it had been made for only her. It brought out the green in her hazel eyes. Like her father, she'd inherited the Walker hazel eyes, courtesy of an Irish great-grandfather. Her light teak coloring came from her mother who was part Brazilian. She could truly say that she'd come from a multicultural heritage.

She knew she was straying away from the point. The thought of meeting Gil Jackson in a personal setting was unnerving to say the least, but she'd get through it. Brenda pulled the velvet dress out of the closet and laid it across the bed. It didn't matter what she wore this evening. It would be her last time in his company.

⊰⊱⟡⊰⊱

"I like that suit, Gillie," Shirley complimented her nephew when she opened the door to him.

"Aunt Shirley, you promised not to call me that."

"I'm sorry, it slipped out."

"As long as you don't let it 'slip out' when Brenda gets

here."

Shirley's eyes twinkled. "You're really looking forward to this evening, aren't you?"

He shot his aunt a warning glance, which she completely ignored.

"There's no need to feel embarrassed."

"I'm not embarrassed, Aunt Shirley."

"Good. It doesn't show weakness to be anxious, Gillie— Gil," she amended. "Brenda should be here any minute."

Gil couldn't totally squash his feelings of unease. The way Brenda glared at him the last time made him apprehensive about this evening. He was curious to know everything there was to know about this woman, and he sensed that it wouldn't be an easy task he'd set for himself.

There was something about Brenda Davis that fascinated him, like a snake charmer's flute does a snake. Everything about her suggested strong emotion, deep passion, and fragile vulnerability. He sensed an intriguing story behind those wary hazel eyes, and he intended to find out all he could about her.

Brenda parked her car in front of Shirley Edwards' house. She noticed the car in the drive was a gold Jaguar. Mrs. Edwards drove a blue Lumina, so it had to mean that the car belonged to Gil Jackson, and he was already inside. Letting out a resigned sigh, she got out of her car and headed up the walk. She wondered how she was going to get through the evening feeling the way she did. Before she could knock, the door opened.

"Right on time." Gil smiled. "I like a punctual woman. Come on in. Aunt Shirley and I have been anxiously waiting for you to get here."

She believed that Shirley genuinely was anxious, but as far as her nephew was concerned, Brenda had her doubts about his motives. She smiled politely and preceded Gil into the hall, where he took her coat, hung it up in the closet, then showed her into the living room.

Brenda liked the charming Victorian clapboard home. A giant hearth fireplace dominated one entire wall of the living room. An old-fashioned burgundy silk double parlor couch set and a cherry-wood coffee table resided on the Oriental rug taking center stage.

Smiling, Shirley came out of the kitchen. "I'm so glad you could come, Brenda. Can I get you something hot to drink, cider, tea, or coffee?"

"A cup of coffee will do me fine." Brenda smiled warmly. "Fall is definitely in the air."

"Gil, you entertain Brenda while I get her that coffee."

He groaned, wishing his aunt wouldn't be so brazen with her matchmaking technique. He could see the adverse affect it was having on Brenda.

"I won't bite you, I promise," he told Brenda.

"I hope not," she answered, purposely choosing to sit on the couch across from the one he suggested.

Gil decided to let that pass. "What made you decide to settle in Long Rapids, Brenda?"

"Don't you think you're being a little pushy considering that we hardly know each other?"

Gil nodded his head in a *touché* gesture. "You see, that's what I want to change. I want us to get to know each other very well."

"What makes you think I want to get to know you at all, let alone very well?"

"I'm psychic."

"Look, Gil, I don't want to burst your bubble—"

"Don't you?"

Shirley chose that moment to return, carrying a tray laden with a coffeepot, cups, sugar, and cream. "I forgot to ask how you preferred your coffee."

"Cream and no sugar," Brenda answered. She had a sneaking suspicion that Shirley had timed her entrance after having eavesdropped on their conversation. Heaven help all single people when matchmakers were determined to change their status.

Gil could almost feel sorry for Brenda. Almost. Except he wanted to get closer to this lady, and he was willing to accept any help he could get toward his goal.

"Gil likes his coffee the same way you like yours. Isn't that an interesting coincidence?"

He cleared his throat. "That pot roast sure smells good, Aunt Shirley."

"I didn't ask what you might like for dinner, Brenda. I hope you like pot roast, dear."

"Pot roast is fine with me, Shirley."

The evening went well until they got to the dessert and coffee following the delicious dinner.

Brenda wasn't sure where she'd put dessert. But when she tasted the Sock-It-To-Me cake, it almost melted in her mouth. "This cake is fabulous. What are the ingredients?"

"It's a takeoff on the ordinary pound cake. The difference is that you pour half of the pound cake batter in the pan, then sprinkle nuts, cinnamon, and sugar before adding the rest of the batter, then baking it."

"It sounds like something even I could tackle without disastrous results."

"I'd be more than happy to help you. Then we could try it out on Gillie, I mean Gil."

Gil's eyes widened in embarrassment.

Seeing this, Brenda couldn't help razzing him about Shirley's little familial slip.

"Gillie?"

"It's my pet name for my nephew since he was a little boy, isn't it, Gil?"

He groaned. What could he do but acknowledge it? "It's hard to get Aunt Shirley to stop calling me that."

"It's hardly a name a big-shot lawyer like you would want to be called."

Realizing the potential for the ruination of her well-laid plans, Shirley asked Brenda, "Would you like another slice of cake, dear?"

"Thank you, no. I don't have room for another bite." Brenda rose to her feet. "I've enjoyed the dinner, and I thank you for inviting me, but I really must be going."

Shirley rose from her chair. "Oh, do you have to leave so soon?"

"We can't take up all of Brenda's time, Aunt Shirley." Gil moved his chair back.

"Well, we'll have to do this again real soon," Shirley said undaunted. "How about a week from today?"

"Oh, I'm afraid I'll have to bow out on that date, Aunt Shirley. I'll be out of town attending a Native American Council meeting."

"You don't have to tell me, Carl is urging you to go with him, isn't he?"

"Now, Aunt Shirley, don't start in on Carl."

"Even though he's kin, he can be cold and unfeeling in certain areas."

"I know it may seem that way, but that's because he's still grieving the loss of his only son."

"What he needs is a good woman to take him in hand. Maybe I should seriously consider helping him find another wife."

"Aunt Shirley!"

"Yes, maybe I should. It's been eight years since Gabrielle died."

Brenda sat stunned to silence at the revelation that Gil Jackson and Carl Wintercloud were related. She hadn't met Carl Wintercloud, but from what Laura had told her about him, she wasn't sure she even wanted to. One thing she hoped was that Shirley didn't put Laura at the top of her matchmaking register where that man was concerned.

"I really have to be going, Shirley. I'll get back to you about the dinner invitation."

"Just don't forget, Brenda. I've really enjoyed your company and so has Gil."

Brenda ached to tell her not to plan on anything happening between her and Gil, but decided to let things ride in the hope that Shirley would eventually ease up on her matchmaking campaign.

"I'll walk you to your car," Gil offered.

"That won't be necessary," Brenda quickly put in.

"Oh, but I insist."

Shirley smiled, voicing her approval.

Brenda had no choice but to let Gil escort her to the car.

Once outside after the door closed behind them, Gil cupped Brenda's elbow. "You really must learn to bow to the inevitable."

"And why would you say something like that?"

"Because it's inevitable that you and I are going to be in each other's company a lot in the future."

"I can see that besides being psychic you're arrogant as hell."

"Flattery just might get you somewhere."

"Of all the—look, Gil, I don't happen to agree with your prediction or your assumption that I'll fall in with your plans, okay? I don't know you and I don't want to—"

Gil stopped, and turning Brenda toward him, kissed her soundly on the mouth, then again more gently, more arousingly, more completely.

Brenda's breath caught in her throat. His first kiss sent volts of electricity shooting through her body. And the second seemed to melt her insides, turning her legs to jelly. And the third...

Gil felt her reaction and ended the kiss, but slowly.

"I'd say this is the best way in the world for a man and a woman to come to know each other."

When Brenda opened her mouth to protest, he placed a finger across her lips.

"And don't tell me you were unaffected by what just happened between us, because I won't believe you."

Dazed, Brenda backed away from Gil. She couldn't believe that she was responding to him like this. What had come over her? Why hadn't she even tried to push him away?

"Why fight the attraction between us? Something very

basic happened."

"No, it didn't," she denied vehemently.

"Honey, yes it did." He drew her into his arms and kissed her again, this time molding his fingers to the back of her head, holding her in place as he explored her mouth.

A moan escaped Brenda and the sound jolted her out of his spell.

No! She couldn't let this happen to her. She broke away and ran to her car.

"Brenda, wait!" Gil called to her. "We need to talk about this."

"There's nothing to talk about. Stay the hell away from me, Gil Jackson." She unlocked her car door and swiftly wedged herself behind the wheel. Her hands shook so badly that only after several tries did she finally succeed in inserting the key in the ignition and driving off.

Gil stared after her until the taillights of her car disappeared as she turned the corner. There were depths to Brenda Davis he'd only begun to plumb. She intrigued him as no other woman had in a long time.

There was fire in the heart of ice, passion inside her body waiting to be awakened. He wondered what could have happened to make her so cold. Some guy had probably hurt her. That had to be the reason for her wary attitude.

Gil slowly walked back to the house. His curiosity about Brenda Davis was stoked. He had no choice but to pursue her. He wouldn't settle for knowing less than everything about this enigmatic woman.

—⋇✧⋇—

Brenda was trembling with shock and fear by the time she reached her apartment. Gil Jackson had managed to slip beneath her guard and arouse her. How could she have let him do that? She'd promised herself that she would never let that happen to her again. The price of caring for someone led to heartache and misery. She couldn't risk going through that again, she just couldn't.

She would have to find a way to discourage him, but how did she go about doing that? Gil Jackson was a lawyer used to winning all the time. She couldn't let him win this time. Her life and her emotional well-being depended on it.

She closed her eyes, waiting for the comforting numbness she had learned to induce, to steal over her emotions. But this time she found it harder than usual. She knew it was because Gil Jackson had affected her so deeply. She couldn't afford to let him get any closer.

The thought of leaving town flashed through her mind, but she thrust it aside. She wasn't running away again. She would stay and face this. Gil Jackson would just have to leave her alone, that's all.

Yeah right, a niggling voice inside her head taunted. *And just how are you planning to make him?*

Later after she bathed and climbed into bed, thoughts of Gil Jackson battled inside her mind. Brenda remembered the taste of his mouth, the sensations he caused to erupt inside her, the feel of his fingers moving through her hair when he kissed her the second time.

By the third kiss her mind had suddenly gone blank and she let herself be pulled into a web of passion the likes of which she had never experienced before. For a moment she had been helpless to resist him. She shuddered thinking about the power he exerted over her senses. Yes, she would definitely have to avoid this man at every turn.

Chapter Four

The moment the tall solemn-faced man entered the Lodge, Brenda knew it had to be Carl Wintercloud. His dual Native American and black heritages were clearly stamped on the harsh planes of face and body. Now that she'd seen him, she could understand Laura's ambivalence. The man *was* intimidating. He reminded her of the fierce warriors she'd seen in the movies. And since he had warrior blood from both sides of his heritage it made him all the more dangerous.

Just then Laura came down the stairs. Brenda noticed a nervous smile, and her heart went out to her friend. She could only imagine what Laura was feeling at this moment.

"Jon-Marc is sleeping," Laura said to Carl. "We can talk about our situation upstairs."

He looked around. "You have a very nice place here. But I'm not convinced it's the right atmosphere to be raising my grandson."

"Follow me, Mr. Wintercloud," Laura said calmly, "where we can discuss it in private."

Brenda watched them head up the stairs with a feeling of trepidation. She wondered if Laura was up to dealing with a man like Carl Wintercloud. He obviously possessed the pride of his dual heritage as well as the looks.

A few minutes later Shirley Edwards came into the lodge.

"Brenda, I want to start a new quilt. The pattern is an old one. I was wondering if you would happen to have it."

"Tell me the name of it, and I'll check in the storeroom to see if we have it."

"It's called a wedding ring quilt."

27

"Is someone in your family getting married?"

"No date has been set as yet, but I want to have it finished for whatever day they decide to marry."

"Then you think it'll be soon." Brenda looked suspiciously at the older woman and wondered if she was referring to the relationship she hoped would grow between her nephew and Brenda. "I'm sure we have one."

After a few minutes Brenda found the pattern and returned to the counter. Carl Wintercloud came tromping down the stairs, Laura following close on his heels.

"We'll just see about that," he said in a loud voice over his shoulder.

"Yes, we will, Mr. Wintercloud," Laura retorted.

"Carl," Shirley called out.

"Shirley!" He cleared his throat. "Ah—how have you been?"

"Better than you, I'd venture to guess." Shirley glanced at Laura's angry face and her cousin's obstinate features. "I'm coming out to the reservation Saturday the same as usual. Are you going to be there?"

"Yes, of course I will."

"Good." She turned to Laura. "I haven't seen much of you lately."

"I've been a little busy with my grandson."

"*Our* grandson," Carl corrected her. "It's not the end of what we discussed, Laura." He left the Lodge, slamming the door behind him so hard that the shop bell sounded like a strangled bird.

Laura fumed. "That man has to be the most stubborn, pig-headed—"

"He can be that and a lot of other things I could name. But," Shirley added, "he does love his grandson, Laura."

"I know he does. Gil promised me that he would at least listen to what I had to say."

"Gil is a lawyer. They're liable to tell you anything," Brenda said. "I wouldn't put much store in what he says."

Shirley gave her a sharp look. "He may be a lawyer,

Brenda, but he is also a very compassionate man."

Aware that she had offended the older woman, Brenda had the grace to guiltily look away.

Shirley paid for the pattern and left without saying another word to Brenda.

Laura gave Brenda a sidelong look. "Shirley is right about Gil. From what I've observed he is a very understanding person. I can't say the same for his cousin, though."

"It's because Carl Wintercloud is Gil Jackson's cousin—"

"That you have such a low opinion of him? You really shouldn't jump to conclusions, Brenda. So far Gil's been fair, not at all biased."

"Maybe not yet, but—oh, never mind."

"Brenda, you're so bitter. Don't let it cloud your thinking."

"I'd better do the paperwork."

A cry echoed through the building.

"And I'd better see to Jon-Marc. The loud voices must have woken him up."

"Don't worry about the Lodge, I'll close up, Laura."

Laura looked as though she wanted to say more, but the insistent crying of her grandson urged her up the stairs.

Brenda was glad for the interruption because she was definitely not in the mood to discuss Gil Jackson.

She'd already offended Shirley and suspected if Gil got wind of it there would be hell to pay. Why couldn't she have kept her opinion to herself?

Because you can't help comparing Laura's dilemma to the one you went through and still haven't gotten over and probably never will.

I've come a long way.

Yes, you have, but have you come far enough? Can you ever overcome not having your son with you?

No. Never.

When Brenda got home, she took out the materials to start

a new quilt. After deciding how she wanted it, she stretched the top layer out over the quilt frame and began working on the design. She found that working on her quilts was therapeutic. It had helped save her sanity after she...

Oh, God, how it hurt to think about the child she'd given up. He was a part of her life she could never get back.

She always managed to avoid people with small children and babies. She'd never touched Jon-Marc. She just couldn't bring herself to do it. Unfortunately she'd already accepted the job at the Quilt Lodge before finding out Laura had a baby. Jon-Marc, whom Carl Wintercloud wanted to take away.

And Gil Jackson was Carl's cousin and attorney.

Gil Jackson.

Why did everything lead back to that man? There seemed to be no escaping him.

The tension at the Lodge had stretched almost to the limit since the confrontation between Laura and Carl. Brenda wanted to ask Laura what her next move would be, but she resisted the urge to get into her business. Finally, a few days later, Laura received a summons to appear in court.

"That man!" She crumpled the offending piece of paper in her fist.

"What's going to happen now?" Brenda asked. "Have you spoken to your attorney?"

"Ella said if it ever got as far as the courtroom it could be a nasty custody battle. I wanted to avoid it, but it seems that the situation is out of my control and will be in the hands of a judge if Carl continues to be unreasonable. It's all or nothing with that man. Gil was so sure that—"

"I told you not to trust Gil Jackson, Laura. He's the man's cousin, for God's sake, which means that he has his own personal axe to grind."

"I don't believe that. Gil is too—"

"Too what? Honest? You're too trusting, Laura."

30

"And you're not trusting enough."

Brenda laughed bitterly. "Oh, I was as trusting as you once, but I learned my lesson."

"You believe that because Gil is a lawyer he's not trustworthy."

"Exactly."

Laura peered at her friend. "It's more than just the fact that he's a lawyer that's bothering you. Whoever the man was, he must have hurt you very badly."

"Let's just say I had my eyes opened and leave it at that."

The shop bell jangled.

Brenda shifted her glance to the door and saw Gil Jackson striding toward them.

"If it isn't the black Matlock in the flesh," she said sarcastically.

Laura gasped. "Brenda!"

"The name is Gil Jackson, Ms. Davis, and I need to have a word with you in private."

"You and Gil can go in the pattern room, Brenda. I'll watch the counter until you're done."

"Laura, I—"

"It's no problem. You go ahead and have your talk."

Brenda wanted to strangle Laura but smiled coolly at Gil and signaled him to follow her. Once inside the pattern room, Gil pulled the door closed.

"I want to know what in the hell you said to Aunt Shirley. She was very upset when I went by to see her yesterday. I told you if you—"

"I didn't purposely set out to hurt her. I care about her too much to do something like that."

"So you say."

Brenda's eyes narrowed. "I think you'd better leave, Mr. Jackson."

Gil came to within inches of her. "And I think you'd better tell me what happened."

"And if I don't, what are you going to do? Beat me?"

A dangerous light glowed in his eyes. "You really don't

31

want an answer to that question. Look, Brenda—"

"I'm sorry if I hurt Shirley's feelings, all right? I'll call her and apologize. Will that satisfy you, *Mr. Jackson*?"

"Nothing short of having you naked, making sweet savage love to you will satisfy me."

He opened the door, then turned. "You make that call. Better still, go by and see Aunt Shirley."

On his way to the front door, Gil stopped at the register to speak to Laura. "I'm sorry that things didn't work out between you and Carl, but I won't give up on you two. I'm going to work on my cousin and try to get him to see that compromise is the only way to go."

"Thanks, Gil. You and Brenda—"

He grinned. "She's another matter entirely. I don't think compromise will work with her. There's a very definite reason why she reacts to me the way she does, and I'm determined to find out why that is."

"I hope you do."

He winked at her. When he looked up and saw Brenda standing framed in the doorway of the pattern room glaring at him, he guessed from her expression, she'd heard what he'd said. He shot her an it-ain't-over-between-us look before leaving the Lodge.

"The sparks do fly whenever you two are in the same room," Laura commented.

"It's because I can't stand him or what he represents."

"You know what they say about hate. It's the darker side of love."

"Not in this case, you can be sure of that."

"Can you deny that you're attracted to the man?"

Brenda didn't answer.

"I thought not."

The rest of the day went by slowly. By the end of it Brenda felt ready to face Shirley Edwards. She wasn't doing it because of Gil's veiled threat, but because she genuinely liked the older woman and thought she owed her an apology.

—⋈◈⋈—

"Brenda! Please, come on in," Shirley said with a smile, moving aside to admit her into her home. "Let me take your coat."

Brenda eased out of her coat and handed it to her. "I apoligize if I offended you the other day."

"I see Gil has been talking to you. I'm sorry if he came on too strong."

"No, it's all right. I shouldn't have said what I did."

"Would you like some coffee or a cup of tea?"

"Tea would be wonderful."

"Let's go in the kitchen and talk."

Shirley's home reminded Brenda of her Aunt Bertha's. The kitchen was warm and cheery and smelled of sugar and cinnamon. Her aunt was forever baking something sweet.

"Sit down, Brenda. What I want to know is why you said what you did?"

"I don't know if I can explain, Shirley."

"I thought you liked Gil."

What could she say to her? Brenda wondered. She couldn't tell her the truth. She cleared her throat. "It isn't that I don't like him. I just overreacted to the situation between Laura and Carl."

"You sure that's all there is to it?"

"Yes. How is that wedding ring quilt coming?" Brenda was sure that Shirley had noticed the way she had sidestepped answering her question when she saw the sage look in the older woman's eyes before she decided to follow her lead.

"Why don't you come into my workroom and see for yourself."

Brenda couldn't get over how beautifully Shirley had worked the quilt. "It's exquisite, Shirley. I hope one day to become as good at quilting as you are."

"You will. It's taken me years and years of practice. I've won the quilter's prize at the county fair eight years in a row."

"I can see why, if this is a sample of your work. You have to show me a few pointers."

"I'd be glad to."

Brenda felt warmed from the inside out by the time she left Shirley Edwards' home. She realized how much she needed the kind of warmth that special lady offered. Being with her was like being with Aunt Bertha. The kind of relationship she and her aunt shared was worlds apart from the one she had with her own mother or father. That unique closeness never existed between them. And after what they had done she was sure it was never going to happen.

Returning her thoughts to Shirley, Brenda smiled. She hadn't gotten away from her without promising to have dinner at her house the following Sunday. The woman was a con artist of the first degree. Shirley Edwards could charm the ducks out of the pond, as Aunt Bertha would say.

The prospect of seeing Gil again after their last encounter was a little frightening. Given Shirley's affinity for match-making, there was no doubt in Brenda's mind that he would be there.

Chapter Five

"Do you really want to go to court, Carl?" Gil asked his cousin.

"If I have to, to get my grandson."

"What's wrong with Laura raising him and you having visitation rights?"

"Visitation rights! I want more than that, Gil. I want to be a part of my grandson's life, take care of him, teach him things about the other side of his heritage."

"You think Laura would stand in the way of that?"

"I don't know what she would do, and I don't want to take the chance."

"I'm the one who suggested a compromise. I should have known better knowing you as well as I do. You've got to be the most intractable human being on the planet, Carl."

"I want my grandson."

"I wouldn't count on a judge giving you custody."

"Why?"

"Because—forget it."

"No, Gil. Tell me."

"Because of the relationship between you and Jason."

Gil noticed the way Carl's expression changed, and he felt sorry he'd brought up the painful reminder, but it had to be faced. "You and Jason were always at odds and even more so before he died and years prior to that when he married Stephanie."

"I know I wasn't a perfect example of fatherhood, but I want to make up for it with Jason's son."

"I understand that, but a judge will look at it differently.

Laura has raised two children. Her son, Robert, is a pillar of the community, and so was Stephanie."

"I don't know what else to do, Gil. I don't see any other solution."

"What about joint custody?"

"I don't think that'll work either. I still wouldn't get to be with Jon-Marc the way I want to."

"It's not all about what you want, Carl. I think Aunt Shirley's right. You've been alone too long and have forgotten how to share."

"Not you too. I hear enough of that from her. I guess you think I should marry Laura." His voice held a note of mockery.

"That would solve a lot of your problems."

"I was only kidding."

"I'm not. Laura is a very attractive woman." Gil smiled. He could tell that his cousin was considering it.

"I promised myself I'd never marry again after Gabrielle died."

"I know you loved her, but it's been eight years, Carl. You have needs like any other man."

Carl didn't answer.

"Think about it."

"What about you? Isn't it about time you got married again?"

For so long the image of his wife Monique had filled his thoughts and his heart, but now since meeting Brenda Davis it was her that he dreamed about. It was her face that constantly floated before his mind's eye during the day.

"Have you been seeing anyone?"

"Not exactly."

Carl gave him a sidelong glance. "What do you mean 'not exactly?'"

"Aunt Shirley has been trying to throw Brenda Davis and me together."

"She's the woman who works for Laura, isn't she?"

"Yes, she is."

"I met her the other day." Carl grinned. "Is she the one, Gil?"

"Get outta here, Carl."

"She's a very pretty woman, if a little prickly. I get the distinct impression that she doesn't like me very much."

"It's probably because of Laura and Jon-Marc."

"I imagine Laura has discussed our situation with her."

"They *are* friends, which is more than what Brenda and I are right now."

"You mean you haven't managed to seduce her yet?"

"Carl!"

"Don't look so shocked. Your reputation precedes you, counselor."

"You make me sound like Don Juan or somebody."

"I know a few women who might believe that about you."

"That's a laugh. Since Monique's death, I've rarely dated. And what with my busy law practice and taking care of my son, I hardly have time."

"What about Alicia Kelly?"

"That was over before it really began. "

"Do you intend to make time for Brenda Davis?"

"That's none of your exclusive business, cuz."

Carl laughed. "I'm outta here. See you in court."

"Carl—"

"I know you want me to change my mind. But don't count on that happening."

—⋙⟡⋘—

It was Sunday, and once again Brenda found herself preparing to go to Shirley Edwards' house for dinner. She pulled out a satin-lined red wool dress. It had a sage-green paisley scarf. It was a little dated, but it looked good on her.

Why was she going to so much trouble? It was after all only a simple dinner invitation.

Yeah right.

No, it wasn't a simple dinner invitation; it was another one

37

of Shirley Edwards's matchmaking attempts. She would just have to treat it like any other dinner invitation and try to somehow discourage the woman from doing it in the future.

It's going to take a miracle to pull that one off. And you're fresh out of them right now.

She and Gil would be in his aunt's company for the entire evening, so there wasn't a chance of them being alone.

You know that with just a look, Gil Jackson can make you feel as though you and he were alone in a crowded room.

How well she knew it.

She glanced at the clock. It was almost time to go.

"Can you ease up on the heavy matchmaking routine, Aunt Shirley?"

"I've gotten her to agree to come to dinner, haven't I? The rest is up to you. If you're the man I think you are, you'll take the proverbial ball and run with it."

Gil looked warily at Aunt Shirley not knowing whether to trust her seemingly self-satisfied attitude. His aunt could be a crafty vixen when she chose.

"Now don't look at me like that, Gillie, you know I don't bite my tongue about anything I have to say."

"A Wintercloud trait no doubt."

"I'd say it runs pretty freely in that side of the family." She looked at the clock over the mantle. "Brenda should be here any minute."

Gil smiled at his aunt. She was incorrigible. He remembered hearing his Uncle John say she was a handful. And the last time he talked to Carl, he had complained about her efforts to find him a wife. Although Gil didn't mind her helping him with Brenda, he didn't want her taking it to extremes. He intended to handle his relationship with Brenda in his own way.

He glanced out the living room window in time to see Brenda drive up. "Here she comes, Aunt Shirley."

The older woman slipped into the kitchen.

Gil met Brenda at the door.

"You're looking exceptionally lovely this evening, Brenda."

"Thank you." His nearness and the intense look on his face made her nervous, yet excited her all at the same time. She came prepared to resist him, but like the last time, found it easier to say than to do.

As Brenda moved to take off her coat, Gil eased his hands over her shoulders. She could almost feel the heat from his hands through the thick layers of cloth. Her heart rate sped up at his close proximity.

"W-Where is Shirley?"

"Putting finishing touches on dinner." After hanging up her coat, he said, "Let's go into the living room. She'll call us when dinner is ready."

Gil motioned for Brenda to precede him into the living room, then walked over to his aunt's stereo. He was glad that he had thought to bring several of his tapes. When he finally got this lovely woman to come to his place, he would play some of his more mellow CD's. Getting her there was half the battle, he thought with a smile.

From where she stood Brenda saw that wicked smile on his face and stiffened. Why couldn't he just...

What? Give up? Dream on.

Gil rattled off the titles and the singers on the tapes. "Which one do you want to hear first?"

"You decide."

"Ah, a woman who likes a take-charge man. I like that."

"You would. Play Luther Vandross."

A knowing, sensual smile spread across his lips. Brenda realized that of all the tapes he'd named, the one she selected was a particularly compelling love ballad and added to that the sexy voice of Luther Vandross...

Gil had baited his trap well, she had to admit, but she wasn't about to get ensnared in it.

"I think I'll go in the kitchen and help Shirley."

"There's no need," Shirley answered from the doorway. "I have everything under control. I have some hot spiced cider for you both to enjoy before dinner." She set the tray down on an end table. "That's some nice romantic music you're playing, Gillie. Why don't you move the coffee table, so that you and Brenda can dance."

Brenda wanted to refuse, but what could she say or do that wouldn't sound tactless or ungrateful. It was clear that Aunt and nephew were in perfectly orchestrated collusion.

Gil grinned at Brenda as he moved the table.

She felt like pouring the hot cider over his head.

He quickly swept her in his arms and whispered in her ear. "Relax and enjoy."

Gil noticed as his aunt slipped out of the room that she was wearing a self-satisfied smile on her face.

As Gil drew Brenda closer, she realized that he was a good dancer, his movements smooth yet sensually arousing. She didn't know how he managed to stay respectfully proper while doing it. He obviously possessed many hidden talents.

As they continued to dance, his movements changed, becoming progressively more intimate. He rubbed his cheek against her hair, his thigh against hers, making her quiver with desire.

Brenda knew it was time to put a stop to this, but before she could, Gil slid his hand up and down her back in slow sensuous strokes causing the silk lining of her dress to slide deliciously against her skin.

He whispered in her ear, "The scent you're wearing is very seductive."

"Look, Gil—"

"And your skin is so soft," he murmured, caressing the back of her hand with his thumb.

When she tried to move out of his embrace, he tightened his hold, marrying his chest to her breasts, meshing his hips and hers together, cradling his aroused flesh in her pelvis.

This intimacy was too much for Brenda, and she squirmed out of his hold. Gil's expression said his desire for her had tested his control, making him momentarily oblivious to their surrounding. She guessed that rarely happened to him.

"The way you responded to me, Brenda, I..."

"I'm sorry if I gave you the wrong impression."

"You didn't. Look, Aunt Shirley has prepared a fantastic dinner for us."

As if on cue, Shirley called them to the dining room.

Brenda glanced at Gil across the table, wishing he wouldn't look at her as though he wanted to make love to her.

Whenever her gaze wandered to Shirley, the woman seemed completely oblivious to the undercurrents swirling around her. But Brenda knew better. Shirley was probably jumping for joy at how well her campaign was proceeding.

Brenda glanced back at Gil and saw his lips twitch and knew that he was aware that his aunt's seemingly innocent demeanor was anything but.

"Isn't Aunt Shirley's fricasseed chicken the best you've ever tasted?" he asked, sinking his teeth into a piece.

Brenda nodded as she watched his lips move over the fork. She never thought watching a man eat could be so arousing.

"Now, Gillie—Gil, I don't want Brenda to think I'm fishing for compliments."

Gil ignored Brenda's snicker when his aunt called him her special pet name. "You know you don't mind receiving them, Aunt Shirley."

"How about some dessert, Brenda?"

"I don't think so, Shirley."

"Surely you don't worry about your figure."

"You're wrong, I do. I have to really watch the calories. You see, I have an insatiable sweet tooth."

"That's one secret you should never have revealed to Aunt Shirley."

Brenda flinched at the mentioning of the word *secret*. Did he believe she was a woman of secrets and hoped to uncover them?

Gil noticed the unconscious gesture. What did this beautiful lady have to hide? He was becoming more and more intrigued by her.

"You stop teasing her like that, Gillie."

Gil groaned. "Aunt Shirley, what am I going to do with you?"

"There's nothing you can do. You've been taught to respect your elders. I am who I am and I'm not likely to change at this late date. "

"What you're saying is that I have no choice but to accept your slips?" he bantered back.

"Now you behave yourself." She gazed at her other guest. "Brenda, when are you going to come again?"

Gil shot his aunt a warning look. "Aunt Shirley!"

"I—I think it's time I left," Brenda said, "I'll have to get back to you about dinner, Shirley."

"You think you could squeeze me into your busy schedule?" Gil asked.

"Gil, I—" she sputtered, completely caught off guard.

"Go ahead, Brenda, dear," Shirley encouraged. "I'm sure you haven't taken time to enjoy any of the perks Long Rapids has to offer. There are some, believe it or not. We may be a small town, but we do have a few things in our favor. You need to give us a chance to impress you with them. You won't find a better guide than Gil."

Brenda hesitated, trying to think of an excuse, any excuse to refuse. "I don't know."

"I do." Gil took her hand in his. "Come on. You have to say yes."

Brenda saw the look of challenge in Gil's eyes and the expectant one in his aunt's. She felt ambushed. Surrounded.

"All right. I'll have to let you know when. I really must be going. You don't need to bother walking me to my car, Gil." She eased her hand from his and headed for the hall closet to retrieve her coat.

Gil was there before she could put her arm in the sleeve and brushing her fingers aside, helped her into her coat, his fingers purposely lingering on the lapels.

"About my invitation—" He gazed intently into her eyes.

42

"Gil, please, don't—"

He caressed her cheek with the back of his hand. "I'll need your phone number and address."

Seeing no other way out of it, Brenda reached inside her purse for a pen and paper. She found a grocery receipt and wrote her address on the back.

"Now was that so hard?" he asked in a teasing tone of voice as he stuck the piece of paper into his pocket.

You have no idea how hard, she thought bitterly, but answered, "No."

Gil opened the door. Brenda turned and calling a quick good night to Shirley, fled down the walk to the sanctuary of her car.

As he watched her get in, Gil frowned. He knew she was trying to avoid getting involved with him. He also knew that her reasons probably had nothing to do with her not being attracted to him. In fact, he suspected it was the exact opposite; she was more attracted to him than she wanted to be.

You may as well get used to me in your life, Brenda Davis, he silently added, *because I never give up on anything I want. And sweetheart, I do want you.*

Chapter Six

"You've been as nervous as a cornered cat all morning, Brenda. What's wrong? Every time the phone rings you jump."

"Nothing is wrong, Laura."

When the shop bell sounded, Brenda whipped around. Relief washed over her when she saw that it was only the Perkins sisters entering the Lodge. She never thought she would ever be happy to see those two.

"From the look on your face, you expected Godzilla or King Kong to come crashing through the door."

Brenda had to laugh. "Godzilla or King Kong I could handle."

"But not one handsome, determined lawyer named Gil Jackson," Laura said wryly. "Somehow I don't think he'd be flattered to know that you put him in the same category with monsters. Why does the prospect of him getting in touch with you have you so stressed out?"

"It doesn't," she answered, knowing that it was, but she resisted the urge to confide in Laura about her growing feelings for Gil Jackson. Only her natural wariness where men were concerned prevented her from responding, and as much as she wanted things to be different she couldn't change them. Her feelings were in total chaos with her insecurities.

It was a few hours to closing, and Gil Jackson hadn't come into the Lodge. For some reason Brenda felt a strange sense of disappointment spread over her. The rest of the day was quiet and uneventful. Deciding she would go home and work on her quilt, she went around the Lodge collecting what she needed to create the story part of the quilt she had recently started.

—❖—

Brenda parked her car in the garage and headed up to her apartment. When she got there, she found Gil Jackson waiting beside her door. Her heart lurched in surprise, and she had to admit to herself that seeing him pleased her. She had missed him.

"How long have you been waiting?"

"Not long."

She shifted her bag to her left arm, so she could insert her key in the lock.

"Give me the bag," Gil said reaching to take it. "I would have waited as long as necessary to see you."

She had asked. "Come on in and I'll make us some coffee."

"I certainly won't turn down an offer like that. It's cold out here," he said stretching out the word *cold*.

Brenda hung their coats in the closet. "Make yourself at home."

Stepping into the living room, Gil took in his surroundings at a glance. The apartment was definitely feminine, though not overly so. There were not the usual frills or laces you might expect. Her apartment, although small, was tastefully decorated. He liked the warm welcoming beiges, mauves, and blues. He sat on a comfortable slate-blue overstuffed couch.

In the kitchen, Brenda was all thumbs. Gil's presence seemed to dominate her tiny apartment even though he'd only been in it a matter of minutes. The coffee machine signaled that the coffee was ready. She placed two cups, cream and sugar on a tray and carried it back into the living room. Gil's warm smile disarmed her, and in spite of herself she found herself relaxing.

"What brings you out in the cold to see me?"

Gil grinned. "I think you know the answer to that."

Brenda felt a frisson of excitement jet through her. "Gil, I—"

"You what?" he said, taking the tray from her hands and

45

setting it down on the coffee table.

"Nothing." She gulped. "Now, getting back to the reason for your visit."

"I wanted to ask you out."

"You didn't need to come by to personally extend the invitation. You have my phone number."

"I know, but I wasn't about to give you an excuse to refuse me and then hang up." He caressed her hand.

She inched away from him.

He grasped her wrist preventing her from moving any further away from him. "I want to get to know you better and let you get to know me. We have to start somewhere."

She wanted to tell him that she didn't want to start anywhere with him, but that would be a lie. Somehow she never wanted to lie to him. Strangely enough what he thought of her was important. Right now, she didn't care to think about why it should matter.

"Are you free Saturday evening?"

"And if I said I wasn't?"

"There are six other days in the week. I'd go on to each one until you agreed."

"And if you ran out of days?"

Gil grinned. "You're something else, aren't you, Brenda Davis?"

"How do you mean that?"

"In a purely flattering way, believe me."

"I bet you tell that to all the girls."

"No, I don't actually. Only to the very special ones, and I believe you fit in that category."

"You do have a way with words, Mr. Jackson, but then you're a lawyer."

"My being a lawyer has nothing to do with what is between you and me."

She wanted to believe that, but experience had taught her flattering words were nine times out of ten superficial and empty.

"There is nothing between us."

"Oh, there is all right, but you're too afraid to give it a chance to grow."

"Your coffee is getting cold."

"About as cold as you're turning while the seconds go by."

"I didn't ask you to come here."

"Go out with me Saturday, Brenda," he persisted, ignoring the bite in her voice.

Although she wanted to say no, she longed to say yes even more. "All right, I'll go out with you. Where do you plan on taking me?"

"Don't be so suspicious. Let it be a surprise, woman. Dress up. That's all the hint I'm going to give you. I'll pick you up at six-thirty."

"I'll be ready. Now it really is getting late."

"Is that my cue to hit the road?"

"Look, Gil—"

He pulled her across his lap and kissed her. A sweet, unexpected languor flowed through Brenda and she moaned.

"Oh, baby," he murmured in her ear, his hands sliding over her breasts, stimulating nerve endings, arousing her young body. "Your skin is smooth and warm, like heated silk."

Brenda began to tremble as hot blood flushed through her veins, rushing into all her pleasure points. She'd never felt this way before and didn't know how to handle it. She'd only known one other man's touch and it hadn't begun to compare to how Gil Jackson made her feel.

"Gil, I don't—"

He slipped his tongue inside her mouth and hushed away her words, then, easing his mouth away a little said, "Don't talk, just feel, baby."

He kissed her again, thoroughly banishing any thought she might have had of stopping him. The fire that blazed up to scorch her scared Brenda and she sought to escape before she was severely burned.

He quieted her struggle. "No, not yet, baby."

"Yes! Let me go, Gil."

"In a moment," he groaned and continued to make love to

47

her mouth, while letting his fingers graze a nipple through her blouse.

Her body throbbed, craving more of his lovemaking, but her mind rebelled against the sensations he coaxed so easily from her. It was as though he was exercising control over her body. She'd let a man do that to her once before and wouldn't allow it ever again.

Brenda wriggled free of Gil's embrace and shot off his lap, surging to her feet breathless and shaky.

The haze of passion cleared and Gil saw the frightened look in her eyes.

Not again! screamed through Brenda's mind. It was happening again! She couldn't let it!

"What's the matter, Brenda? I know you want me."

She couldn't deny it, she did want him, but she didn't dare give in to those feelings. "I think you'd better leave."

He wanted to stay, but... "All right. But I still expect you to go out with me on Saturday."

"Maybe we should cancel."

He cupped her chin. "Not a chance, we're going out to dinner," he said firmly, allowing no possibility of debate on the subject by moving his mouth over hers again in a quelling kiss. "I'm a patient man up to a point."

Gil let her go and headed for the door. "Saturday, Brenda. Don't even think about changing your mind." With that he left.

Brenda stood in the middle of the room and closed her eyes. He made her feel completely surrounded, with no avenue of escape. But she knew deep down that she didn't really want to escape him, and that frightened her more than anything.

⟶≈⋐⊱≈⟵

Gil sat at his desk the next morning in his office whistling as he reviewed a long involved legal brief.

"What's got you in such a good mood, cousin? It can't be

your work. Whatever it is share the wealth," Carl teased from the doorway.

"Carl, come on in. Luck is with me, my man. I just happen to have convinced a certain reluctant lady to go out with me."

"Anybody I know? Brenda Davis finally said yes, huh? Shirley said you'd asked her out several times and she had refused."

"You could ask Laura, and we could make it a foursome."

"As for Laura, I really can't—"

"It's only two weeks to the court date. The two of you still haven't made any progress toward—"

"Finding a solution to our problems? No, we haven't." Carl put his hand up. "Now I know what you're going to say, and I don't want to hear it."

"You're going to hurt the one person you claim to love if you don't try harder to find a way to share him with his grandmother."

"You don't think I've tried?"

"Not hard enough, Carl. Call her."

"What am I going to say?"

"How do you feel about Laura?"

Carl walked over to the window and gazed outside. "I care about her."

"I think it's more than that. Why don't you try working a little of that Wintercloud charm on her. I can tell that she's not immune to you. You're both free, normal and over twenty-one."

"What does being free, normal and over twenty-one have to do with it?"

"You're not over the hill because you're forty-five. Laura's only forty-two. You and she could have a fulfilling marriage."

"You're as bad as Shirley."

"In this instance I think Aunt Shirley has the right idea. You need a woman in your life. I know you loved Gabrielle, but she's dead and you're very much alive."

"Gil, I—"

"Why don't you try a little courting, cuz?"

"Advice from on high?"

"Not at all. You're my cousin and I want to see you happy."

Saturday arrived and Gil came to pick Brenda up. She was ready and they left for the restaurant. Minutes later a hostess came to show them to a table by the window, overlooking a small pond.

Heritage House, a restaurant and inn, though contemporary in its approach, remained respectful to the original theme and seemed a natural and appropriate descendant of the way it looked long ago. The hostesses, waiters and waitresses all wore late nineteenth-century period dress.

"This is a surprise!" Brenda exclaimed.

"A pleasant one, I hope. I believe you'll enjoy yourself."

"I love the atmosphere...It's rustic and yet modern at the same time."

"The venison is delicious and the old-fashioned cherry cobbler is excellent, but Aunt Shirley's is to die for."

"I'll let you order for both of us."

He grinned. "A wise choice."

A waiter arrived to take their order.

Gil looked handsome to the bone in his dinner clothes, Brenda observed. Several of the women at other tables were eyeing him appreciatively. He seemed totally oblivious to them.

"Have you lived in Long Rapids all your life, Gil?"

"Yes, I was born and raised here. Fresh out of law school, I moved to Johannesburg to practice law at a prominent African firm for a few years, but I missed home and family and decided to came back."

"And you never married?"

"I did. My wife died two years ago. We have a four-year-old son named David. Right now he's spending time with my twin sister, Carol, and her family in Omaha. Since Monique's death I haven't gone out much. Aunt Shirley has been trying to fix me up with her eternal matchmaking, but I hadn't found a woman who interested me."

When he gazed deeply into Brenda's eyes as if to say "until now," she suddenly felt uneasy. A serious relationship with him was definitely not a subject she wanted to think about. And the fact that he had a son the same age as the one she'd given up only added to her distress.

"What about you, Brenda Davis? Why isn't a gorgeous woman like you married with a couple of kids?"

She looked away. "I guess I never found Mr. Right."

Gil had noticed the way she clenched her jaw when he hinted at being seriously interested in her. He wondered again if she'd had a special relationship that went awry.

"Long Rapids is a little off the beaten track. You don't seem to me to be the small-town type of girl."

"What is 'the small-town type of girl'?"

He smiled. "You've got me there. It's just that—never mind. You're obviously enjoying living here. That's all that counts, I guess. There's a hayride next Saturday. Want to go?"

"A hayride? You've got to be kidding. I thought they only happened in farm towns and in old movies."

"They're real all right and a lot of fun. Come on and go with me."

She laughed. "All right."

"I like to hear you laugh, Brenda. He placed his hand over hers. "You need to do it more often."

Their dinner arrived. Just as they began to eat, Brenda saw a hostess showing Carl and Laura into one of the restaurant's private dining rooms. "I don't believe it!"

"What don't you believe?" Gil asked, following her line of vision. When he reached the end of it, he smiled. "I see my cousin is doing what I suggested."

"Buttering Laura up for the kill." Brenda shot to her feet. "I should have known you would resort to anything to see that your cousin gets what he wants."

"Just what are you accusing me of?"

"You know damn well what. I was beginning to think you were different. It was all an illusion. Believe me, I won't make that mistake again. Please take me home."

"Sit down, Brenda." He put his hand on her arm.

"If you won't take me home, I'll get a taxi."

"I said sit down," he said firmly.

Brenda jerked her arm out of his grasp. She saw that people were beginning to stare, so she did as he said. "I don't want to stay here with you," she gritted out.

"I want to know why you're going off like this. What's wrong with Carl taking Laura out to dinner? You call yourself her friend. Don't you want them to work things out?"

"Of course I do. To your first question, there is nothing wrong with Laura going out with him if it isn't the first step in a master plan you and he cooked up to get Jon-Marc away from her."

"You really think I'd—I guess you do. Do you have this low opinion of me in particular or all lawyers and men in general?"

"You lawyers are all alike underneath. Winning is all you care about. Not the people you hurt in the process."

"What happened to make you so bitter, Brenda?"

"I don't want to discuss me, it's Laura I'm concerned about."

"I think it's more than that."

"It's not that I don't want them to work things out. It's Carl's methods and your motives."

"My motives? You think they're suspect!"

"Just take me home, Gil."

"I think I'd better. We're going to have to talk about this."

"There's nothing to talk about. I don't think we should see each other again."

"I don't happen to agree. What's between Laura and Carl is their business, but what's between you and me is ours."

"You're entitled to your opinion, just as I'm entitled to mine."

"You're right about that. You may as well eat, Brenda, because I don't intend to let this delicious food go to waste."

She wanted to pitch it over his head and stalk out of there, but, instead picked up her fork and began to eat.

For all the justice they did to the meal, Gil wished they'd left. Watching Brenda's stiff, unbendable attitude made his stomach churn. What was the matter with the woman? He began to realize what a challenge she was going to be. Did he want to pursue her? The answer was yes.

They drove up in front of Brenda's apartment building. She unfastened her seat belt and hastened to get out of the car.

Gil put a hand on her arm. "Wait. I'm coming in with you."

"I don't think that's a good idea."

"You don't give an inch, do you? Well, that's just too bad because I'm coming in with you anyway."

Brenda shrugged, and pulling away from him, got out of the car and started up the walkway.

Gil sprinted to catch up to her. "Brenda, I don't want to be at odds with you."

"I don't see that there's any choice."

"I believe there is. Why don't you tell me the reason you hate all lawyers?"

By the time they made it to her apartment, Brenda felt reasonably certain that he wouldn't leave without an explanation. She unlocked the door and moved aside to let him in. She turned on the light, then took his coat.

"What happened to me is personal and I don't care to go into the details. Suffice it to say, I've had dealings with lawyers who for their own selfish motives betrayed me. They pretended to care about me and my situation, but the bottom line is that they cared only about the rewards they would reap at my expense."

"They sound like unethical bastards. But all lawyers aren't like that."

"Yeah, right."

"You can't tar all lawyers with the same brush."

"Can't I? Look, Gil, I don't want to get into word games with you. No matter what you say, I won't change my mind about that."

"What did these lawyers do?"

"It's over and done with. Let's forget it."

"Obviously you haven't and can't. There's a man who hurt you in this too, isn't there? Whatever happened between the two of you has nothing to do with us."

"I keep telling you there is no *us*."

When Gil reached for her, his hands sent shivers of passion quivering through her. She twisted in his arms, arching her body, trying to evade the effect he was having on her. But there was no way she could avoid him. Gil drew her closer, then lowered his mouth to hers. His tongue was a velvet paint-brush tracing the sweet fullness of her lips. He was so persuasive, she opened to him, allowing him to stroke freely.

Her thoughts floated and her senses reeled.

He drew her inches away from him. "And you say there is nothing between us. Stop lying to yourself, Brenda. And please stop lying to me."

Dazed by her response to him despite her anger, Brenda pulled out of his embrace. "I'm not lying. Anyone can be seduced."

"You admit that you can be, then?"

"What's the point of this conversation? We simply aren't right for each other, that's all. Period. Can't you let it go at that?"

"No, I can't. I think we *are* right for each other. Do you want me to prove it to you?"

"Because you can make me respond to you doesn't prove anything; only that we are two sexually healthy people."

"It goes beyond that and you know it. I'm not going to give up on you, Brenda, so you may as well get used to it. I'm here to stay, baby. I'll pick you up on Saturday. You're going on that hayride with me."

"Gil, maybe—"

"Later, Brenda."

Chapter Seven

Brenda couldn't believe she had agreed to go on a hayride of all things. Her very sophisticated social-conscious mother would be scandalized. Smiling at the thought, she walked over to the closet and pulled out an old pair of jeans and a big white, cable-knit pullover sweater. Brenda had to search through the bottom of her closet to find the only pair of western boots she owned and had worn just once.

She glanced in the mirror wondering what to do with her hair. She ended up plaiting it into a single French braid. Brenda glanced at the clock. Gil would be there in a few minutes.

How would it be between them since their last date? She hadn't mentioned seeing Carl and Laura at Heritage House to Laura. She entertained the hope that her friend would volunteer the information, but since she hadn't, Brenda assumed that nothing was resolved or that she just didn't want to discuss it.

The ringing of the doorbell brought her out of her absorbing thoughts, and she went to answer it. A grinning Gil stood framed in the doorway.

"You ready?"

"What if I told you I was allergic to hay? What then?"

"I'd say we would have to make a pit stop at the drugstore on the way to the farm."

"I should have known you'd have an answer for that. I suppose if I were to say I wasn't ready, you'd drag me out."

"Kicking and screaming." He smiled, tilting his western hat at a rakish angle. "Since you're such a smart woman, ma'am, I'm sure those tactics won't be necessary."

She wanted to be indifferent to this man, but he wouldn't let her. Darn him. He was nothing short of gorgeous in his western boots and expertly cut jeans, which molded his flat stomach, lean hips, muscular thighs and calves to perfection. He had on a red plaid shirt, brown leather vest and sheepskin jacket.

"Let's call a truce and just enjoy ourselves today, Brenda. Okay?"

"Okay."

He led her outside.

"If you're looking for my car, you won't find it. I borrowed my cousin's Land Cruiser."

"I still can't believe I let you talk me into this."

"We'll have fun, you'll see."

And they did. When the hay wagon finally returned to the farm, Brenda was chilled but felt exhilarated. A crowd of people were playing and kidding around in the barn. Gil found an unoccupied corner, tossed Brenda into a hayloft, and joined her.

"I'll get straw in my mouth, you idiot."

"Idiot? *Moi*? Oh, you're going to pay, woman." He wrestled her down and drew her hands high above her head. He molded their bodies together, chest to chest, hip to hip, thigh to thigh. As he gazed into her eyes, his features eased into a sensually arresting expression.

"Gil—"

He pulled straw from her hair and brushed a stray stalk away from her mouth, then hungrily covered her lips with a devouring kiss. He groaned. Her womanly scent mixed with the heady fragrance of her perfume was driving him crazy. "Brenda, you're so fine, girl."

His words not only made her forget any thought she had of resisting him, but made her respond with reckless abandon to his kiss. He nuzzled her neck and the sensitive area behind her ear. Her moan of pleasure echoed in his head. Suddenly Brenda felt him stiffen and clear his throat.

"I think we'd better suspend this until another time."

"Huh?" Brenda was momentarily disoriented.

"As much as I'd like to have a roll in the hay with you, unfortunately we're not alone," he said, looking around to find knowing smiles and several pairs of curious eyes riveted on them.

Brenda's face flushed with embarrassment, and she pushed Gil away.

"Just when I thought I could find the proverbial needle in a haystack," he said, smiling into those curious faces.

"You're crazy, if you think they bought your explanation." Brenda laughed.

Rising to his feet, he pulled her up. "Mr. Owens is probably just about ready to start the barn dance."

"The what?"

"The barn dance. It's not your usual run-of-the-mill barn dance. This one has a little soul added to it."

"How is that possible?"

"You'll see. This is a special occasion. We have a couple of celebrities here: Bonnie Raitt and Delbert McClinton."

"I see what you mean. I like her and that duet she does with Delbert McClinton. It's a great combination of country and soul. You didn't tell me that anyone famous was going to be here."

"Bonnie has relatives in Long Rapids. Once a year, she comes here to perform. I hear music now. I think they're about ready to start the sing-along."

The singers performed *A Good Woman Needs a Good Man*. Brenda felt as though Gil had arranged that particular song just for them.

"I know what you're thinking, but I didn't, I promise. Scout's honor," he said, raising two fingers to his forehead.

"Scout's honor, huh? Were you ever a Boy Scout?"

"Actually, no," he said sheepishly.

Brenda shook her head and laughed. The man was incorrigible.

They dug into the food. There was every kind of barbecued meat, baked beans, potato salad, and many different desserts ranging from pumpkin bread to apple pie. There was an apple-bobbing contest and a taffy pull for the kids.

"I've never done anything carefree like this in my life."

"I said you'd enjoy yourself," he said in his best country accent. "Did I lie? If I tell you a mule is going to lay an egg you'd better start building a nest."

Brenda giggled. "Where did you ever hear a corny saying like that?"

"I'll have you know I learned it at my granddaddy's knee. It's one of his favorite sayings."

"I would like to meet him."

"Don't worry, you will. He's still alive and kicking."

Brenda had never met either of her own grandfathers. One had died years before she was born and other the year she was born. She was sure they had been nothing like she imagined Gil's to be. His family sounded like hearty, down-to-earth kind of people if his Aunt Shirley was any example.

"What's going on in that pretty head of yours, darlin'?" he drawled.

"Nothing. I'm having a good time."

"It's a pleasure watching you loosen up. Now if I could change your mind about a few other things—"

"You can't. So don't even try, all right?"

The stubborn, determined look on her face warned him to go slow, but he was a perverse man when challenged. It was buried in his genes, he guessed. "Don't you know by now that I'll try anything to get my way with you?"

She was sure that he would do just as he said, and she knew she would have to do everything she could to see that he didn't succeed.

"I'm ready to go."

He grinned wickedly. "Sounds like a good idea to me. Your place or mine? Do we listen to music? Watch videos? TV? What?"

"Gil."

"Don't tell me you're not going to invite me in?"

She could tell by looking in his eyes that he knew exactly

what she was thinking. If she didn't invite him in, it would make her seem ungrateful. Talking about laying on guilt trips. She guessed it was the lawyer in him.

During the ride back to her apartment, Gil tried to draw Brenda out by getting her involved in conversation. But most of the answers she gave him were monosyllabic ones.

Brenda's mind was steeped in the realities of a past she'd tried so hard to forget, but knew she never would in a million years.

"Though I insist on walking you to your door, I'm not coming in with you, Brenda."

She looked at him in surprise. "I don't understand you."

"You will in time."

Minutes later Brenda watched the Land Cruiser pull away from the curb and wondered what he was up to. He could have insisted on coming in with her, but he hadn't. Gil Jackson had her confused. He made no secret of the fact that he wanted her. She had been so sure that seduction was going to play a big part in his strategy. Why hadn't he come in?

He hadn't mentioned anything about wanting to see her again either. She'd been telling herself that was what she wanted, especially knowing that he had a young son. And the possibility that a relationship between them could become a reality wasn't something she wanted to think about.

All day Sunday Brenda worked on the squares for her new quilt. She found herself putting Laura and Carl's situation into it. She used beads and feathers, cut out gray storm clouds, added spears and a painted African mask denoting Carl's dual heritage in one square.

The tall Indian figure of Carl Wintercloud began to take shape. Why was she doing this? Why was the situation he and Laura were going through preying so heavily on her mind that she felt she had to exorcise it by unfolding it in the quilt?

She started her story quilts with the people involved using

things from their heritage and background. She realized that she needed more information about Carl. Outside of asking him, Gil or Shirley would have to provide it. To deal with either one of them could be a sticky proposition.

And what about Laura?

Laura had been walking around with her head in the clouds for days since she'd had dinner with Carl. Could she be weakening, changing because of Carl's and Gil's influence? She couldn't possibly be considering letting them talk her into giving up her grandson!

The situation mirrored her own more and more. Brenda knew she couldn't stand by and let Laura go through the same kind of pain she had, experiencing the regret and guilt over a wrong decision.

Monday morning, shortly after opening the Lodge, Brenda left the shelves she'd been straightening and walked over to where Laura was dusting the memorabilia rack.

"How are things going between you and Carl Wintercloud? I know it isn't any of my business, but—"

Laura smiled. "It's all right. I found that there are depths to the man. I'm beginning to understand his feelings about Jon-Marc, his heritage, the plight of the nearly extinct Native American and their fight to preserve it in the present and future generations."

"I see they've been brainwashing you. Surely you're not thinking about—"

"Giving Carl custody?" Laura finished. "No, but maybe there is a way we can both share our grandson without fighting. I don't have anything specific in mind yet, but—"

"Short of marrying the man I don't see how—surely you're not considering doing *that*!"

"Marriage."

Brenda could tell by Laura's expression it wasn't a novel idea. "You don't have to go that far unless you're falling in love with him. Are you?"

"I—am attracted to him, maybe more than attracted. But marriage—"

"Has he hinted around that he might be considering it?"

"No, but Gil believes—"

"Gil!" Brenda's eyes narrowed with suspicion.

"He didn't say it flat out, but he links us together in a familial way every time we talk."

"Subtle subterfuge, I'd say."

"It would solve our problem. That way we could both oversee Jon-Marc's future."

"Surely, you aren't serious about this, Laura?"

"Carl hasn't even asked me, Brenda."

"Somehow I think he will. He wants his grandson, and I think he and Gil will go to any lengths to get him, even if they have to sacrifice you in the process."

"Marriage isn't a sacrifice, Brenda. There is still such a thing as a marriage of convenience."

Brenda didn't want to argue the point with her. After work, she intended to go see Gil Jackson and give him a piece of her mind. A very large piece.

Laura wasn't thinking straight, but she, Brenda, was going to protect her friend's interests. Didn't Laura know that once she was married to Carl Wintercloud he could take Jon-Marc from her should things not work out between them. Brenda was sure Gil hadn't mentioned that possibility to Laura.

Brenda had phoned Gil's office before going there to find out the time of his last appointment. She arrived just as Carl Wintercloud was leaving.

"Miss Davis," he said politely.

"Mr. Wintercloud," she answered frostily.

He frowned. "You don't like me very much, do you?"

"I don't like anyone who hurts my friends. I consider Laura my best friend."

"I'm not seeking to hurt her. I just want to be a part of my grandson's life."

"So you and Gil have cooked up a scheme to get you what

you want."

"Miss Davis—"

"I'll handle this, Carl," Gil said from the doorway of his private office. "I'll get back to you later in the week."

Carl hesitated. "All right." He glanced at Brenda. "Miss Davis, the last thing I want to do is hurt Laura." Then he left.

"If you would come into my office, Brenda." Gil waved his hand for her to precede him inside. "You can go on home, Denise," he said to his secretary. "I won't be needing you for anything else this evening."

Denise nodded. "Let me take your coat, Miss Davis."

"I'll do that," Gil said and watched as Denise left his office.

Brenda handed her coat to Gil, and he hung it up on a coat-rack by the door.

"Sit down, Brenda."

As Gil circled his desk, she did a quick study of her surroundings. It wasn't at all what she expected. His office was very utilitarian. The furniture was sturdy but in good taste. The walls were done in warm brown colors. Wall-to-wall bookshelves lining the room were filled with many bound volumes of law books. His desk, which dominated the center of the room, stacked with files and reports. A floor-to-ceiling window behind his desk took up one entire wall.

He waited until she took her seat before sitting down in his chair. "All right, what brings you here, Brenda?"

"I'm on to you and Carl Wintercloud, and I won't let you get away with it."

"Get away with what?"

"You know good and well what."

His brows arched. "Are you accusing me of something?"

"You're absolutely right I am. I expected better from you than this, Gil. I was beginning to trust you."

"What you think I've done has changed your mind, I take it?"

She shot to her feet. "Leave Laura alone, Gil. That baby is where he belongs."

Gil rose from his chair. "Carl has as much right to that

child as Laura does. I'm only trying to help them work something out that can be beneficial to everyone concerned."

"You make it sound so simple, when you know it isn't. Laura is alone and vulnerable. You and Carl are taking unfair advantage of that fact."

"You don't know what you're talking about." He circled his desk and came to stand in front of her.

"You slick lawyers are all alike and—"

Gil grasped her upper arms. "Are you accusing me of using unethical means to—"

"If the glove fits."

"It's not really Laura's problem that has you so ticked off, is it, Brenda?"

"I don't know what you're talking about. Of course it is."

"I don't think so." His voice softened. "I think you've taken more than just a friendly concerned interest in this. You're making it personal."

Brenda flinched, looking away.

"I'm right, aren't I?"

"I just don't want to see Laura suffer."

"Like you did? Or somebody close to you. Tell me about it, Brenda. Get it out in the open so we can deal with it."

"There's nothing to deal with. I've said what I came here to say." She jerked out of his hold and headed for the coatrack to retrieve her coat.

"Wait!"

"I don't want to talk about this anymore."

He put a hand on the door. "I'm not letting you leave here until you do. Now come back and sit down."

Brenda bit her lip to still its trembling. She felt trapped. There was no way out except past Gil. He was a lawyer. She was sure he wouldn't understand if she tried to explain.

"I've had dealings with two lawyers, both of whom betrayed me."

"You've mentioned them before. And?"

Tears slid down her face. "I just can't go into it. I can't."

Gil pulled her into his arms, guessing that it must have

63

been a traumatic experience if it still hurt her this much.

"Brenda, did you turn these men in to the Bar Association?"

"No, they were too smart for that. I can't get into this."

"All right, it can wait. I can see you're in no condition to talk rationally on the subject. But don't think this is the end of it. I do intend to have some answers from you, Brenda. Are you—can you drive yourself home?"

"Yes, I'll be all right."

"I'll call later to make sure you got home okay."

"It's not necessary."

"I think it is."

Gil walked her out to her car and helped her inside. "Take care, drive carefully, Brenda. Later."

Brenda sat in her living room listening to music, thinking about what had happened in Gil's office. She was so vulnerable to this man and she couldn't understand why. She'd tried not to get involved, not to encourage him, but it hadn't done any good. There seemed to be a chemistry working between them that had nothing to do with their personal lives and wasn't influenced by her past.

She was attracted to Gil Jackson despite her aversion to his profession, and despite the fact that he had a four-year-old son. Knowing he was a lawyer should have stopped her in her tracks, but it hadn't. She should have been wary of his easy charm and handsome good looks. She was wary, but not wary soon enough apparently. She'd been charmed by a man like that once before and was evidently still susceptible. Lord, she couldn't let herself be drawn into another relationship like that, but how was she going to put a stop to it?

The phone rang.

"Brenda."

"Gil."

"I told you I'd call. Are you all right, baby?"

She wished he wouldn't call her that. "I'm fine."

"I've been doing some thinking since you left my office and I had a talk with my cousin. We decided that both you and Laura need to understand a few things. Carl is inviting both of you out to the reservation."

"The reservation?"

"Yes. We think that you both need to become familiar with our shared heritage."

"What does that have to do with Jon-Marc?"

"It's a part of his heritage too. Now will you come out there with me on Saturday?"

"All right."

"Wear jeans and your boots. I'll come by Saturday morning at eight."

"Why so early?"

"Will I be cutting short your beauty sleep? Carl and I want you and Laura to get a fair overall view of Indian life from the start of a routine day."

"You've really got me curious."

"Until tomorrow, Brenda."

Shirley came into the Lodge the next morning and walked over to where Brenda stood arranging a quilt on the display rack.

"I'm so happy to hear that you're going out to the reservation. It happens to be one of the Saturdays I spend with the children."

Evidently Gil couldn't wait to spread the word. She was glad Shirley would be there as a kind of buffer between them. "Gil and Carl think it's a good idea for Laura and me to go."

"It is, believe me. My father was half Chippewa and my mother an eighth Kiowa. Gil's mother is my youngest sister. I can remember living on the reservation when I was a little girl. Times have changed since then, but the life of the Native American Indian still isn't an easy one.

65

"And Brenda, you need to understand that part of our heritage. It's a part of Gil's, too, if a smaller part than Carl's. A visit to the reservation will help both you and Laura understand the men in your lives."

"I can't see how going there will change anything," Brenda argued.

Shirley refrained from saying anything more on the subject. "I think I'll take a look in the miscellaneous box for things to decorate my wedding ring quilt."

The word *wedding* made Brenda nervous. It was one institution she wanted no part of. It implied commitment, family. Children.

She had wanted that once. She'd wanted it more than anything in her life. It was a dream that changed into a nightmare. Her life had evolved into a living hell because she dared to make her dreams come true.

She was into reality now. She no longer believed in dreams or love. If you didn't get involved, you didn't get hurt. That was the course she intended to follow.

A mental picture of Gil flitted through her mind, and she shook her head to clear it. Men always complicated a woman's life. The last thing she needed in her life at this point was complications. And she spelled Gil Jackson with a capital *C.*

"I've found what I need." Shirley held up two giant flat rhinestone cloths that emulated the diamonds on the female ring, which are meant to denote forever. The wedding rings of the male and female dominate the center of the wedding ring quilt.

Brenda rang up the sale, then watched as Shirley left the Lodge minutes later. Shirley Edwards was a born matchmaker, which meant that she believed in happily ever after. Brenda knew that life was rarely that ideal. She had come to realize it early in her adult years, and she was unlikely to forget the lesson she had learned.

Chapter Eight

Carl and Laura were already in the backseat of the Land Cruiser when Brenda climbed inside Saturday morning. She thought it odd that Gil should be doing the driving since the vehicle belonged to his cousin, and he was riding in there with them. She struck up a conversation with Carl and Laura before seating herself on the front seat beside Gil.

"You sure your eyes are open?" Gil teased Brenda. "It is kind of early in the morning."

"I'll have you know I've been up for hours."

"I think you've put me in my place."

"I believe she has, cousin," Carl quipped.

It was a quiet half-hour ride out to Leech Lake Reservation.

Gil smiled as he took in the signs of autumn that had already begun to manifest themselves. It was his favorite time of year. The days were beginning to shorten and the night to lengthen. There was every indication that there would be a sunny fall. This day reminded him of the times he'd spent on the reservation with his cousin when he was a little boy. Carl was ten years older and had made sure his younger cousin knew that part of their shared heritage from a realistic standpoint.

The sugar in the maple trees they passed was turning the leaves a rich red. In a few weeks the ash, walnut and oaks would start to shed their leaves.

Brenda too found herself caught up in the change of seasons. It reminded her of the times she'd spent with her aunt Bertha in Delaware. The atmosphere was similar, the smell of autumn in the air, bringing with it a kind of excitement. She

67

was actually looking forward to going to the reservation.

As they entered the reservation grounds which were partially made up of woods, Gil knew that soon it would become a tapestry of rich ambers, golds, reds, and greens with acorns popping underfoot.

A glowing light would fill the woods and drift down from the canopy of tree leaves above. Deeper into the season the sharp-sweet scent of lobed heptica would be wafting through the air. White-tailed deer would add splashes of fall color to balance the picture.

Several miles into the reservation grounds, they came to a gate and Gil waved to an old Indian doing carpentry work on the fence. When they arrived at the main building, Shirley Edwards and a group of girls between the ages of six and eleven came out on the porch. They were dressed in colorful shirts and jeans. Their dark braids gleamed in the soft early morning light. Copper-tinged faces ranging from varying shades of pale brown to Gil's rich brown coloring smiled back at them.

Brenda could see how the mixing with different races had diluted the look of the Indian. Brenda began to understand why Carl Wintercloud was so determined to have his grandson, to instill in him what he knew of their disappearing culture. She could tell by the expression on Laura's face, she had reached the same understanding.

Brenda wondered what effect this visit would have on the situation between Laura and Carl. When she glanced at Gil, she saw that he was studying her just as intently.

"I'm glad to see you, Brenda, and you too, Laura," Shirley exclaimed. "I think you both will be interested in seeing what the girls and I do."

Gil grinned. "Go ahead and show them, Aunt Shirley. Carl and I will wait until you come back to begin the tour."

A few minutes later Brenda couldn't help admiring the quilts in the crafts building Shirley used to teach quilt making to the girls. She showed them the progress the children had made in their quilting and the varying stages of completion.

"The children have such vivid imaginations. A lot of their ideas are wonderfully creative. I always remind them to include their heritage and never forget their Indian blood and to always be proud of it. I feel such a sense of accomplishment when I leave here."

"Jon-Marc is a part of this," Laura said absently.

"Yes he most certainly is. It's important that he know it and a lot more. Carl and Gil are probably growing impatient to show you around the rest of the reservation. They want you both to have a clearer picture of the life of the Native American."

Brenda and Laura left the building feeling differently than when they walked in.

"Are you ready to begin?" Carl asked.

"Yes we are," Brenda answered for them both, eager to see more.

"I think we should start with the school," Gil suggested, holding out his hand to Brenda.

"That's a good idea." Carl took Laura's hand and followed close behind them.

Gil pointed out the new modern elementary, junior high, and high school buildings.

"When I attended here, those buildings were little more than shacks," Carl said.

Gil cleared his throat. "Carl and I are gathering funds and supporters as well as contributing our own money and time to the construction of a trade school here on the reservation. I make myself available for any legal advice that might be needed."

Brenda said, "I'm impressed."

"So am I," Laura added, a dawning respect for Carl Wintercloud evident in her voice and her eyes.

As they walked, Carl talked about the conditions around them.

"The landscape is harsh in places and living was very hard. Scorching summer heat, brutal winter cold, and isolation from the other communities made the reservation an even tougher place to live.

"My father, as our tribe's chief, fought against overwhelming odds. Unemployment was high. And according to independent studies today, it has reached eighty percent or higher on some reservations. As a result, depression, alcoholism, and child abuse, both physical and psychological, are commonplace."

Both Brenda and Laura were stunned by that revelation. They had no idea. Brenda found herself feeling compassion for Carl Wintercloud as well as respect.

She felt ashamed of some of the things she'd thought and said about this man who was Gil's blood cousin. She glanced at Gil. He was a part of this in every way. He obviously didn't give just lip service. He and his cousin were making a difference.

She realized that he was not like the lawyers she'd had dealings with. He was an ethical lawyer and a compassionate man. And she had a new respect for him and his ideals. She asked herself how she could have been so wrong about him.

Because you have your own prejudices and let them get in the way.

"It used to be a place where children had little hope for a better life," Carl continued, "but not anymore, if Gil and I can help it."

"We want you to see the new hospital," Gil said proudly.

Brenda and Laura followed him and Carl down a dirt road. After several yards, the road took a twist. When the land dipped slightly, Gil took Brenda's elbow and Carl, Laura's. Ahead of them was a modern medical facility. There were men paving the road leading up to it.

"The road should be completely paved in a few weeks," Carl explained, pride glowing in his dark eyes.

"What my cousin failed to say is that he is using men from his timber harvesting and construction businesses to complete the work. Everything you see here is the result of his efforts to make a difference for our people.

"Many of the women of the tribe refused to go to a hospital to have their babies and the others with health problems would not go to them either, so he vowed to change that attitude by building one on the reservation, staffing it with people of Indian descent. Carl has kept that promise."

Gil pointed out several other projects underway. By the time they had finished the tour, both Laura and Brenda had different opinions about the men in their lives.

Gil drove to Carl's house to get his own car to take Brenda home. Brenda watched Carl and Laura. She suspected that something monumental had happened between them, and wondered where her relationship with Gil was headed.

—⋙⬧⋘—

Gil parked his car in front of Brenda's apartment building and turned to her. "So what do you think of my cousin and me? Do you still find us suspect?"

"You know I don't."

"Do I?"

"Look, Gil, I know you have every reason to be put out with me and my attitude, but there are reasons."

"I know there are. One day you'll progress to the point where you can confide in me."

"How do you find time to be so involved in the Indian improvements?"

"I'm not just an advocate for the rights of Americans of African descent and Indian rights. I'm an advocate for civil rights. Period. Don't you see that all people's rights need to be protected, not just Indian, Black, or Hispanic. All people have rights. Don't let me get started, I've been known to get extremely long-winded."

Brenda was beginning to see more than Gil knew. She was beginning to see that all lawyers were not alike. And all men weren't like the one who had nearly destroyed her five years ago. Gil Jackson was special and he was interested in her. Because of knowing him, so much had happened to change her.

71

What about his child? If their relationship evolved to the point of marriage, would she be able to handle raising his son knowing hers was forever lost to her? Could she be the kind of mother the boy needed?

"What are you thinking?" Gil asked.

"How wrong I've been about so many things."

"You know this calls for a celebration. I want to take you to St. Paul to a special supper club I know. The owner is a friend of mine. Andre will give us the royal treatment. You want to go there and party with me, baby?"

"Are you sure you want to take me out after the way I've acted toward you and your cousin?"

He leaned over and kissed her. "I wouldn't have asked if I didn't want to, girlfriend. Get dressed up, I intend to wow you, woman."

It had been so long since anyone had done that. And so long since she wanted to be wowed.

"All right."

"I'll come for you at seven. It's an hour and a half drive to St. Paul."

"I want to apologize again for misjudging you."

He grinned. "As long as you now know that I'm for real, I forgive you."

Brenda rushed out to buy a new dress and accessories after leaving the reservation. Later she lay on her bed, her hands stacked behind her head, thinking long and hard about her life. It was shaping up differently than she'd originally planned, and that was because of Gil. He refused to let it remain ordered and predictable. He was the excitement she needed to feel like a woman again.

All her fears and insecurities were still there, but relegated to the back of her mind, where they belonged. Since meeting Gil she was more like the woman she used to be. She felt freer somehow.

How would he feel once he knew all there was to know about her? She had made some serious mistakes in the past and paid a very high price for them. She'd sacrificed her soul, and she would feel the pain for the rest of her life.

Was it fair to inflict herself on him with all her hangups? If their relationship reached the point where she had to tell him everything, would she be able to do it?

Brenda slipped into a sleek black dress for her evening out with Gil. It was a short, figure-hugging fine wool-knit with silver-sequined peach-colored roses around the neckline of the dress. Brenda knew she looked good in it and she was sure Gil would like it. She decided to wear her hair down in a slightly curly style.

Brenda had put the finishing touches to her makeup when she heard a knock at the door. She wet her lips and, swallowing down her nervousness, went to answer the door. When she opened it, she found Gil leaning against the jamb.

"You look fantastic, Ms. Davis." He straightened, the gleam in his eyes clearly revealing that he liked what he saw.

"So do you," Brenda murmured as she took in the handsomeness of her date. The front of Gil's coat was open, revealing his black tux. And Brenda had to admit that he was fine in it. The white material of his shirt contrasted attractively with the deep brown-copper coloring of his skin. His eyes shone black as onyx, passion sparkling in their depths.

"Are you ready to go?"

"Yes, I am. Would you like to come in and—"

"Don't tempt me, Brenda, or we won't make it to St. Paul."

Brenda smiled. "Am I that much of a distraction?"

"You know you are. Now get your coat. Please."

The Candlelight Club was everything Gil promised it

would be, Brenda thought when they walked through its elegant frosted-glass double doors. A giant chandelier dominated the ceiling of the huge dining area. The artificial candles in it looked liked the real thing. The soft glow it gave off lent the impression of pampered royalty.

There were candelabra sconces and tables strategically spaced along the circular wall. Antique-lace tablecloths covered each table and on them white candles sat in crystal-and-brass holders. The chairs were covered with beige silk upholstery. The champagne-colored carpet beneath their feet sank as they walked across it.

The decor was most definitely romantic. The ever-present sound of glasses clinking together gave the impression that a continuous celebration was going on. The romantic music ranged from mellow jazz to sultry ballads and contemporary songs. A subtle scent of jasmine filled the air. Everything about the place spelled romance with a capital *R*.

The waiters wore silk shirts, black satin cumberbands with tuxedo pants, and waitresses wore gaily colored organza blouses with black silk sashes at the waist of slim tuxedo skirts, with black net stockings complementing the outfits.

Gil and Brenda were immediately ushered to a table near one of the bay windows overlooking a lake.

Gil laughed when Brenda commented on the lake. "Lake? The majority of Minnesotans call any puddle of water a lake, therefore giving credence to the state's nickname 'land of ten thousand lakes.'"

"You have no imagination."

"Oh, but I do. Right now I'm imagining how you would feel in my arms when we dance. Care to dance?"

"Don't you think we should order first?"

"You can't blame a guy for being eager to snuggle with you, Brenda."

"Are you really that eager?"

"Honey, yes," he said, caressing her cheek with his fingers, his gaze as soft as his touch.

Brenda gasped at the intimacy of the gesture. Her heart

racing, she found herself completely carried away by the contact as a tingling sensation started in the pit of her stomach.

A waiter came to take their order, breaking the spell. "Would you like to start with Crème Maria, sir?"

"Celery Soup." Gil glanced at Brenda.

"Sounds wonderful."

"Would you like for me to order the rest of our dinner?" he asked her.

"Yes, please do. My French is rusty, I'm afraid."

"They do have menus in English."

"No. I prefer to let you order. It's more romantic to order in French." She smiled at him.

"When you smile like that, you take my breath away." He cleared his throat. "Do you like seafood?"

"Yes, I—nothing." She almost told him she was a native Chicagoan and was used to it. It was the first time she'd felt this easy in a man's company since—

Gil finished giving the order to the waiter. "We'll have the tossed green salad. Perch à la meunière. Stuffed mushrooms. And a white Bordeaux. For desert Pineapple Crown."

"Pineapple Crown?" Brenda asked.

"It's a gelatin mold made of pineapples, crushed strawberries, and champagne."

"Sounds fabulous."

"Oh, it is. Wait'll you taste it." He spoke to the waiter. "Is Andre available?" The man nodded. "Would you ask him to come to our table, please?"

"Yes, sir." Taking the menus, he walked off.

"Is André from France?"

Gil laughed. "No. He was born and raised in New Orleans. We met in college when I attended LSU. We've kept in touch through the years."

"How did he end up in St. Paul?"

"It's a long story." Gil glanced over her shoulder. "Here he comes."

"Gil, it's so good to see you. It's been a while. André's eyes glittered when he looked at Brenda. "Who may I ask is this ravishing creature with you?"

"André Varnoux, Brenda Davis."

"André." Brenda noticed that for a moment Gil seemed uncomfortable and wondered why. She flashed André a smile. He was a handsome, dark-skinned Creole of average height with magnetic brown eyes and a warm, charming smile.

"Have you ordered?" he asked.

"Yes, we have, André," Gil said. "Please join us."

"I would like to, but I'm with a very charming lady at the moment."

"Anyone I know?"

"No, she's new in town."

"Have you staked your claim already?"

"Why do you ask? Are you worried that I might stake a claim on this lovely woman beside you?"

"No woman is safe around you, André"

"I'm flattered to hear this." André grinned. "Enjoy your dinner. And I'll see you both later."

Brenda watched him weave his way between the tables. "He is a very charming man, isn't he?"

"Has he charmed you, Brenda?"

She gazed into his eyes. "Not as much as you have, Gil."

"I'm relieved to hear it." He smiled. "Ah, our dinner has arrived."

❖

"The dinner was everything you said it would be," Brenda said later.

"They're playing our song."

"Our song?"

"Yes." He pulled her to her feet.

"I wasn't aware that we had one."

"Oh, weren't you? *Forever, For Always, For Love*, by Luther Vandross."

As he drew Brenda closer, his nearness made her senses whirl. She found herself becoming totally entranced by this man. Dancing with him was a purely sensual experience. She practically floated back to the table after the song ended.

As soon as they were seated, a wine steward came to the table.

"We'd like a bottle of your best champagne," Gil said.

After they'd gone over the wine list and the man left, Brenda whispered, " Do you think we should?"

"The point of the evening was to celebrate. If it will make you feel better I'll have them pack it in ice, so it'll still be cold when we get back to Long Rapids. All right?"

"All right."

Chapter Nine

As they drove back to Long Rapids, Brenda thought about how the evening had progressed. Her heartbeat quickened at the thought of Gil and that bottle of champagne chilling in the styrofoam ice bucket in the trunk. There was no way she could let him drive home if they drank the entire magnum of champagne, which meant that he would be spending the night. She wondered if she was really ready for this.

Gil noticed her preoccupation. "I can always take the champagne home, and we can drink it another time."

Those words told Brenda he was sensitive to her feelings, and it made her love him.

Love him!

Yes, love him.

She realized that was exactly how she felt about this man. When had it happened?

It started the moment you saw him walk through the Lodge door.

Tears rolled down her cheeks at this stunning revelation.

Gil saw them. "Brenda?"

"It's all right, Gil. I'm all right. It's been a long time since I've felt this right."

"Then why are you crying?"

"These happen to be happy tears, because that's what I am for the first time in a very long time."

"Can I take some of the credit for this outburst of happiness?"

"You can take all the credit, Mr. Jackson." It would be more than just a celebration of her changed opinion of Gil as a lawyer and a man. It would also be a celebration of her re-entry into life as a young passionate woman. A woman who had fallen head over heels in love with this man even though she'd fought tooth and nail against doing so.

After reaching Brenda's apartment, Gil killed the engine. Turning toward her he gazed soulfully into her eyes.

"If I take this champagne in with me, you know what it'll mean."

"Yes, I do."

"And?"

"And I still want you to come in, Gil."

"Are you sure?"

"Yes, I'm very sure."

Gil leaned toward her and kissed her lips.

Brenda moaned, closing her eyes, and reveling in the taste of his mouth.

He moved his lips away from hers.

"Keep that up and we'll never make it inside to enjoy the champagne. And I can tell you that making love out in this weather might prove to be a chilling experience."

"Putting an altogether different construction on the meaning of chill. Right?" She unfastened her seat belt. "I think it's time we went inside, don't you?"

"Yes, I sure do. And you don't have to worry about protection."

"I'm glad you thought of it."

Gil took the champagne and ice bucket out of the trunk, then walked around the car to open Brenda's door.

She smiled up at him. "I see chivalry is still alive and well."

"Yes, it is, my lady." Gil gave her a mock bow, then guided her up the walk to her apartment. When they reached her door, he took the keys from her fingers, handing her the ice bucket while he unlocked the door.

Once inside, Brenda hung their coats in the closet. "I'll get the glasses. You can start the fire."

"Sounds like a fair deal to me. My Boy Scout training

should come in handy."

"I thought you told me you were never a Boy Scout."

"Ah, yeah. I'm busted. Actually, my cousin taught me all I know about building fires."

Brenda laughed. "Luckily, you won't have to draw on those skills tonight. I use only the kind of logs that come in a package at the grocery store. All you need to start it is a match."

"And you say I have no imagination."

Brenda shook her head and walked into the kitchen. Returning to the living room minutes later with glasses, she found that Gil had the fire blazing, with cushions from the couch romantically arranged in front of the fireplace. And he was searching through her collection of CDs.

"I'll have to bring some of my CDs over."

"Should be enough there to suffice for tonight."

He held up a few for her approval.

She checked out his choices. "Vanessa Williams, Brian McKnight, Glen Jones, Luther Vandross. I like your choices, Mr. Jackson."

"I hope you like me half as much," he said, putting CDs in the player. He turned to her, and taking the tray, set it down on the coffee table.

"Oh, I like you at least half as much." Brenda noticed that he had loosened his tie, taken off his jacket and draped it across the back of the couch. To her, at that moment, he was the sexiest male on the planet. She reached out and slipped his tie from around his neck and tossed it on top of his jacket. The glowing dark eyes gazing into hers were like embers, smoldering hot with desire and expectation. Her insides responded with a quiver.

From the first moment they met, Gil Jackson disturbed her in every way, and nothing that had happened since then had changed that. If anything, those disturbing vibes had intensified. She could feel the barriers she'd erected around her heart thawing, melting away.

Gil cupped her face in his hands, bringing her lips to within inches of his. He closed his eyes and gently married their mouths in a soul-joining kiss.

Brenda's heart jolted and her pulse pounded. A lurch of anticipation skittered through her body as his tongue delved inside her mouth, stroking the walls, caressing the sensitive roof, arousing her senses to titillating life. She found herself wanting more from this man, much more.

With a groan he ended the kiss and slipped his arm around her, drawing her into his body.

"Oh, Brenda, how I want you, girl. I want to come inside you, feel your tight, wet heat surrounding me."

She moaned at his stimulating words, burying her face in his neck, instinctively moving her body against his. She felt a shudder pass through him. And like electricity surging through a power line, Gil transmitted his desire into her, causing lightning sensations to sizzle through her.

He pulled down the zipper of Brenda's dress and eased his fingers inside, gliding them over the smooth heated surface of her back, glorying in the feel of incredibly soft bare skin.

Seconds later Gil slipped the dress off one shoulder, baring it so that he could rain kisses there. When he felt her tremble, he bared the other shoulder bestowing equal attention there.

"Gil."

"Yes, sweetheart. If you want me to stop, tell me now."

"No, don't stop. I want you as much as you want me."

"I don't think that's possible." He hungrily covered her lips again, devouring their softness, then suddenly raised his mouth from hers to gaze into her eyes. "The champagne awaits."

"It can wait a little longer," she murmured, getting out of her heels.

"It can certainly keep longer than I can." He returned his mouth to hers yet again. The champagne forgotten for the moment, he slowly lowered them both to the carpet.

Brenda returned his kiss with enthusiasm.

"I don't think we need champagne to inspire us, do we?"

"No. You've already gotten me high on you, girl."

"I have?"

"You want me to prove it to you?"

"I thought you were."

The CD *We've Only Just Begun (The Romance Is Not Over)* by Glen Jones began to play.

"I think my man Glen Jones says it perfectly."

"You mean to tell me you're the kind of man who lets another speak for him?"

His answer was a heart-devouring kiss primed to devastate. "Does that answer your question?"

She gasped for breath. "It definitely does."

"Would you like an instant replay?"

"I think I would." She drove her fingers into his hair. "In fact I know I would."

He recaptured her lips, more demanding this time, if that was possible. She returned the kiss with wild abandon. He groaned, leaving her mouth, kissing his way from her face to her neck, across her shoulder. Shivers of ecstasy followed the contact of his mouth on her skin.

Gil lowered the dress to her waist, then undid the fastening of her strapless bra. He touched his lips to her nipple in a thrillingly possessive gesture, teasing the tip until it stiffened into a hard peak. When he eased his mouth over to excite its twin, he heard Brenda whimper, and watched as she restlessly moved her head from side to side. He could feel the sensations of pleasure as they undulated through her body.

He started peeling the dress down the rest of her, taking her slip with it, enjoying what his fingers uncovered as they made their descent to her feet.

"Baby, you're so beautiful."

When she felt his hand start to rove up her leg, Brenda put her hand over his. "Enough. Now that you've had your fun, it's my turn."

"Honey, by all means. You have my permission to go ballistic."

And she did, starting with the quick removal of his shirt.

Once she had freed him from its confines, she couldn't help

stroking his bare chest, nor could she resist caressing his male nipple. She unbuttoned his pants and slipped her hand inside the waistband of his briefs, splaying her fingers across his sex.

"Baby, do you know what you're doing to me?"

"I hope I do."

"If you want to make the night last, I think you'd better move your hand."

She lowered her lashes and smiled. "Maybe now would be a good time to open that champagne."

Gil reached for the bottle and after popping the cork poured them each a glass.

"To us." He clinked his glass against hers.

After taking a sip, Brenda eased the glass away from her mouth. "Now, get more comfortable, Gil. Take off your shoes. All the better to remove your pants later, my dear."

"Said the she-wolf. Am I your dear, Brenda?"

"You most definitely are, and more."

"How dear and more am I?"

"You want me to show you? All this time I thought you were born in Minnesota not Missouri."

"No more subterfuge, woman."

"No, because I'm ready to finish what we started." She set her glass on the coffee table.

"And just what have we started?"

"I think you know."

She watched as he set his glass down next to hers and thought there was something so intimately romantic seeing them side by side, hearing the crackle of a fire and the sound of soft music filling the room, mingling with the scent of male musk floating up her nostrils.

He molded his fingers to the back of her head, moving his lips over hers lightly teasing the soft supple surface. Her senses swirled and skidded as pleasure clamored inside her.

She could feel the warmth of his fingers on her skin through the filmy material of her panty hose and helped him free her from them.

"Now you." She eased him out of his pants and briefs.

"I like it when we're both equally naked."

She caressed his hip with her hand. "You're an equal opportunity man."

"Do you want me to hire you?"

"In what capacity?" She rubbed her fingers across his sex.

He brushed his fingers over her breasts. "What position are you applying for?"

"Lover."

He kissed her eyes.

"What are your qualifications?"

"I haven't much experience, but I'm more than eager to learn. Are you willing to take me as an on-the-job trainee?"

"Most definitely and I think your training should start immediately." He eased his hands around her to explore the delicate slope of her back, caress her small waist, the firm softness of her thighs and buttocks. Have mercy, she was all woman. She had intrigued him from the start. And she did so even more now.

Brenda moaned softly as he lowered her to the carpet and slid his body over hers, easing her thighs apart, stationing himself between them. She trembled at the contact.

When Gil moved his lips over her breasts and circled the taut brown nipple with his tongue, Brenda cried out, arching her back, squirming beneath him.

A tormented sound fled his throat.

She trailed her fingertips up and down his back. Wrapping her legs about his hips, she massaged the back of his thighs with her feet, sensuously abrading them against his hair-roughened skin.

He wanted to take his time bringing her to passion but when she began to move her body against his, he felt on the verge of losing what little control he had left.

"Oh, sweet darling," he murmured, moving his fingers down her belly to her femininity, stroking the wet nub of desire hidden just beyond its folds.

Brenda cried out, bucking against his fingers, proof of her desire creamed over his fingers. She opened herself more fully for his invasion. And invade her he did, not wildly, but slowly, sensuously, sliding himself inside her slippery heat.

"Gil, oh, Gil. Please! Baby, please!" she rasped.

The ragged sound of her building passion undid the last fragile hold he had on his control. He removed his fingers and with one powerful move thrust deeply within her, letting her welcoming heat envelope him completely. The shock of unadulterated pleasure reverberated through him when he felt her hot swollen passage clench tightly around him, electrifying him to stillness.

If shock rendered him temporarily motionless, it had the opposite effect on Brenda. She moved frenziedly, repeatedly against his pulsing hot organ.

The sensations began to intensify, storming his brain. His body suddenly jerked into action, blending in harmony with the rhythm she set.

Gil's movements grew more frenetic, directing volts of ecstasy through her, firing every nerve and receptor, repeatedly transmitting sensual messages to her brain. He uttered endearments into her ear but she was too far gone in her desire to reach fulfillment to understand the words, only the hungry passion in his voice relayed their meaning.

"Oh, Gil, baby, now!" burst from her lips.

He kissed her, then thrust hard and deep. A burst of sensations exploding inside her, she molded her body tightly against his.

"Brenda, oh, baby, yes, yes!" An identical explosion blasted him as he spilled himself deep inside her. A male shout of triumph tore from his throat, echoing through the room.

Tremors quaked their bodies until every last spasm quieted and they lay spent in each other's arms.

Chapter Ten

Gil kissed the top of Brenda's head. "You were fantastic, baby."

She caressed his chest with her lips. "So were you."

Sensing a subtle change in her mood, a kind of tension he couldn't quite put his finger on, he asked, "You're not sorry we made love, are you?"

Brenda gazed at him, gently touching his lips with her fingertips. "No, never."

"Then why do I get the feeling that you have regrets."

"I don't have any regrets about what we shared. I just never thought to get this involved with anyone, certainly not this fast."

"You got involved with some other man as quickly and he hurt you, didn't he?"

Her smile wobbled. "I don't want to talk about it."

"You say something like that and expect me not to want to talk about it!"

"I'm just not ready, Gil."

The pain in her eyes and the plea in her voice convinced him to back off.

"I don't want to pressure you, Brenda. You'll tell me when you're ready. I can be a patient man when I have to be, but don't make me wait too long. Okay?" He smiled. "Do you think the champagne has gone flat?"

Brenda returned his smile and reached for the bottle. "Luckily I recorked and put it back in the ice bucket before we became—ah, preoccupied."

He kissed her forehead. "I have to say that it was a worthy

preoccupation."

She laughed. "A worthy preoccupation to which you dedicated your full attention. I'll testify to that."

He kissed the tip of her nose. "I rest my case," he said taking the bottle of champagne from her fingers and drawing her into his arms. "You go to my head more effectively than any champagne ever could."

"I'm just as high on you, Mr. Jackson. I wouldn't mind if you wanted to take me higher."

"Oh, I definitely want to do that." He wrapped her legs around his hips and entered her, easing himself deep, glorying in her tight warmth, he cried out. "Brenda, you feel so good, girl!"

She moved against him, softly groaning as the pleasure of having him inside her took her higher. And to think she had tried to escape this!

Gil shifted Brenda on top. She gasped when he embedded his manhood deep inside her to the hilt. And then moments later set a slow, sensuous rhythm of flesh sliding in and out of flesh, again and again, until the exquisite friction of his movements nearly drove her crazy.

"What are you doing to me, Gil?" she whispered breathlessly.

"I'm loving you out of your mind."

"Turnaround is fair play." Brenda began to set her own rhythm with every rotation of her hips. "I intend to love you just like that."

"You have no idea how much I'm looking forward to it. In fact I can hardly wait."

They were soon lost in their lovemaking.

⇥∗✦✧∗⇤

Several hours later, Brenda raised up on an elbow and gazed into Gil's sleeping face. She never thought to love like this. The only other relationship she'd had couldn't begin to touch this.

Gil was an exciting, generous lover and most of all a very special man. And he deserved the truth, but could she tell him all of it and expect him to understand? Expect to keep his respect? She shifted her gaze to the fireplace and stared into the flames.

"Come back, sweet darling," he whispered in her ear.

Brenda blinked at the sound of his voice. "Gil." She smiled. "I haven't gone anywhere."

"Not physically maybe. I wouldn't let you do that, you know." He pulled her back into his arms. "This floor is getting kind of hard. Do you think we could go to your bedroom?"

"You have to have your creature comforts, huh?"

He kissed her with his eyes, then did a follow up with his lips. "You're the only creature comfort I have to have. And what a beautiful creature you are to have."

"You're a gilt-tongued rogue, Mr. Jackson. It's not every woman who'll let you get away with calling her a creature and find herself loving to hear you say it."

He caressed her breast. "You're not every woman though, are you, baby?"

Brenda stood up and held out her hand to him.

She was beautiful in all her naked glory, like a goddess, he thought, rising from the carpet, taking her hand, letting her lead him to her bedroom. She could lead him just about anywhere and he would go without hesitation. He was fascinated by this woman and yet he still didn't know very much about her, not nearly enough anyway. She was a mystery that he intended to solve one day.

A beam of sunlight spilled over Gil's face, gently waking him the next morning. As he opened his eyes, a feeling of well-being covered him like a warm blanket. The heady scent of perfume, lovemaking and woman wafted up from the sheets to tease his senses. He reached for Brenda, but found the bed empty.

The Price of Love

empty.

The smell of coffee brewing drifted into the room. He smiled, and throwing back the covers, left the bed and went in search of his woman.

From the doorway, he watched as Brenda took bacon and eggs from the refrigerator, then set them on the kitchen counter. He found himself fantasizing about seeing her domestically occupied like this every morning for the rest of their lives.

He stepped away from the doorway, came up behind her, wrapped his arms around her waist, and squeezed. "You feel nice," he said burying his face in the feathery wisps of hair along her temple, while breathing in its delicious scent.

Brenda felt his aroused manhood pressing against her buttocks. "So do you," she said, inhaling his unique male musk, rubbing her cheek against his. "How do you like your eggs?"

"Like my women."

"Oh, and how is that?"

"Over easy."

"Gil!"

He kissed her neck. "You did ask."

"Is that back or front?"

"Any way that pleases us both."

He slipped her robe off her shoulders, watching it slide down her body to the floor.

Brenda gasped when she felt his long lean fingers caress her nipples.

He turned her to face him. "Brenda?"

"Yes."

No other words were needed. He shoved the bacon and eggs aside, and raising her onto the counter, parted her thighs, easing between them. When he moved into her wet, silky depths, he heard her moan of pleasure and felt her pliant flesh quiver and mold around him. He groaned, lifting her from the counter still intimately joined to him and headed back to the bedroom. Any thought to breakfast was suspended until later, much later.

━━◆━━

"I see you've worked up quite an appetite after our last—vigorous, ah, exercise session," Brenda said, watching as Gil tucked into his breakfast with gusto.

"I admit it was hard work but somebody had to do it."

Brenda flailed him with a dish towel. "You're impossible."

His gaze smoldered. "I hope not too impossible for a certain lady."

"You want some more coffee? More eggs, Mr. Impossible?"

"I'm hungry, but not for more breakfast. I'm hungry for you, love. You're food for the gods. And right now, you make me feel downright omnipotent."

"Flattery will get you just about anything."

"Really?"

"Really," she said huskily, wrapping her arms around his neck.

"In that case I'm going to have to become more creative when exploring my options."

━━◆━━

Gil noticed that Brenda wasn't really paying attention to the movie on television. There was a faraway look on her face. He was curious to know what she was thinking. When she found him studying her so intently, her mood seemed to lighten and the look disappeared.

"Heavy thinking?" he asked.

"No. The movie is gone off." She left the couch to turn the set off. "How do you want to wile away the rest of the day? And don't tell me you want to spend it in bed."

"I must confess it's the first thought that came into my mind, but I'll make it easy for you and let you decide. What do you usually do on Sunday?"

"I usually work on one of my quilts, read, or watch television."

"You're more than just a clerk at the Quilt Lodge. You actually quilt yourself?" He looked astonished.

"Yes. Why do you find that so strange?"

"You're so young. I relegate that kind of hobby to people Aunt Shirley's age or older."

"The Gray Panthers, a movement for seniors' rights, would have you drawn and quartered for saying a thing like that. I can see your aunt as their president. And I don't think that because you're her nephew she would waive punishment."

"In that case I withdraw my supposition."

"Spoken like a true lawyer," she said, her voice tinged with a hint bitterness she couldn't camouflage.

"What is it with you and lawyers, Brenda? Every time the word is mentioned your mood changes."

"I told you I have my reasons."

"But you haven't gone into any detail. Look, Brenda, it's not good keeping things bottled up inside you. It can brew into something ugly, permanently molding you into a bitter, lonely person. I've sensed that you were coming out of your shell, don't regress now. As the old saying goes, 'You've come a long way, baby, to get where you've got to today.'"

"Maybe you're asking more of me than I can give. I sense that you'll demand everything from a woman, and I don't know if I can handle a relationship like that. And what about your son? I've yet to meet him."

"Now that you've got me all figured out, I'll tell it like it really is. I'm not trying to pressure you, Brenda. But you're right about one thing, I won't settle for anything less from my woman than I'm willing to give to her in return. As for my son, I know he'll love you."

She believed Gil when he said he wouldn't pressure her, but knowing his expectations, his show of patience was still a subtle form of pressure. He was a father who loved his son. She wondered if he could really understand why a mother who loved her son could give up her child? In any case, she wasn't ready to tell him her story.

"I can leave if that's what you want, Brenda."

"I don't want you to go."

"It's all right for me to make love to you, but you can't trust me with your feelings, or your heart?"

"When you say it like that—" She kneaded her bottom lip with her teeth.

He put a finger across her abused lips.

"You blamed the fact that this all happened so fast as a reason for your reluctance. We can take it slow, but it won't change the outcome. I want you to be mine, Brenda Davis. Heart, body and soul. I want you to understand that from the jump."

"Gil, I—"

"Don't decide right now. Take a few days to think about it. But for today, can you put it in a lockbox and turn the key?"

He replaced his finger with his lips, kissing her tenderly on the mouth, then, rising from his chair, held out his hand. "There are still several CDs we haven't listened to yet. Come on."

They spent the rest of the day in a state of companionable truce. When the day altered into night, drawing their time together to a close, Gil pulled Brenda into his arms and returned to caressing her lips with his own.

"You know, you have the sweetest lips in the state of Minnesota."

"Only Minnesota!"

He grinned. "Should I have said the world?"

"Not unless you know this to be true from personal experience."

"Not so much from personal experience. I'm just a good guesser. Walk me to the door, baby."

"Gil, about what you said earlier—"

"You don't need to say anything else. You feel the way you feel. It's just that I want to know why you feel that way, so I can understand you better. Now don't get that funny look on your face, baby. I told you I could wait. And I'm a man of my word. You're going to come to know that about me." He bent to kiss her again. "I'll call you. You do believe me when I say

I can be patient and that I can be understanding?"

"I—I'm trying—I want to."

"But it's damned hard for you, isn't it? I'd like to ring the necks of the people who hurt you."

She smiled. "My hero, my champion."

"You'd better believe it. Good night, Brenda."

"Good night, Gil."

Brenda watched him go with a feeling of trepidation. She'd once trusted a man completely and he'd nearly destroyed her. Could she give herself body and soul to Gil?

I don't know. I'm so confused. I love this man and yet...I'm not ready to take that final step.

Chapter Eleven

"Brenda. You've been a million miles away all morning."

"Did you say something, Laura?"

Laura smiled. "What's up with you, girlfriend?"

"I'm in love with Gil Jackson."

"You say that as if it is a fate worse than death."

Brenda turned to face her friend. "I didn't mean for it to sound that way. It's just that I feel so—"

"Fragile? Vulnerable? Exposed?"

"I see you understand how I feel."

"Yes," Laura answered with a commiserating nod. "I certainly do."

"Does that mean that you and Carl—"

"I've tried to deny my feelings where he's concerned, but I can't any longer. I love him," she admitted softly.

"Are you going to marry him?"

"He hasn't asked me yet."

"Oh, he will. When he does, are you going to say yes?"

A look of pure love lighted Laura's face. "Yes, I am." She studied Brenda. "How about you? If Gil—"

"Whoa! Things haven't progressed to that stage yet. I don't know if they ever will."

"If you love him, I don't see why it wouldn't."

The shop bell jangled.

"Here comes Shirley. I'd better prepare for a grilling." Brenda laughed. "And don't you look so smug, Laura Carson. She's going to get you, too."

"That sweet old lady?"

"They're the worst kind, didn't you know?"

"Brenda and Laura, just the people I want to see."

"What did I tell you?" Brenda cleared her throat. "Shirley, it's good to see you."

"It's good to see you too, dear." Shirley looked past Brenda to Laura. "Are you and Carl becoming better acquainted since going on that tour of the reservation?"

"Yes, we sure are. I, ah, need to check on Jon-Marc. It's good to see you again, Mrs. Edwards."

"Please, call me Shirley, Laura. I have a feeling that we're going to be a lot closer in the not-too-distant future, if I know Carl Wintercloud." She smiled that sweet knowing smile.

Brenda watched Laura's retreating figure. *Coward*, she silently berated her friend for leaving her to Shirley's tender mercies.

"How may I help you this morning?" she asked the older woman.

"You're wearing the same glow my nephew is wearing these days. Something going on between you two that I should know about?"

"Shirley, I—"

"You don't have to say anything. I'm happy for you both."

"Shirley, we—"

"You may as well call me Aunt Shirley."

"Now wait a minute. We haven't—"

Shirley patted Brenda's hand. "You will, dear. You will. Take my word for it. I can hardly wait to tell the rest of the family. His mother, my sister Sara, his father, Durant, and especially Granddaddy Turner will be so pleased. I don't know whether you and Gil or Laura and Carl will be the first to get married. I've already finished one wedding ring quilt. I'm so excited! I'd better get started on the other quilt right away."

The woman wouldn't let her get a word in edgewise. Brenda wanted to tell her that things weren't that settled; that it wasn't a foregone conclusion that she and Gil would marry. She wanted to tell her that she had some serious problems to resolve before she could consider a future with Gil.

As Brenda watched Shirley thumb through the new yarn catalog, her thoughts shifted to Gil. He seemed to be every girl's dream. So had another man in her life, but she wouldn't think about him or how he had hurt her.

The phone rang.

"Quilt Lodge, this is Brenda, how may I help you?"

"There are a number of ways you can help me, lovely lady."

"Gil!"

"You miss me?"

"I just saw you the other day."

"I'm crushed that you haven't missed me."

"I didn't say that I hadn't missed you. I did. I do."

"Allow me to refresh your memory this evening, Ms. Davis. I'll even throw in a memorable dinner."

"McDonald's?" she said suspiciously.

"Actually I was thinking more along the lines of Chinese take out."

"Gil!"

"Only kidding. I want dinner to be a surprise."

"You aren't even going to give me a hint, are you?"

"No. I'll be by your place at six-thirty."

"I'll be waiting."

Brenda stood with the receiver in her hand and a smile on her face for long moments after Gil had hung up the phone.

"You definitely have that look, Brenda," Shirley remarked.

Brenda blinked, coming out of her reverie. "What look is that?"

"The look of love, dear. It's in your eyes. You're in love with Gillie."

Brenda put the receiver back on its cradle. "Did you find everything you wanted today?"

"You can't hide your feelings by dodging the subject. You young people, honestly—" Shirley shook her head.

Time seemed to drag for Brenda. Six-thirty couldn't come soon enough to please her. She kept watching the clock. Finally closing time arrived.

"Don't drive too fast in your haste to get home." Laura teased.

A knowing smile spread across Brenda's face. "Carl wouldn't be keeping you company tonight, now would he?"

A heated flush splashed Laura's face. "Yes."

"Maybe you'll be the one to receive the wedding ring quilt Shirley has already finished."

—✦—

Minutes later, at her apartment, Brenda pulled a kimono-style caftan from her closet in anticipation of Gil's visit. Then she began to wonder whether she should wear it. She didn't want to seem overeager.

When the doorbell rang, she jumped. Nervously patting her hair, she answered the door.

"Don't you look beautiful. Nothing like having my own personal geisha."

She bowed. "What did you bring this humble geisha to eat, Gil san?"

"A truly hungry woman, I love it," he said, holding their dinner just out of reach of her impatient hands.

"Smells exotic."

"Do you like oysters?"

A revolted look came into her face. "You didn't—"

"No, I didn't, gotcha." He grinned. "You don't care for oysters, I take it?"

"Can't stand them."

"They're supposed to heighten your sexual awareness."

"I don't need oysters to do that. Just seeing you turns me on, Mr. Jackson."

"I'm flattered to hear it, Ms. Davis."

"Just don't let it go to your head. All right?"

"Sorry, it's too late. You already go to my head, Brenda.

97

Now guide me to your kitchen so I can warm up this master-piece."

—❦◆❧—

"You've surprised me all right," Brenda said wiping her mouth with a napkin after they finished their dinner.

"How did you like the lobster?"

"It was delicious. I've never had it prepared this way."

"It's called Lobster Sunset. I had a hell of a time convincing Heritage House to fix this unusual takeout order."

"Is the cook male?"

"Yes, as a matter of fact."

"That explains it then. If the cook were female, you would have charmed her into it, no problem." When he smiled at her, it melted her insides.

"Thanks for the compliment. Let me help you clear this away."

"We can do that later."

He arched a brow. "You have something more interesting in mind?"

"Oh, yes, I definitely do."

"Do I get a hint?"

"You don't need one."

"I don't?"

"No, you know exactly what to do."

—❦◆❧—

Later as they lay in bed, Gil traced the curve of Brenda's breast with his finger. "You're so soft and cuddly."

"Is that all."

"Oh no, there's more."

"More?"

"Yes, much more. I think I love you, Brenda Davis."

The three most precious words in the world to Brenda and for reasons she didn't care to dwell on, she didn't relish hearing them just now.

"Did I say something wrong?"

"No, you didn't."

"Then why the sad, faraway look?"

She didn't answer.

"Someone else say those same words and ended up not meaning them?"

"Gil, I—"

"It's all right. I'm here to stay and I intend to keep telling you that until you believe that I'm for real."

"You're a most persistent man, aren't you?"

"To the bone." He sealed his vow with a kiss. "I want you to meet the rest of my family. I've already told my mother about you."

She tensed. "You have?"

"Umm. She can hardly wait to meet you and neither can my father and grandfather. It's not every day I bring a woman I'm interested in home for their approval. They've been very protective of me since my wife's death."

Brenda felt so special. But she was a little afraid too. Did going to meet his family mean that—

"Is Sunday good for you?"

"I don't know."

"You have something else planned?"

"No."

"Then it's settled, you're coming to dinner at my parents' house on Sunday."

"Are you always such a decisive man?"

"Always, sweetheart. No woman wants a man who isn't in control of his own destiny."

"You're so philosophical this evening."

"Does it impress you? Do I impress you?"

"Yes, it does and you do impress me, very much."

"The question is do I impress you enough."

"Enough for what?"

"This." He took her lips in a slow, soul-stirring kiss guaranteed to curl a woman's toes.

And it did and more, much more. It proved to be a prelude to yet another episode of exquisite lovemaking.

—◦◦◈◦◦—

After Gil had gone, Brenda lay in bed wondering if his family would like her. He'd told her that he had a twin sister and two brothers. All except one lived out of state. His sister lived in Omaha with her husband and three kids. His middle brother, Richard, an architect, lived in upstate New York. Only his younger brother Dylan lived in Minnesota. He was a doctor at Long Rapids Memorial, but also helped out at the reservation hospital.

She'd told Gil so little about herself. Would his parents be eager to know more about her family and her background?

Brenda closed her eyes. Her past was so painful. Would anyone understand why she'd done some of the things she'd done, made some of the decision she'd made? Would Gil?

He had a child. Gil had every right to know about her past. She had to tell him sooner or later.

—◦◦◈◦◦—

As he drove home, Gil thought about the woman he loved. He knew positively it was love he felt for Brenda. He'd loved Monique, but he'd never felt for any woman what he felt for Brenda. She was an enigma, true enough, but not for long. He'd get her to open up to him, and he'd help her deal with her fears and insecurities once he knew what they were.

When he first made love to her, he knew it had been a very long time since she'd made love. She was almost as tight as a virgin, yet she wasn't a virgin. He could tell by her responses that she wasn't that experienced either. He sensed that he had only skimmed the surface of her passion. Every time he touched her, she trembled with desire and need.

He didn't think he'd find another woman to love after Monique. Of all his aunt's matchmaking attempts, he was glad he had waited for Brenda. He believed that this lovely woman was meant to be his. Now, if he could just convince her of that, he'd have half the battle won.

His granddaddy, Turner, would like Brenda, and she him. Turner was one of the most down-to-earth persons he'd ever known. And at eighty-two years old, he was an excellent judge of character. Turner still had an eye for beautiful women and ways to charm them. His manner of putting people at ease would impress Brenda. He'd make her relax in his company.

Gil realized that he was going to need all the help he could get to disarm this wary lady.

Chapter Twelve

As Gil drove, he sneaked occasional glances at the woman seated next to him. She looked beautiful in her gray wool dress.

"How many times does that make?"

Brenda turned toward him, a blank expression on her face. "What?"

"That you've checked your makeup or patted your hair?"

"Gil, I'm nervous about meeting your family."

"Don't be, they'll be as crazy about you as I am."

"How can you be so sure?"

"Aunt Shirley already is. Brenda, sweetheart, calm down. Everything will be all right, you'll see."

She snapped her compact closed and shoved it back inside her purse. "I sure hope so."

"It will be, baby, trust me."

Trust. She'd heard that word before and once again it beckoned to her to give it another try. Brenda knew that without trust, love didn't stand a snowflake's chance of surviving in the blazing desert.

As they headed for his parents' home, Brenda noticed that his family lived quite a distance from the city in a wooded area. It was amazingly beautiful here. You could see a part of the river in the distance as it threaded in and out of the landscape like a long ribbon.

"How do you like it?"

"I like it. I can picture you as a little boy growing up here. It's not far from the reservation, is it?"

"This is part of the land my mother and Aunt Shirley inher-

102

ited. You see, during the time when so many peace treaties were being broken after the civil war, my great-grandfather found gold hidden in caves near the reservation."

"Really!"

"Yes. He used it to obtain the land. Since Indians couldn't purchase land during that time, he had my great-grandmother do it, thereby managing to pass it down to my mother and aunt and eventually to me and my brothers and sister since Aunt Shirley never had any kids."

"What about the family on your father's side?"

"My father's grandfather was one of the first successful black trappers in Minnesota. He and his wife had migrated from Louisiana to Minnesota shortly after the end of the civil war."

"You certainly know a lot about your roots."

"I don't know very much about yours, though. Care to enlighten me?"

"There's not that much to know," she said evasively.

Gil stayed silent for a moment. He sensed from the look on her face that she didn't really want to talk about it, but he waited for her to elaborate. When she didn't, he said, "Whatever there is to know about you, I want to know it because I love you, Brenda. I want to know everything about your life and your background."

She hesitated, but seeing the patient yet determined look on his face, she began. "My great-grandfather came to America from Ireland and settled in New York. He met my great-grandmother, a runaway slave who had successfully made her escape from a plantation in North Carolina. They moved west to Chicago, where he found work in a small meatpacking company. Eventually, he owned the company and passed it on to my grandfather, who nearly lost it during the Depression."

"How did he manage to hold on to it?"

"According to my father those were lean times for him and Aunt Bertha. They lost their mother at an early age from the Spanish influenza. My grandfather sold the meatpacking business and opened a small hotel. Through diligence and hard work, he was able to send my father to college. When my father returned home after graduation, he took over the running of the hotel. Several years later he met my mother."

"You have a look of the exotic about you."

"I got it from my mother. She is the daughter of a Brazilian immigrant and a Black Belisian mother who made their way to Chicago and settled there. She and my father fell in love, got married and ran the hotel together. I arrived on the scene fifteen years later after they'd given up any hope of ever having a child."

"I'd say that's a lot to know. Do your father and mother still own the hotel and live in Chicago?"

"Yes." She didn't mention that they owned a chain of hotels.

"Did they spoil you rotten?" He laughed.

She smiled wryly. "To the core."

"What made you decide to leave Chicago? Long Rapids is a far cry from the life you were used to."

"A whole world apart. It's one of the reasons why I left."

"You're a country girl at heart, right?"

"Right. Is that your parents' house over there?"

Gil looked in the direction she indicated. "Yes, it is." He wanted to know more personal details about Brenda, but decided not to push it. He'd gotten her to reveal more than he ever expected. The rest could wait.

Brenda glanced at Gil. What she'd told him seemed enough to satisfy him for the moment. She couldn't let him know what she'd carefully left unsaid, she just wasn't ready for that.

Will you ever be?

A large two-story log cabin-like house grew larger as they neared it. This was no ordinary house. There was a driveway leading to a natural rock wall enclosed courtyard with a raised deck that resembled the battlement of a castle.

"My father designed the house. Isn't it magnificent?"

"Yes, it certainly is. Is he an architect?"

"One of the best in this part of the country. And I'm not

just saying that because he's my father."

"I believe you. The house is so unusual. It gives the concept of the log cabin a different interpretation."

"He's considered a man of vision," Gil said proudly.

"Not unlike his son. I thought it came from your Indian heritage."

"No. My father is part Creole, Haitian, and African."

"There should be no bigotry in this country where color and race are concerned, considering that everyone is part of so many different cultures."

"You would think so, wouldn't you. I see my mother peering out the window."

Brenda tensed at his words.

"Relax, everything will be all right." He placed a large gloved hand over her small one. "They won't eat you, Little Red Riding Hood."

She laughed. "You idiot. Of course they won't."

"I try to help the woman and she insults me. Women!"

Gil activated the electric gate opener, then drove through to the courtyard. As he helped Brenda out of the car, she saw a stand of birch trees on the right, and to the left a flagstone staircase that ascended to the deck level. They climbed the stairs and crossed a ten-foot-long bridge to the house. Underneath, a creek flowed.

The concept fascinated Brenda. Gil's father had literally turned his home into a castle of sorts even though it was constructed of wood, not stone.

The large oak door opened just as they reached it. Two smiling people greeted them. Gil's mother looked as Indian as her husband did not. They were a very handsome couple. Gil, Brenda saw, had been endowed with the best in looks from both parents. It made her wonder what his sister and brothers looked like.

"I'm Sara Jackson, Gil's mother. You must be Brenda Davis, the young woman he keeps raving about." Sara extended her hand.

Brenda took off her glove and shook hands. "I'm pleased

to meet you."

Gil's father stepped forward. "Durant Jackson, Gil's father. I never knew my son was the king of understatement. He said you were attractive, but what he didn't tell us was that you were such a ravishing beauty."

The ability to charm apparently ran in the Jackson family, Brenda surmised. "Thank you for saying that."

"It's only the truth," she heard a strong, raspy male voice say. "I'm Turner Jackson. This young rascal is my grandson. Come on in here so I can get a good look at you, girl."

"Now, Granddaddy."

Turner ignored his grandson and said, "Never mind him." He leaned on his cane and held out his other arm to Brenda.

She wrapped her arm around it and smiled at Gil who hunched his shoulders.

"Don't you monopolize all Brenda's time, Dad," Durant scolded.

"You trying to tell your old daddy how to act, Durant Jackson? I've probably forgotten more than you'll ever know about enchanting the ladies."

Durant shot his wife a rueful look as they followed his father and Brenda into the living room.

Gil suppressed the urge to laugh at his grandfather's temerity. He certainly had a way of getting right to the heart of things. Age definitely had its advantages. And Turner Jackson took advantage of every one of them.

Brenda felt relaxed in Turner's company. He was exactly the way she thought a grandfather should be. He was witty, warm, without an ounce of pretension of any kind. She felt right at home with the Jackson clan.

Turner seated Brenda beside him on the couch before the fireplace. Gil sat down next to her on the other side.

Turner grinned at his grandson. "You've done yourself proud again, Scamp."

"Grandaddy!"

Turner rapped his cane across Gil's foot. "Don't interrupt your elders. Now, as I was about to say before I was interrupted, although Brenda's nothing like Monique, I feel she's right for you, Scamp. She's a real beauty too." He grinned engagingly at Brenda, taking her hand in his and bringing it to his lips.

She cast Gil a speaking glance. She returned her attention to his grandfather and had to admit that he was a handsome old devil. She bet he had been quite a ladies' man in his younger days. He could still charm the birds out of the trees, she silently amended, taking in his thick shock of splendid white hair and his alert, sparkling coffee-dark eyes.

The warmth from the Jackson family spread through Brenda, making her feel like she belonged. She didn't expect to take to them this quickly.

Gil was pleased that his plan to bring Brenda out of her shell was working. He knew he could count on his family's help, especially his grandfather's. The old brazen devil loved women.

"Brenda," Gil said in an aside, "There are horror stories I could tell you about that wicked cane of his. When I was ten years old, he used to brandish it like a sword."

"A sword!"

"If we didn't do as we were told, us kids would feel the wrath of his cane across our shoes. He would say that feet in a hurry to do mischief needed slowing down."

Brenda remembered another old saying Gil had told her he'd learned from his grandfather, about a mule laying an egg and building him a nest.

"Don't let him fool you," Turner confided. "I was only acting out of self-defense. As a boy, my grandson happened to be a mischievous little scamp. Never could pull the wool over my eyes, though."

"I bet he tried, didn't he?" Brenda chuckled.

Turner patted her hand. "I see you know him pretty well."

Brenda gazed at Gil. "I'm getting there," she said softly.

They all sat down to a simple dinner of baked chicken, field peas, mashed potatoes, and homemade dinner rolls. Dinners with Brenda's own family may have been more elegant, but they were definitely never this comfortable and warm.

When they'd all finished eating, the family congregated in the living room for coffee, dessert and conversation.

"This dessert is fabulous, Mrs. Jackson," Brenda glowingly remarked. "What do you call it?"

"Cherry Jubilee. You really like it?"

"I sure do."

"Then I'll have to put some in a container so you can take it home with you. If you want me to I can give you the recipe."

Gil moved closer to Brenda. "If you don't watch it, Mama will have you fat as a butterball before you know it. I feel sorry for you if you have a sweet tooth."

Brenda groaned. He would have to say that. He knew she did.

Turner didn't miss that look. "She could stand to put on a few pounds, in my opinion." Turner glared at Gil. "Only dogs like bones, scamp. Real men like flesh on their women."

"I'll remember that, Granddaddy."

"See that you do. This little girl needs feeding and loving up." He arched a silver brow. "You listening to me, boy?"

Gil laughed. "Hanging on your every word, Granddaddy."

"Impudent puppy," Turner grumbled under his breath.

Brenda smiled at the exchange. Taking a cup of coffee, she walked over to the fireplace to look at the array of family pictures proudly displayed on the mantle.

Gil came up behind her. "Mama's monster museum," he quipped.

"Shame on you, MaGil Jackson. I'll have you know that all my children are good looking, including you."

"I have been duly chastened. This is my sister, Carol," he pointed to a picture of his twin. "And her husband Wayne and their three boys, Mike, Curt, and Stevie." He moved on to the next picture. "These are my brothers Richard and Dylan." Gil smiled broadly at the next picture. "And this is my son, David."

Brenda's heart stopped when she got a good look at the little boy. The blood drained from her face, and she felt a trembling begin deep inside her body. Her mouth went dry. She nearly choked on her coffee.

She had to be wrong. It just couldn't be! Pain lanced through her brain.

Those eyes! That face, so like—

Surely fate couldn't be so cruel!

The cup slipped from her fingers, crashing to floor. Brenda looked apologetically at Sara. "I—I'm sorry!"

"It's all right. Accidents will happen."

A frown worried Gil's forehead. "What's the matter, Brenda? Are you feeling sick? Talk to me, sweetheart!"

She swallowed around the lump in her throat. "I think you'd better take me home."

She swayed on her feet. Gil's arms came up protectively around her to steady her.

"Maybe you should go upstairs and lie down," Sara suggested.

"No, please, I'd just like to go home."

"If she's feeling that poorly, maybe you should take her to the hospital, Gil," Durant suggested. "Your brother's on duty tonight, isn't he?"

"No hospital," Brenda said quickly. "All I really want to do is go home."

Sara started toward the closet. "I'll get your coats."

"You'd better take good care of her, Scamp."

Concern molded Gil's features. "I intend to, Granddaddy."

"I'm sorry to spoil everyone's evening," Brenda apologized.

"You didn't." Durant smiled reassuringly at her. "I hope it's nothing serious."

"Get out of their way, Durant, so Gil can take the child home," Turner groused.

Brenda felt guilty about leaving like this, but she just couldn't stay after—A flaming arrow of pain shot through her head, making her draw her breath in sharply. Nausea began to bubble and dinner threatened to erupt from her stomach.

Gil helped her into the car, then slid behind the wheel. He noticed the perspiration beading above her upper lip. Her hazel eyes had darkened, dull with misery, the pupils dilated. He wondered what could have caused her condition.

When they reached her apartment, he guided her up the stairs to her apartment.

"You don't have to stay with me. If I lie down, I'm sure I'll feel better."

"Are you sure you don't want me to take you to the hospital?"

"No. It's just a headache and the excitement of meeting your family, I guess."

Gil believed the headache part of her explanation, but not the rest of the reason she gave. He knew the symptoms of shock when he saw them. He'd seen enough people go into shock while testifying on the witness stand. He searched his brain trying to figure out what could have put her in this state. One minute she was looking at the family pictures; the next she—

"Gil, there's no need for you to worry. Really."

"When I've made sure you're all right, then I'll leave, not before." He held out his hand for her keys.

With a weary sigh, Brenda handed them to him. She felt too miserable to argue. She didn't know how she was going to get through the next few minutes or the rest of her life for that matter.

Sensing her distress, Gil took her coat and made her sit down. "Is there anything I can get you before I go?" he asked, hanging her coat in the closet.

"No." She sat down gingerly on the couch.

"Want me to tuck you in?"

She grimaced. "Any other time and I'd love to take you up on your offer, but—"

"But tonight you're not feeling up to it. I understand." He bent to kiss her forehead. "I'll call you in the morning to see how you're feeling."

"All right."

"Take care, baby."

"Good night, Gil." Brenda gave him a wan smile.

Only after he had been gone a few minutes did she break down. All the pain and misery she'd stored deep in her soul came gushing out in a torrent of tears. When she could finally gain control of herself, she went into the bedroom, and with shaking hands, pulled a small metal box from the top shelf of her closet.

She opened it. Tears slid down her face when she lifted out a piece of paper and the frayed picture of a newborn baby.

Brenda stroked the photo and gazed at the hospital record. This was all she had of her child. "Could it be I've found you at last, my baby?" She sniffed, closing her eyes.

Joy at the thought that it could be true surged through her. She was sure that David was her son. He was the image of his father, Hudson Caldwell, and he had the Walker hazel eyes.

But what if he isn't your son.

"What if I've made a mistake?"

Had Gil and his wife really adopted her child?

She had to know for sure. If she continued her relationship with Gil, she'd have to tell him who she was. And if she was the mother of his adopted son, how would he feel about her then?

But what if she wasn't David's mother? How could she make sure? The courts had denied her access to the files.

Brenda studied the hospital record. She'd deliberately left off the father's name. He didn't deserve to be on it, not after what he'd done. Memories invaded her mind, and suddenly she was Sheila Walker, naive college girl—

She'd just found out she was pregnant and was eager to share her news with her baby's father, Hudson Caldwell, the man she loved.

They'd known each other nearly six months, had been lovers for four. He swept her off her feet the day she met him. She was so happy thinking about the baby she carried, so sure Hudson would be too. He had told her over and over how much he loved her.

Hudson was a portrait painter and had a studio-loft apartment with a view of the Chicago Bridge. He had just begun to make a name for himself, and she was finishing her senior year at Northwestern University. She spent her spare time with him. They rarely went out. If they did, it was to go on picnics in Gary, Indiana, or to a special nightclub in Racine, Wisconsin, and afterward spend the weekend.

Sheila hadn't minded not seeing people. She was so in love with Hudson, being near him was enough for her. If he was a little secretive, aloof, or moody, she put it down to his artistic temperament.

When she discovered she was pregnant, she didn't doubt that he would want the baby and insist that she become his wife.

She'd bathed and perfumed her body and made it her business to look as attractive as she could. She'd ordered his favorite dinner and had the table set with candles and a bottle of champagne chilling on ice.

"I smell Shrimp Devine," Hudson said when he entered the apartment.

"There is nothing wrong with your sense of smell."

She launched herself into his arms, and he swung her around.

"What's the special occasion?" he asked, kissing her lingeringly.

"It's a surprise, but I'm not going to tell you what it is until you've had your dinner."

"If I have to wait that long we may not get to eat. I want you very badly, Sheila," he said caressing her breasts, then sliding his hands over her hips, bringing her closer by pressing her buttocks.

She closed her eyes, glorying in the joy of his love.

"I don't want the food to get cold, Hud."

Reluctantly, and with a groan, he let her go.

Sheila took pleasure in watching him eat. When he finished, he drew her into his arms.

"I bought some champagne to celebrate."

112

"Celebrate what, love?" He kissed her neck, moving his lips to the sensitive area behind her ear.

"Hud, we're going to have a baby." She felt him stiffen.

"What did you say?"

"I found out yesterday that I'm six weeks pregnant. Darling, we're going to have a child." She smiled happily. *"Do you want a girl or boy?"*

Hudson violently shoved her away from him.

"Damn it, I don't want either one. You have to get an abortion."

Her heart stopped, and she stood frozen in place.

"Hud, I—" She gulped. *"You can't mean that!"*

"I do. I know of a doctor who'll—"

"I can't believe you're asking me to do this! I love you. I'm carrying your baby."

His expression turned ugly, and he laughed. *"What do you expect me to do? Marry you?"*

"Hud, I—"

"Sorry, sugar, I'm already taken."

"Already taken? What are you saying?"

"I'm taken as in already married."

She stumbled backward as though he'd punched her in the stomach.

"You, but—Hud—you can't be."

"But I am and have been for the last sixteen years. So you see why you have to get an abortion. Once you've done that, things can go back to the way they were," he said reaching for her.

She couldn't believe that just a few minutes ago she was so happy, and now she felt betrayed, used, and destroyed. Then it came to her why things were the way they had been between them. Why they hardly ever went out anywhere, and only when she had insisted, then only to out-of-the-way places or out of town altogether.

She had been such a fool.

She shoved him away. *"Things can never be the way they were, Hudson. I'm not going to get an abortion."*

"You have to, damn it."

"I don't and I'm not. If you don't want to have anything more to do with us, fine."

She stalked into the bedroom and started gathering her things.

Hudson followed.

"You're not going anywhere until I make you see that an abortion is the only way to go."

"Oh, I'm leaving all right. You've used me for the last time, Hudson. I thought you loved me."

"You're good but not the best I've ever had, and you won't be the last."

His words gutted her heart and shattered her soul. She realized that he never really cared for her as she cared for him.

"Don't think about going to my wife, Sheila," he warned.

She stared at him. Who was this callous stranger? How could she have ever believed she loved this man? She took the key to his apartment off her keychain and threw it at him.

"Don't worry, I won't go to your wife. I feel sorry for you, Hudson. One day she'll find out what kind of man you really are. Then she'll leave you and you won't have anyone. I just wish I could be there to see it. You're a low-down, selfish bastard."

"Am I? What do you think you're carrying in your belly?"

"God, how I hate you," she ground out and slammed out of his apartment.

She tried to tune out his cruel words and unfeeling look, but it was no use. When she got to her car, she climbed inside, slumped over the steering wheeling, and cried. She never thought she could hate anyone as much as she hated Hudson Caldwell. She promised herself that she would never allow another man close enough to hurt her that much—

With difficulty, Brenda shook off the effects of the painful walk down memory lane and folded the hospital record, then picked up the photo and lovingly rubbed her fingers across the picture of her baby. There were no words to describe her feelings at this moment. He was a part of her and yet—

114

Brenda closed her eyes. The pain in her head threatened to rival the one in her heart. She wished she could blink them both out of existence. She had to find out if David was really her son. She didn't think she could go through the pain if he wasn't her baby. Or if Gil rejected her.

She opened her eyes, then placed the birth record and the picture back in the box before setting it on the dresser.

Her eyes ached. The dull throbbing at the base of her skull was building into one of the awful headaches she was so susceptible to, blurring her vision, threatening to take the top of her head off. The headaches had begun when she was eight years old. She recalled clearly their onset because it was the day her parents sent her away to boarding school.

Brenda stumbled into the bathroom to the medicine cabinet. Her hands shook so badly she could barely screw the cap off the bottle of painkillers.

She'd never told anyone about the headaches. She endured the agony in silence until one day when she was eighteen the pain became more than she could bear, and she had to go to a doctor who described painkillers.

Brenda reached for the glass on the sink, filled it with water, and took two of the tablets. Somehow, she managed to drag herself to bed. She closed her eyes and waited for the pain relievers to kick in.

The headaches had all but disappeared until—until she'd given up her son. Afterwards she managed to control her stress by not getting involved, by mentally distancing herself from the pain. Now—

There was no way she could go in to work in the morning. She opened her eyes and glanced at the clock on the nightstand. It was only a few minutes after nine. She reached for the phone.

"Hello."

"Laura, this is Brenda."

"You sound awful. What's wrong?"

"A migraine headache, and I won't be in to work in the morning."

"Are you taking anything for it?"

"Yes, I have some tablets, but it usually takes a while to recover. I hate to leave you in the lurch."

"I can handle things at the Lodge until you're feeling better. Take care of yourself. If there is anything I can do, don't hesitate to call me, okay?"

"Thanks. Good night, Laura."

Brenda lay still until the pain subsided then she undressed and put on her nightgown. If not for the tablets, there was no way she could sleep. Soon she felt herself drifting into a deep medication-induced sleep. Her last thought was of Gil's son, who might also be her son.

Chapter Thirteen

Just as Gil started to leave his office, Carl walked through the door.

"You on your way to court, counselor?"

"No. As a matter of fact I'm on my way to visit a sick friend."

"Brenda Davis?"

"How did you—Aunt Shirley." Sometimes Gil forgot how close his mother and aunt were. They told each other everything. Their lines of communication were up there with Western Union and Money Gram.

"I ran into Shirley at the bank about an hour ago. It's not anything serious, is it?"

"I don't know. I tried calling Brenda earlier and got the answering machine. Then I called the Quilt Lodge and Laura said Brenda wasn't coming in today. Said she was suffering from a migraine headache."

"I feel for her then. You should get her some of Benicia's headache remedy tea."

"I'll drop by the reservation when I leave here. Now why didn't I think of that?"

"Because a man in love rarely thinks straight. I should know."

"You and Laura?"

"Yes." Carl grinned. "I'm going to ask her to marry me."

"I'm happy for you, cuz. I hope everything works out for you both."

"Me too. I'd better not keep you from going to see Brenda."

Gil sent his cousin a sidelong glance. "It's amazing, the

change that's come over you lately."

"Blame it on the rain. Or a certain lovely lady. I never thought I'd fall in love again."

"You deserve it more than anyone I know. It's been a long time since Gabrielle died. I'd say you are overdue for some happiness."

"Spoken like a true cousin, or a man who's in love himself."

"Get outta here, man."

Carl grinned. "I'm on my way."

Gil raised his hand to knock one more time when the door to Brenda's apartment opened at last.

"I was beginning to worry. Are you feeling any better?"

"Yes, thank you." Brenda still felt a little groggy from the pain relievers. At least they had dulled the pain and taken the edge off the trauma of last night's discovery. "What time is it?"

He glanced at his watch. "It's almost one-thirty."

"I didn't realize it was so late. Come on in."

Brenda looked a little ragged, Gil thought. "I bet you haven't eaten anything, have you?"

"No, but you don't have to—"

He led her into the living room and helped her down on the couch. "I'm into taking care of you. Can't you get that through your head, woman?"

She smiled weakly. "I'm beginning to."

"Good." He made her lie on the couch, propped her feet up, and pulled an afghan over her before going to the kitchen to see what he could fix her to eat.

A short time later, he returned with a bowl of soup, crackers, and a cup of tea. "The soup isn't my mother's but it'll have to do."

"I'm not complaining. What are you doing here this time of the day?"

"Visiting a sick friend."

"Very funny. Don't you have to be in court or something?"

"Not this afternoon. Did you feel the headache coming on last night? Is it when you began to feel sick?"

He'd given her the perfect excuse, although only a temporary stopgap one. Knowing where her son was had opened up a Pandora's box. But was he really her son? She had to know the truth.

And if David was her son, would it be just the beginning of her pangs of distress, taking the form of headaches as well as heartaches? When she looked at the food, any thought to eating it vanished.

Gil pushed the cup of herb tea toward Brenda.

"Carl swears by this Chippewa headache remedy. According to him, it won't leave you groggy like the pills the doctors prescribe."

Brenda sipped the tea. "Tastes like mint."

"That may very well be in there. I have no idea what any of the magical ingredients are. Carl used to have a lot of those headaches right after his wife died. Could the cause of your headache be more psychological than physical?"

"I don't know what you mean."

"I think you do. You seemed all right, then all of a sudden—"

"My head is beginning to throb, Gil, I think I'd better go back to bed."

"Whatever it is that's bothering you won't disappear, Brenda. It'll still be there after the pain subsides. Trust me, baby. I can only help if you tell me what's wrong."

This was the moment she didn't want to face. What should she do? She just couldn't bring herself to tell him the truth or ask him if his son was adopted.

Gil saw the indecision in her face. What was it? Why wouldn't she confide in him?

"I have to be getting back to the office, but I'll call you when I get home. I put the rest of the tea in the tea canister. Now, let me help you back to bed."

He reached for her hand. When he pulled her to her feet and slipped an arm around her waist, he felt her tremble. He didn't understand her. What could have happened to her last night? But he didn't ask, only helped her to bed and kissed her good-bye.

—※◈※—

Brenda heard Gil clearing away the dishes then put them in the dishwasher before he left. He was a caring compassionate man. He was the man she loved with all her heart.

If you love him you owe him a little honesty.

Tears spilled down her cheeks. Yes, she did owe him that. She would have to tell him the truth eventually, there was no getting around it.

Brenda continued to drink the Chippewa tea headache remedy throughout the afternoon and evening. By the next morning all signs of her headache had disappeared. The tea had worked miracles. She called Laura to tell her she'd be in to work.

As luck would have it her first customer was Shirley Edwards.

"Gil has been so worried about you, Brenda dear. I'm glad to see you back at work." She frowned. "You still look a little peaked to me."

"Now don't fuss, Aunt Shirley," Gil said from the doorway.

Brenda turned. She hadn't heard the shop bell. She forced a smile to her lips. "I'm glad to see you."

He wondered if she really meant it. There was something about her smile that—Maybe he was just being paranoid.

Laura came downstairs with Jon-Marc in her arms.

The old pain squeezed Brenda's heart like a vice. Being around babies, especially little boy babies, made her uneasy. The memory and the guilt over giving up her own always seemed to hover near, torturing her mind and heart.

"I forgot something. Will you take Jon-Marc for a minute, Brenda?" Laura put him down.

120

There was nothing she could do but take his hand. She checked the misery invading her soul and blinked back tears. She even forced a smile when she saw Gil watching her.

"Oh let me have him, Brenda," Shirley insisted, "This little fellow needs to get to know his relatives."

Brenda's uneasiness receded and the tension holding her loosened its grip when Shirley took Jon-Marc's hand and walked over to the window.

"It's too bad that Aunt Shirley never had any children. She does have a way with them."

"Yes, she sure seems to."

"When we get married and have kids, she's sure to spoil them rotten as she has David."

"Gil—"

"I know it's early days to be talking about kids when I haven't officially proposed." He grinned. "But, I like thinking ahead."

Ask him about David, the voice of reason urged Brenda.

"Gil, I need to—"

He silenced her with a quick but potent kiss. "I'll be by your place at six-thirty. Got to go." He glanced at his watch. "I have an appointment in thirty minutes. But I had to come by and see you."

She would ask him this evening, she thought grimly.

—∗⟨❖⟩∗—

"What is it, baby?" Gil stroked Brenda's hair as they sat before the fireplace after their meal.

She snuggled closer and put her arm around his waist. "I'm a lucky woman."

"I'm the lucky one."

"I'm not the only woman who believed that."

"Are you concerned that I'll compare you to Monique?"

"Well it—"

He laughed. "You're unique, Brenda Davis, and I love you for just being you."

"How did she die?"

He paused before going on. "It had been snowing and the streets were icy that day, but Monique was determined to go and pick up David's birthday present. The car went into a skid, she lost control, and crashed into a truck. She was killed instantly."

"How awful," Brenda gasped in horror.

"Yes, it was awful." He sighed. "David was in the car with her, but luckily his car seat was anchored in the backseat."

"You must have been devastated."

"I was. It was an impossible time for me and David. I don't know what I would have done if I didn't have my son."

"He must look like your wife. He doesn't favor you at all."

"I imagine he does resemble his biological mother and father. I wouldn't know. I've never seen either of them. Monique and I adopted David when he was five days old. A colleague of mine had a lawyer friend who knew of an unwed mother who wanted to find a good home for her baby."

He gazed into the fire. "Monique and I had tried for years to have a child. When she finally did conceive, she had a miscarriage. We discovered later that she could never conceive another child as a result of complications from the miscarriage."

"How sad."

"It was more than that for Monique. We tried in vitro fertilization and she carried the baby several months before losing it too. Eventually she had to undergo a hysterectomy. She was one of the most courageous women I have ever known."

"So you decided to adopt," Brenda probed gently.

"Yes. We had gone through conventional methods and found that we would have to wait. It seems that there is a shortage of black babies to adopt. I didn't want Monique to wait that long for a child after all she had already gone through. When my colleague suggested contacting his friend, we jumped at the chance. Months later, just before the adoption was to be finalized the natural mother tried to take him from us."

Brenda heard the lethal anger in his voice and cringed inside. But at the same time she was thrilled at finding out for sure that David was her child.

"I'm glad we never met the woman." His features clouded over with pain and bitterness. "She nearly drove Monique to a nervous breakdown," he gritted out. "But we managed to keep our son. I'm ashamed to say that I'll always hate that young woman for what she tried to do to us."

Brenda's voice was unsteady. "Maybe she genuinely regretted giving her child up."

Gil kissed the top of her head. "You're so wonderfully compassionate, Brenda Davis. It's one of the reasons why I love you so much. You were a real friend to Laura, making her pain your own. But your compassion is misplaced where David's natural mother is concerned."

"You sound so bitter."

"I can't help it. The woman's own parents provided evidence that she wasn't emotionally fit to raise her child. Do you have any idea how hard it must have been for them to put the welfare of their grandchild first? They cared more about the child than that young woman did. She didn't care that she would be disrupting his life."

"How can you be so sure? There could have been extenuating circumstances that you knew nothing about."

"I doubt it. She certainly didn't give a damn about mine or Monique's feelings. I can never forgive her for her selfishness, especially the pain and misery she caused my wife."

The word *never* echoed through her head. And Brenda felt her insides freeze at the condemning tone in Gil's voice.

She cleared her throat. "How did you and David manage?"

"If not for my family—" His voice faded. "Right now, David is spending time with my sister and her kids. Since she has all boys, David fits right in. He needs the sense of belonging and warmth my sister and her family can provide. Don't get me wrong I want him with me, but he needs to be around children his own age."

"You could send him to preschool or a day-care center."

"No, I couldn't. I refuse to do that. Besides, Aunt Shirley is a retired school teacher and she studies with him. She says that he is exceptionally bright for his age. He is reading already. I spend as much time with him as I can."

"I can see that you are a devoted father."

Gil lifted her hand to his lips. "I'm going to be a devoted husband to you, Brenda. All you have to do is agree to be my wife."

"I believe you," she said softly, but didn't make any promises.

"I love you, Brenda." He gazed into her eyes as his lips caressed the back of her hand.

"And I love you." She reached up and pulled his face down to hers and kissed him.

"When David gets back, I want the two of you to get to know each other. I know he'll grow to love you as I do."

The sharp edge of panic cut into her heart. She had a chance to know her own child, be a mother to him. Did she dare take it? Did she dare not to?

You must tell Gil the truth. Do it now or you'll regret it.

I can't, not yet. Our relationship needs time. I need time to get to know my child.

You're fooling yourself, girlfriend.

I'm not. I'm not.

"Brenda?" Gil frowned. "Are you all right? You look a little peaked."

"I was wondering how I will feel when I meet your son. And whether he will like me."

"He'll love you, baby, so stop worrying. I'd better be going. I have an early court case in the morning or I'd stay and keep you warm all night."

She loved this special man so much, she thought, watching him as he put on his coat.

"I hate saying good-bye to you, Gil."

"After we're married you won't ever have to again." He smiled warmly. "That I can promise you." He opened the door. "I'll call you tomorrow."

"I'll be waiting."

Brenda closed the door and leaned back against it. Gil was everything she ever dreamed about in a man, though she hadn't dreamed about one for a long time. She didn't think such a man existed, at least not for her. She had promised herself she would never get involved again. Now look at her, she couldn't get more deeply involved if she tried.

Brenda walked over to the fireplace and stared into the flames. She was sorry that Gil's wife had died, but she couldn't deny her feelings of joy. David was truly her son. She could have it all. It was so near, she could almost taste it. She could have a husband she loved and the child she'd given up.

What if he finds out who you really are? What then?

Who's to tell him?

You're playing Russian roulette with your heart.

I know, but I don't want to lose my son. And I can't lose Gil. I can't and I won't.

Chapter Fourteen

When Gil got back to his office after leaving the court-house the next morning, there was a message to phone his mother.

"I want you to bring Brenda with you to our Thanksgiving dinner," his mother told him when he called her back.

"You liked her, didn't you?"

He could hear the smile in her voice. "You knew we would. She's a lovely girl. Will we be hearing wedding bells in the near future?" She rushed on not giving him a chance to answer. "Your granddaddy is especially taken with her and can hardly wait to see her again. He thinks you hit the jackpot. He said so in just those words."

"I'll bet he did." Gil laughed. "If he were forty years younger I would have to consider him serious competition for Brenda's affections."

"Then I was right about the wedding bells?"

"I haven't asked her to marry me yet, but I plan to. She wants to meet and get to know David first, and then there are other reasons too." He didn't want to think about the possibility that she might decide not to marry him when he did seriously ask her. "I'll see if I can convince her to come for Thanksgiving dinner. She may have made plans to spend the holiday with her family."

"From talking to her, I gathered that she and her family aren't that close. She seems a little lonely to me."

"She is a bit of a loner, but I intend to change all that," he vowed.

—⋙◈⋘—

Brenda heard the phone ringing as she walked into her apartment and ran to answer it.

"Hello!"

"Baby, you sound out of breath."

"Gil. I wanted to reach the phone before it stopped ringing. I just got in."

"I hope you didn't do any shopping for dinner because I want to invite you to my place."

"You're bored with my collection of music and want me to listen to yours."

"Actually that isn't the reason I want you to come over, but if it's the inducement I need to get you over here, that'll work."

"You're incorrigible."

"Incorrigibly crazy about you, sweetheart. I'll be by to pick you up in fifteen minutes."

"All right. I'll be ready."

Brenda hung up her coat and headed into her bedroom to find something to wear. She was in an up mood just knowing Gil loved her. Seeing him would round out her day.

—⋙◈⋘—

Gil cast an appreciative look over her figure when he walked through the door. "That's a nice sweater you're wearing, ma'am."

"Thank you, kind sir."

"You don't need to thank me. And I'm not being kind. I was thinking that you would look even better with it off," he said reaching for her, drawing her into his arms to kiss her.

"We'll never make it to your place if you—"

He interrupted the flow of her words with another kiss. "You talk too much, woman. And they accuse us lawyers of doing that." He felt her stiffen. There was that animosity about his profession again. "You're right, we'd better get going."

127

Brenda had tried to master her reaction to the word *lawyer*, but found that she couldn't, even when she knew he was only joking. What must he think about that? What must he think of her? "I'll get my coat."

They rode to his place in silence. This would be her first time going there. She didn't know what to expect. It certainly wasn't the beautiful house she saw. His father must have designed it, she thought. It was a different take-off on the log cabin design his father had used on his own home. This was more modern.

As though reading her mind, Gil said, "Yes, my father's fine hand is obvious, isn't it? We pooled our ideas on the design. There is a guest bedroom and four family bedrooms and a huge playroom for the large family I hope to have one day." He glanced purposefully at her. "With a little help, of course."

He stopped the car and turned to Brenda.

"Monique never lived here, if that's what you were wondering. The house was only in the planning stage when she died. I have a second chance at love, to have that large family. And I want it with you, Brenda," he said caressing her cheek.

Family?

That word was precious to Brenda. She never thought to ever have one before she met Gil. Now she wanted it with this man more than anything, but—

"Do you like it?" he said, starting the car and driving on.

"It's magnificent." She gasped at the sight of the three-tier set of steps that curved at every level like an elegant spread of cards as it ascended to the house. A perfectly landscaped shrub garden flanked either side of the steps.

Gil drove past them up the sloping drive. He helped Brenda out of the car and they headed along the flagstone path leading to the front door. As Gil unlocked the front door, Brenda observed that there were plenty of windows.

Gil turned on the light. Brenda's eyes widened at the sight of the enormous natural rock fireplace that took up one entire wall of the living room. A huge area rug in front of the fireplace was made from fake tiger skin with several huge matching pillows scattered on the floor.

From the looks of things, Gil had evidently planned a romantic dinner. The coffee table arrayed before the fire had two place settings. Small three-branched candelabras were waiting to be lit on each of the oak end tables.

The decor of the room was a mixture of the Indian and African cultures. Art objects from each, such as blankets, hangings, and carved figurines dominated the room.

Gil took Brenda's coat, then removed his own and hung them in the closet. As she continued a further study of the room, she saw that he had a stereo system and entertainment center built into another wall.

"You weren't kidding when you said you had everything," she said in an awed voice when the list of his CDs came up on a mini wall monitor. "Is the rest of the house this fantastic?"

He grinned. "You want the royal guided tour tonight?"

"Maybe just a mini one. I am kind of hungry, besides being curious to see what your kitchen looks like."

"It's pretty functional, I'm afraid. I have a housekeeper who comes in three days a week. Otherwise, David and I are on our own unless my aunt or mother takes pity on us and we get invited to eat with them, which they do quite often. Are you considering applying for the job?"

"Which one?"

"Wife, lover, mother, housekeeper, cook. Whatever you like. All five if you like. Don't you want to feed me, clean my house, have my babies, be my lover? Not necessarily in that order."

"I especially like one of the above."

"Oh? And which one might that be? I only seem to remember one that's a definite." He stroked her breast. "Maybe I need a memory-refresher course with hands-on demonstrations."

"I meant cook. Lead me to your kitchen, Romeo."

"Actually, the one you picked isn't the one I remember and

going to the kitchen certainly isn't where I wanted the demonstration to take place."

"You promised me dinner, and I intend to see that you keep that promise."

"You are one persistent lady, Ms. Davis."

"You'll find out how persistent I can be in other areas—later."

"Later?" he said huskily. "That sounds promising."

"To the kitchen, Action Jackson."

Gil liked seeing Brenda this way. She definitely needed him in her life as much as he needed her in his. From the doorway, he watched her checking out the dinner Mrs. Arnold had prepared for them. It was as though she belonged there.

"My mother wanted me to extend an invitation to you to come to Thanksgiving dinner. I told her you might have plans to visit your family."

"I haven't made any plans to spend the holiday with them. Your son is going to be there, isn't he?"

"He'll be back in Long Rapids before then."

"I'd be happy to come to dinner." She lifted a bowl out of the fridge.

"They—your parents—may decide to come visit you."

"I doubt that very seriously."

Gil realized that his mother had been right. There was definitely a lack of closeness between Brenda and her family. He was curious to know the reason.

Sensing that Gil had picked up on her antipathy toward her parents, she said, "This looks good. What is it?"

He let her change the subject. "Mrs. Arnold's famous Tourangelle salad."

"Tourangelle salad?"

"It's made with string beans, tomatoes, and new potatoes. The ingredients to her sauce, which makes the salad so good, is a well-kept secret."

"Sounds intriguing."

"Wait until you taste her braised lamb. It's to die for."

Brenda smiled up at him, and his heart did a funny little

flip-flop. God, she was beautiful. And how he loved her.

—◆—

After dinner, Gil chose Luther Vandross's latest CD, *Your Secret Love*. When she came back from the kitchen, Gil seated himself on the floor then poured her a glass of wine. He leaned back against the couch, nestling Brenda deeper in his embrace as he gazed into fire.

"What upset you at my parents' house, Brenda?" he asked gently.

She knew this was coming, and she would have to choose her words carefully.

"It was being with your family, knowing that the relationship with my own was—is nothing like it and never will be."

"You want to talk about it?"

"It wouldn't do any good." She sipped her wine.

"You'll never know until you try."

She sighed. "My parents are wealthy, part of an elite social society in Chicago. I'm their only child. I've always had everything a child could ever want, except—"

"Their love and affection."

She considered his words. "I think they love me in their own way."

"But not in the ways you want or need to be loved."

She nodded. "When I was eight, they sent me away to boarding school. All their friends were doing it." She laughed. "I guess it was the 'in' thing to do at the time." Her thoughts drifted to happier times. "I looked forward to the summers when they allowed me to visit my Aunt Bertha in Delaware. I was always closer to her than to my parents."

Gil heard the regret in her voice. He sensed there was more to it than that. He could see the pain in the depths of her expressive hazel eyes. What horrible experience had she gone through with her parents, he wondered.

"I convinced them to let me attend college at Northwestern University, though they weren't hot on the idea. They wanted

131

me to go to one of the prominent women's colleges." She cleared her throat. "I reached my senior year without mishap, until I met Hudson Caldwell."

Gil tensed. "He's the one who hurt you, isn't he?"

"Yes," she said quietly and put her wineglass down because her hand had begun to tremble and she didn't want to spill it.

He tightened his embrace. "If it's too painful, you—"

"I need to talk about it." She paused gathering her composure. "W—we became lovers and I got pregnant."

Gil felt the urge to say something but didn't. He waited for her to go on.

"He wanted me to have an abortion. I refused. It was then that he told me he was married. I—I told my parents about the pregnancy but not the name of my child's father. They were more vehement than Hudson that I have the abortion. They tried to—" Her voice broke. Tears streamed down her face. She wiped them away. "When I refused to do as they said, they sent me to live with Aunt Bertha. After the baby was born, they and their lawyer began a campaign to convince me to give my baby up."

Gil frowned. That explained her reaction to lawyers. "And did they succeed?"

"Oh, yes." She sniffed. "I finally decided that they were right and did what they wanted."

Gil wanted to say something. But what could he say to ease the pain she must have experienced at giving up her child. It explained the compassionate look she'd given him when he mentioned the unwed mother. It explained more than that. It explained her seeming aversion to holding Jon-Marc's hand. The look on her face when she saw the photo of his son. And, finally, why she didn't want to become involved with him. Her reluctance to make a commitment.

"Brenda, look at me."

She turned her head.

"I know why I love you so much. You're one hell of a woman."

"You mean you don't hate me for what I did?"

"No, my darling girl. It took real guts to do what you did and an incredible amount of strength to pick up and get on with your life after that soul-destroying experience. Most women would have broken after going through something like that."

He just didn't know how close she'd come. That was one period in her life she never wanted to think about.

"After we're married, I'll give you another child, as many children as you want. I know it can't replace the one you gave up, but maybe it'll help make coping with the loss easier. I noticed your reaction to Jon-Marc. I could tell that you love children by the fond look you gave him, but something was holding you back from showing it. I never dreamed it could be anything like this. I love you, Brenda Davis."

"And I love you."

He held her close. This woman he loved had been through hell and survived. He was going to spend the rest of his life making it up to her by giving her all the love he had to give.

Brenda felt lucky to have Gil. A voice inside her urged her to tell him all of the truth. But she couldn't, not yet.

Chapter Fifteen

As Gil stoked the fire, Brenda watched in fascination. This man was what she needed to make her whole. He was not just warm and loving, he was much more than that. When he turned to look at her, the glow of his smile caused a meltdown of her senses.

She belonged to him, and him alone.

She realized that he was an ethical man not at all like the other lawyers she'd encountered. Brenda wondered how she could have ever thought otherwise, considering the fairness with which he'd dealt with Laura, Jon-Marc, and his own cousin.

Would he feel compelled to reach deep inside himself to be fair when he learned of her relationship to his son?

"Such a serious look," Gil teased.

At the sound of his voice, her somber expression eased into a smile. "I'm always serious about you."

Gil joined her on the floor. "I like the sound of that." He let his gaze rove lazily over her. "You're beautiful, baby."

"I'm glad you think so." She traced a finger along his jaw, to his lips.

He took her finger into his mouth and caressed the tip with his tongue.

As she gazed into his dark eyes, she found them to be as arousing as his tongue felt. Ripples of excitement began to build inside her.

This man was devastatingly appealing. She realized that from the moment they met, and those feelings hadn't diminished despite what she had learned. It was so easy to get lost in his gaze. She didn't really want to be found. The delicious heat infusing her body had nothing to do with the fire blazing in the hearth.

"Oh, Gil."

"Yes, Brenda?" he murmured huskily.

She tingled when he said her name like that. His lips left her hand and moved up her arm past her shoulder to her collarbone. She felt his hands against the back of her head. When he drew her face to his and kissed her lips, a soft moan escaped her, and she slipped her arms around his neck, bringing him into closer contact with her body.

He laid siege to her lips again, this time deepening the kiss, urgently soldering their mouths together as though they were two pieces of hot metal created specifically for that joining. His fingers sought the soft swell of her breasts through the sweater, homing in on her nipples. He felt her quiver at the brush of his thumbs across the sensitive tips.

Gil moved to undo the buttons of Brenda's sweater, slowly releasing each one. Wanting to feel her warm naked skin, he quickly unhooked her bra, freeing her breasts for exploration. He'd come to know her body only recently, but it was as though he'd known the feel, the scent, the warmth of it forever and could never get enough of touching her.

He trailed his lips over her skin, dropping kisses along the path of her throat to the fragrant valley between the heavenly peaks of her breasts, letting his tongue enjoy the rapture of their taut softness.

Brenda cried out his name, arching her back. He groaned, his aroused body hardening in pleasure-pain so acute, it rendered him speechless. He removed her sweater entirely, skimming his fingers over her ribs, then sliding them around and up her back.

Slowly, he lowered her to the rug and gazed into her passion-glazed eyes, their hazel color appearing to be more green than brown. He loved this woman more than life. She fascinated him. Every time he touched her he was lost.

Brenda watched Gil unfasten the button on her skirt, then

peel it off. Next went her slip and panty hose.

Now that she was completely bare, he started the sensuous journey up her body. The touch of his fingers sliding up her calf to the inside of her thigh was so titillating it made her gasp and open her legs. When she felt him insinuate his fingers through the dark forest of curls concealing her femininity and stroke between the delicate folds of flesh, Brenda closed her thighs, trapping his hand. He smiled when she arched against his fingers.

"You ready for me, love?"

"Oh, yes, yes," Brenda cried desperately. When he brushed the sensitive nub of her desire again and again, she closed her eyes, reveling in the ecstasy he was giving her. Then the stroking stopped. She opened her eyes and found that Gil's expression had stilled, his attention riveted on her mouth.

Her voice shaky and breathless, she whispered, "Now. It's your turn. I want you naked and just as eager as you've made me."

He pulled his sweater over his head and unbuttoned his shirt, revealing his incredibly masculine chest. Brenda couldn't resist kissing his nipple. She felt triumphant when she heard him groan.

A tremor of pleasure lowered the timber of his voice, rendering it barely audible. "You want to continue the job?"

"You have no idea how much it would please me, Gil."

"I definitely want to please my woman."

She slowly undressed him. Resting her weight back on her heels when she had removed everything but his briefs, she began rubbing her fingers across them.

"Is feeling going to be enough for you, baby?"

"No."

He lifted his hips so Brenda could pull his briefs off.

She sat staring, entranced by his aroused manhood.

"I take it you like what you see?"

"You look good enough to eat."

"Want a bite?"

"I couldn't stop with just a bite. I'd want to devour the

whole thing," she whispered in a sultry voice.

"Sounds wicked."

"I feel incredibly wicked at this moment."

"Baby, indulge yourself," he whispered, his voice lowering, thickening with passion.

"You know what an insatiable sweet tooth I have."

"It's nothing compared to mine."

He brought her body down over his so they were touching, thigh to thigh, hip to hip and chest to chest. Gil joined his lips to hers in a bone-melting kiss.

Moments later, Brenda felt the throb of his manhood against her femininity, so eager to gain admittance to the gates of paradise.

Gil thrust deep inside her. A low mating sound rumbled in his throat, then he reversed their positions.

Brenda brought her legs up around his hips and began to move with wild urgency, arching her body upward to meet his.

The rub of the soft tiger fur beneath her when Gil moved against her was erotic. She could almost hear the primitive beating of an ancient ritual drum in a wild jungle scene. It was as though their hearts were picking up the sensuous rhythm and passing the message to the rest of their bodies.

Just after Brenda heard Gil's breath go in a sound that was part sigh, part moan, she felt him sink deeply inside her, and she locked her legs around his. The momentum carried him deeper, causing the ecstasy to sizzle through her veins and singe her senses.

"Oh, Brenda, what are you doing to me, girl?"

"Loving you out of your mind."

"Mind? What mind? You've just burned it to ashes."

He captured her mouth, devouring any answer she might have given.

"You take my breath away," she gasped.

"I'm savoring it and you. I love you, Brenda."

"And I love you, Gil."

"I don't want anything to come between us."

"I'd say there wasn't much chance of anything doing that

right now."

"Smart ass. I mean it, Brenda. If there is anything, anything at all you need to tell me, please don't hesitate to come
to me with it. I want you to promise me that."

"Gil, I—"

"Say it. I want to hear you say it."

"I promise." She kissed him. "You're so special."

"So are you."

He bent to take a nipple into his mouth, laving his tongue
over it again and again.

Gil's sensual stroking sent tingling sensations into
Brenda's loins. Her hold around his waist tightened and she
began to rock against him.

Gil placed his hands on her buttocks, drawing her closer,
embedding himself deeply, as far as he could go. When her
contractions began they were fierce and strong around his
flesh, the pleasure unbelievable.

"Yes, oh, yes, like that," she cried out.

Gil picked up the chant as they moved against each other.
The drumbeat grew louder and their movements more frenzied. The flames flicking their senses blazed ever hotter, ever
higher. Suddenly the dance reached a climax, ecstasy bursting
over them, showering them with sparks as though from actual
fireworks.

—❈—

Later, Gil stared in awe at his woman as she lay asleep in
his arms. She was passionate beyond his wildest fantasies. He
had loved Monique and believed he could never love again,
but he'd found Brenda.

When he thought about how Hudson Caldwell had hurt her,
he saw red. If he ever got his hands on him—

He heard Brenda sigh and saw the sleepy smile curve her
lips. "Having a happy dream, baby?"

"Oh, yes, happier than you would ever believe."

"Was I in it?"

"Oh, you had the leading role."

He crushed her to him. Then he kissed the hollow of her collarbone and moved his lips up her throat, detouring to the sensitive space behind her ear.

When he reached her lips, she drank from his as if she was a woman in the desert, parched from lack of water. He was her never-ending wellspring; she would never drink her fill of this man. She would thirst for him until the end of time.

He slipped over her again. She closed her eyes glorying in his possession.

"Open your eyes, baby. I want to see them when you lose control and fly apart."

"Do you promise to reassemble me?"

"As many times as there are stars in the heavens."

Her eyes darkened when he took her over the edge. He gave a male shout of triumph and followed her into oblivion.

Sometime later they ascended from the aftermath of their lovemaking, and Brenda gazed at the clock over the fireplace. Her brows arched in surprise. It was two-thirty in the morning.

"Gil, I've got to go home."

"You can't go."

"I can't?"

"No, ma'am."

"But I have to go to work in the—in a few hours."

"I'll get you there in plenty of time, sweetheart." He caressed her cheek with his own.

"But I have to change."

"I know." He kissed her and brushed a thumb over her nipple.

"Gil, I—oh, don't do that or I'll—" she whispered.

"You'll what?"

"I'll be tempted to make love with you again."

"Anything wrong with that?"

"No, but—"

"No buts." He slanted his mouth over hers. "Anymore objections?"

She smiled, batting her eyelashes. "No, Your Honor."

"Saucy wench."

"You love me."

"I most certainly do."

A soft savage sound came from his throat, then he made love to her again.

The next time Brenda woke up, she heard a shower running. Gil appeared and held out his hand.

"Let's shower together."

"It sounds good to me."

Several hours later, Gil took Brenda home to change for her workday. He was tempted to play hooky from the office and go back home. But if his woman could go to work after the night they'd spent, he could do no less.

His woman.

Gil loved the sound of that.

Chapter Sixteen

"You're virtually glowing, showing all the signs of being deeply in love and happy about it this time." Laura smiled knowingly at Brenda.

"Oh, I am."

Laura started humming the wedding march.

"Have you and Carl set a date for your wedding?"

Laura laughed. "I was humming the wedding march for you."

"Me?" Brenda's brows arched.

"You have that look."

"What look is that?"

"You know, the one of blissful euphoria."

"Oh, *that* look," Brenda said dreamily. "I love him so much."

Laura hugged her. "I'm happy for you."

"I never thought I'd ever be this happy."

"Why not? You deserve happiness as much as anyone."

"There's a lot that you don't understand."

"You're going to help me to, though. Right?"

Brenda frowned. "I do need to confide in someone other than Gil. There are things I just can't tell him right now." She sighed. "After the Lodge closes I'll stay and we can talk."

⊷≺✧≻⊶

The day literally flew by for Brenda. Closing time came almost too quickly, she thought, as she watched Laura turn the closed sign around and lock the door. Brenda wasn't looking forward to talking about her past. She hadn't been last night either, but she had opened up to Gil.

Laura took a sip from the cup of coffee she'd just poured. After hearing Brenda's story, she asked, "Are you sure you're David's mother?"

"Yes."

"You've been through hell, haven't you?"

"I'm not the only one. Gil's wife went through much more. I can't help worrying about his reaction when I tell him the whole truth. He has practically canonized the woman since her death. And it's not just that. He may see my agreeing to marry him as a scheme to get my son, not because I love him."

"You aren't doing it for that reason, are you?"

Brenda sighed. "No."

"Now I understand why you always managed to distance yourself from Jon-Marc."

"I didn't think you noticed."

"Oh, I did."

"And you weren't offended?"

"I wondered sometimes, but now that I know the reason, I understand. Getting back to my question."

Brenda walked over to the rocking chairs in front of the fireplace and sat down. Laura dropped into the other.

"I never wanted to give up my son in the first place. You have no idea how much it hurt and the misery I've suffered since. Oh, God, Laura—" Tears slid down her face.

"You empathized with me when Carl tried to take Jon-Marc from me. If he had succeeded, it would have been like giving your son up all over again."

Brenda wiped the tears away with the heels of her hands. "Pretty close."

"When you tell Gil the truth, he'll—"

"Understand and forgive? I put his wife through hell, Laura. He loved her very much. When you watch someone you love suffer, can you really be that forgiving to the person who caused it?"

"I don't know. You might."

"You didn't see his face when he talked about David's real mother. What I saw was pure hatred. I wanted my baby, but I didn't want to hurt anyone."

"I know what you mean. Carl had that same look when the judge ruled against him and I walked away with Jon-Marc the first time we went to court. I realized then how much getting custody of his grandson meant to him, but I couldn't give Jon-Marc up. I loved him too much."

"So you see how impossible that idea is."

"I can see Gil's side as well as yours. And I sympathize with you both. What are you going to do?"

"I don't want to hurt my son or Gil."

"I know you don't, but at some point you'll have to trust in Gil's love for you."

Brenda knew Laura was right, but she was afraid. Trust was something she had a hard time dealing with after her experience with Hudson, then her parents and their lawyer. And finally the lawyer whom she trusted to help get her baby back and had betrayed her.

Yes, she had a problem with trusting.

"I know it's easy for me to say, but you'll have to force yourself to do it anyway. Or risk losing the man you love."

"Thanks for listening, Laura."

"I don't have a problem with it, believe me." Laura's mouth widened in an earnest smile. "I just wish I could do more to help."

"Believe me, you've helped." Brenda glanced up the stairs. "Jon-Marc has been a angel. We haven't heard a peep out of him."

"Don't speak too soon."

"He's a good boy."

The subject of her praise punctuated those words by letting loose an ear-splitting scream.

"I'd better be going so you can look after him. I'll see you in the morning."

"Think about what I've said, all right?"

"I will."

※◆※

Over the next week, Gil kept Brenda busy exploring the countryside surrounding Long Rapids, visiting the reservation, and spending time with his grandfather. It was as though he understood her mood and adjusted his campaign to win her trust completely. He was so generous with her, it made her feel guilty for keeping anything from him.

"A penny for your thoughts, pretty lady," he said when they drove back to her apartment after seeing a movie they'd both wanted to see.

"I thought they stopped making them. In any case, I'll tell you what my thoughts are for free. I was thinking of how devotedly you care for me."

"It's a labor of love, sweetheart. Is that all you had on your mind?"

"What do you mean?"

"There's a sad expression that mars that lovely face every now and then. You were thinking of your son, too, weren't you?"

"You into mind reading as a sideline, counselor?"

"Only yours. I'm interested in everything about you.

She leaned over and kissed him.

"What's that for?"

"General principle."

"You've been around my grandfather so much, you're beginning to sound like him."

"He's a sweetheart. And I like him very much."

"The feeling is mutual, I can assure you."

"Are Carl and Laura coming for Thanksgiving dinner?"

"No. Carl decided to take Laura and Jon-Marc to the reservation for Jon-Marc's first Indian Thanksgiving. It's something to see. I'll take you next year."

"I'd like that." She couldn't help wondering if she would still be in Gil's life by then, once he knew the truth. She still

144

couldn't bring herself to tell him everything. She didn't know if she could take it if he turned away from her in disgust.

Gil didn't miss the shift in Brenda's mood. That sad expression was back. But there was nothing he could do to remove it. And until Brenda confided in him, he was helpless.

Brenda ached to confide in Gil, but she was so afraid of losing him if she did.

"Are you all right?" he asked.

"Yes. I just get in these melancholy moods sometimes. They'll pass."

"They'd better. There's no room for them in our lives."

"No?"

He kissed her lightly on the forehead. "No, sweet Brenda."

She found his optimistic attitude contagious and couldn't help responding with a spontaneous smile.

"That's better. You up to having some company this evening, Ms. Davis?"

"As long as the company is you."

"Who else?"

Just then Gil eased the car in front of her apartment building and cut the engine.

"You do know how much you mean to me?" He gently caressed her face and stroked her hair.

"Yes, I do."

As he lowered his mouth to hers, she closed her eyes, glorying in the contact of his lips on hers.

"The things you do to me, Ms. Davis," he rasped.

"You do the exact same things to me, Mr. Jackson."

He kissed her again. "I'm glad to hear it. Now let's go inside and I'll build a fire."

"Presumably in the fireplace."

He grinned wickedly. "To which are you referring?"

"Oh, you're terrible."

"Not as terrible as I'd like to be."

"And how terrible is that?"

"Let's go inside so I can show you."

Chapter Seventeen

Brenda stood watching the heavy white snowflakes fall against the window of the Quilt Lodge. There was only one week left before Thanksgiving.

"Brenda."

"Yes, Laura," she answered turning away from the window.

"You okay?"

"Oh, yes. Just woolgathering."

Laura laughed. "I haven't heard that expression since I was a little girl."

"You can thank Mr. Turner Jackson. If you're around him long enough, his homespun sayings rub off on you."

"He is a charming old gentleman, isn't he?"

"Yes." Brenda smiled. "I couldn't love him more if he were my own flesh and blood grandfather."

"I have a feeling that you're going to fit right into the Jackson family."

"Laura, how can you know that?

"I can't, but one thing I do know is that a friend is suffering, probably needlessly. Haven't you heard that the truth will set you free?"

Brenda arched a brow. "One of Granddaddy Turner's favorite sayings?"

"No, something I've learned through experience and heartache. And it was a hard lesson. It won't be an easy one for you either, but it's best if you do it."

Brenda watched her friend reorganize the shelves. She knew Laura was right, but she didn't want to face that decision yet.

Gil's sister and her family were bringing David home. They were set to arrive later today according to Gil, and he wanted her to come to his house this evening to meet them.

At the thought of meeting her son today, her mood brightened. Her heart was threatening to fly from her chest and her nerves to tangle and knot impossibly. In other words, she was a walking wreck. She'd longed for this day since giving up her son. Now that it had finally arrived, she didn't know how to feel, how to react.

Brenda walked over to Laura. "I'll bet you've been wondering since I told you the truth, what kind of woman I am to have given my baby away."

"You're the kind of woman who wants what is best for her child. Stop punishing yourself like this. You did what you thought was right. You were young and under the controlling influence of your parents. I'm surprised you came away from that wrenching experience a whole person."

"I almost didn't. I spent two years under psychiatric care in a private sanitarium."

"But you survived. Doesn't that tell you something? You're a strong woman, Brenda Davis."

She smiled. "You have a way of always making me feel better."

"I'm glad. That's what friends are for. Right?"

"You're the best."

⊰≕❖≕⊱

When Brenda drove up in front of Gil's house, she saw a van in the drive parked next to Gil's car, and another car as well. She wondered who else was there. Her heartbeat sped up and her breathing came fast and jerky. She nearly slipped on the icy ground when she got out of the car.

Gil came out to meet her. He noticed that her hazel eyes were enormous in her small face. He took her in his arms and found that she was trembling.

"Don't worry. David is going to love you, Brenda."

147

She smiled nervously up at him. "I hope you're right."

"Does it bother you so much meeting him because David is the same age as your son?"

"I'd be a liar if I said it doesn't."

Gil realized how fragile the woman he loved was feeling and how brave. He remembered her reaction to holding Jon-Marc. And later when she admitted why it was so hard for her to be around little boys. He groaned, his sister had all boys.

"You'll get used to my sister and her brood," he reassured her. "You'll like her."

"I'm sure I will. She's your sister, isn't she?"

"My brother Dylan, the doctor in the family, has been dying to meet you since the family has been singing your praises. Not to mention yours truly." He grinned.

Brenda sighed. Gil Jackson was a wonderful man, and for now he belonged to her. If she could help it, he always would. If she could help it.

Gil hung Brenda's coat in the closet, then guided her into the living room. What she saw took her breath away. Four little boys ranging in age from three to seven were sitting Indian style around the fireplace, while a young woman, the female version of Gil, sat telling them a story.

Brenda gazed from one child to the other before settling on the one she believed to be her son. She knew it had to be him because he looked even more like Hudson Caldwell now than he had in the picture. Her heart stopped for a moment, then started beating again, but faster.

Gil urged her closer and cleared his throat. His sister stopped the story and smiled up at him, then shifted her gaze to Brenda.

"Carol, I'd like you to meet Brenda Davis. Where is Wayne?"

"In the kitchen as usual. You know how he loves to cook."

"And mess up," Gil complained.

"The results are always worth the cleanup, Gil."

"For you maybe, but I'm the one who always ends up doing all the work afterward."

"Poor baby," Carol answered with mock sympathy.

"So this is the paragon you've been going on and on about, brother," came a deep masculine voice.

"If you were ever in doubt, this is my brother Dylan," Gil said to Brenda.

She wanted to focus her attention on the people in front of her, but her eyes strayed to her son. She wanted desperately to touch him, hug him, tell him she was his mother and that she loved him, but she couldn't.

"Come over here, boys," Gil called to the children.

Carol's three sons came without hesitation. David hung back.

"Mike, my oldest nephew, is seven. Then there's Stevie, who's five. And Curt, three." Gil signaled to his son. "David."

"Yes, Daddy," he said in a shy, low voice.

"Come here. There's someone special I want you to meet."

Brenda swallowed hard. She remembered seeing the pictures of herself at his age. Her son's eyes were so much like hers had been. They were an unusual shade of brown that would lighten to hazel as he grew older. It was a trait peculiar to the Walkers.

She shifted her gaze back to Gil and studied his expression, wondering if he suspected that David was her son.

No. He couldn't possibly. Not yet.

"David, this is Brenda Davis, the lady I've been telling you about."

"Pleased to meet ya," he said, lowering his eyes.

"I'm pleased to meet you, David." Brenda smiled. Her hand shook slightly as she reached out to the boy.

David went to Gil's side and pressed his body against his leg.

"He's shy with people he doesn't know. Give him time, Brenda," Gil soothed. "When he gets used to you, you'll have to peel him off you."

Brenda sincerely hoped so.

Carol's husband, Wayne, came out of the kitchen wearing

a chef's apron. Brenda liked him immediately. He wasn't at all what she expected. He was six feet four if he was an inch. Although he looked like a linebacker for a pro football team, he had the gentlest eyes she'd ever seen. Next to him, Carol looked tiny and fragile though she was average weight, standing five feet seven or so.

"He's big, but harmless," Carol said with a giggle.

"I resent that," he grumbled good-naturedly, "I think."

Brenda felt as at home with Carol and her brood as she did with the other members of Gil's family.

Dylan Jackson walked over to her. He grinned charmingly. "My brother always was the lucky one. He would have to see you first."

"I did see her first," said Gil. "So don't get any ideas, little brother."

Brenda shook her head. Flattery was definitely a Jackson trait. Gil's brother Richard was probably like the rest of the Jackson men.

While Carol and her sons, and Dylan and Gil played Scrabble before the fireplace, Brenda sat beside David. Wayne went back to the kitchen to put the finishing touches to his masterpiece.

What did she say to her son to break the ice?

He held a toy airplane and fiddled with the wings.

"You like airplanes, David?"

"Yes, ma'am. I wanna fly one when I get growed up. Great-Granddaddy Turner said I can be anything I wanna be."

"He's right. He's a very special man, isn't he?"

"He sure is," David said proudly. He looked up at her. "You know my great-granddaddy?"

"I sure do."

David smiled at her. Her heart turned over and tears stung her eyelids. She couldn't believe this beautiful little boy was her son. Oh, how she longed to hold him in her arms, but knew she would have to wait. And waiting was going to be hell.

Wayne announced that dinner was ready.

When David decided to take a seat next to her, Brenda's

heart swelled with joy. She smiled fondly at her son as she watched him tuck into his food.

Gil, on her other side, said, "He chose to sit next to you. I'd say you've worked some of your special magic on him, making yet another Jackson male your slave."

"Are you jealous, Gil?" Brenda teased.

"Maybe just a little. It would seem that none of us Jackson men are immune to you."

"I agree with that," Dylan inserted. "Richard is the only one who hasn't fallen under her spell, and that's only because he isn't here and hasn't met her yet," he said with a grin.

Later, after Dylan had gone home and Carol and Wayne were upstairs putting the boys to bed, Brenda and Gil started on the clean up.

"I told you I'd end up cleaning the kitchen," he grumbled, stacking the dirty plates on the counter. "When I know Wayne is coming, I should hide all the pots and pans and dishes."

Gil looked beseechingly at Brenda. "Please, won't you take pity on me and agree to be my wife, sweet maiden?"

"Oh, Gil, you nut. Who's to say after I marry you, I won't make you do the same thing."

"You're a cruel woman to joke about something like that."

"I love your sister and brother-in-law. The kids are great too. I especially love David. He's so sweet."

"I told you, you two would hit it off. Now getting back to my proposal. I was serious, you know."

She turned toward the sink and started putting the dishes in the water.

"After what you've been through with Caldwell, I can understand your reluctance where commitment is concerned, but, baby, I love you. I'd never hurt you."

"I know you wouldn't intentionally, but—"

"You've got to learn to trust in my love for you as I trust in yours for me." He wiped his hands on a paper towel and brought them to her shoulders and kissed the nape of her neck.

He trusts you, echoed in her head.

She didn't deserve it because she was keeping something from him that she knew he had a right to know.

You've got to tell him the truth.

She grazed his hand with her cheek.

"I do trust you, Gil."

"I need proof."

"How can I show you when my hands are elbow-deep in soapsuds?"

"That means I have you at my mercy, doesn't it?"

"What are you going to do to me, master?"

"This." He turned her to face him and lowered his mouth to hers.

Her body quivered with desire when he eased his tongue inside her mouth merging it with hers. She moaned and slid her arms around his neck.

Gil was oblivious to the fact that she was getting his shirt wet. All he could think was how wonderful she tasted and how right she felt in his arms.

"You two had better get married very soon," Carol said from the doorway.

Gil slowly left Brenda's embrace. "I agree with you. Now, if I can just convince my lady of that."

"David wants you to tuck him in," Carol said. "According to him, you're the only one who can tell special bedtime stories. He really missed you, Gil, not that he wasn't happy to spend time with his cousins and his favorite aunt."

"His *only* aunt," Gil said wryly, then turned to Brenda. "I'll just be a minute, baby. Don't run off before I get back."

"I won't." Brenda longed to go up with him and help tuck her son in, but it would have to wait until another time.

"You love my brother, don't you?" Carol asked.

"Yeah," Brenda said with a sigh. "I do."

"I was worried about him for a while. He's been so lonely since Monique died. Oh, he's had women chasing him, but he buried himself in his practice and kept himself busy helping

Carl with reservation business and other projects."

"Shirley mentioned that."

"You know, it's the first time I've seen him this interested in a woman to consider marrying again. My brother deserves to love again. I liked Monique, but I like you, too. I sense an inner strength about you, Brenda Davis. I think that's what drew him to you."

"You don't even know me."

"I feel I do. I size people up very quickly. Carl says I possess the powers of shamans from both our cultures." Carol laughed. "Gil calls it the double whammy." Her expression turned serious. "I can sense a certain sadness about you too. My intuition is rarely wrong."

Brenda plucked a dish from the water and started drying it.

"Gil can be as good for you as you can be for him, but I'll tell you one thing about my brother. Although he is compassionate and gentle, don't cross him. If there is something you need to tell him, don't keep it from him. Tell him soon, Brenda."

Brenda had an eerie feeling that Carol knew she was keeping something important from her brother and was warning her of the possible consequences if she ignored that warning. She agreed with Carl about Carol's powers.

"I haven't frightened you, have I?" Carol asked. "Carl and Gil say I have a habit of doing that when I speak my mind."

"No, you haven't."

"Good, I wouldn't want to do that. I'll help you finish cleaning up my husband's mess." Carol laughed.

"The way he cooks, I'd forgive him anything."

"I do."

Gil and Brenda were alone at last. Carol and Wayne had gone up to bed minutes earlier. Brenda snuggled in his arms as they sat on the tiger skin rug, his back propped against the seat of the couch, both enjoying the warmth from the fire.

"I think it went well with David, don't you? You know, he always prays for a new mother since he lost Monique. He misses that special closeness a child shares with his mother."

"That doesn't mean that he'll accept me as a substitute."

"David told me he thought you were pretty. And he was pleased that you liked his great-granddaddy. You scored points with him there. I'd say it looks promising that he will."

"I owe Granddaddy Turner my thanks."

"What about me? Don't I get a reward?"

She kissed him. "Of course you do. It's getting late. I'd better go."

"If you married me, you'd never have to leave," he said in a gently persuasive voice. "I'd take you upstairs to our bedroom and make love to you all night every night."

"You make it sound so tempting. Is that a subtle form of bribery I hear in your voice, counselor?"

"You have to admit the inducement appeals to you. It's the first time I haven't heard that certain animosity in your voice about my profession. You can even kid about it now. You've changed, Brenda. May I assume that I'm the reason for it?"

"You can."

"You seem happier tonight than I've ever seen you."

"I am, Gil." She glanced at her watch. "I really have to go."

He drew her into his arms and kissed her deeply. "Something to remind you of what you're missing."

"Any more and I'll melt in my boots."

Gil walked her out to her car.

"Carol and Wayne and I want to take the boys on an outing on Saturday. Want to tag along?"

"I'd like that."

"Pick you up about noon."

—◈—

As Brenda drove home, she was filled with hope for the future. All she had to do was say yes to Gil's proposal and all her dreams would come true. But the thought of keeping the truth from him lay heavily on her conscience. Guilt plagued her night and day. But did she dare risk losing everything by telling Gil the truth?

A sudden sharp pain sliced through her temple. She gripped the steering wheel until the pain subsided. She wanted to make up to her son for giving him away. Would he one day hate her when he knew the truth? And there was her guilt about what she had done to Gil and his wife when she tried to get her son back.

A dull throb began at the back of her head. She had to tell Gil the truth. She couldn't live with herself if she didn't. It would undermine their marriage. But how did she go about it? What could she say? How could she say it?

"Oh, Gil, I happen to be the bitch who tried to take your son away from you and caused your wife such misery."

What would she tell her son?

"I'm the woman who gave you away after you were born. I'm back now to take your adopted mother's place."

She had to stop thinking like this. Here was her chance to make amends. But what if, in his anger, Gil refused to let her?

That doesn't make what you did right. Tell him, girlfriend.

I will. I'll just have to find the right time.

Will that perfect time ever come?

Brenda had no answer for that question.

Chapter Eighteen

"For years, Mr. Jasperson has raised Llamas for their fur. He has a lot of young ones and allows children to come to the petting zoo every Saturday," Gil explained as he walked Brenda out to Wayne and Carol's van Saturday afternoon.

"He sounds like a nice man."

"Oh, he is. He let us wild Jackson children do that when we were growing up."

"Were you really wild, Gil?" she asked.

"Didn't Granddaddy tell you?"

"I guess that must be the reason he calls you Scamp."

"If we have daughters, I'll have to teach David a few pointers," he said loud enough for Carol to hear.

"He tortured me unmercifully when we were little, Brenda."

"Yeah, right," Gil shot back. "Don't let her meek exterior fool you, she used to wrestle her brothers to the ground, no problem. Ask Dylan. He was the baby, and she didn't even show him any mercy."

"I couldn't afford to, Brenda, they would gang up on me. And my twin here would show *me* no mercy," she said innocently.

Brenda, smiled shaking her head. As an only child, she had often imagined what it would be like to have brothers and sisters. She would have welcomed the chance to argue, fuss and fight with them.

She climbed inside the van and moved into the empty seat beside her son. She wanted him to have brothers and sisters one day.

"I hope you don't mind if I sit here with you, David."

"No, I don't mind. You're nice just like Daddy said."

Gil sat across from them. "I'm an unsung hero, what can I say?"

"What's a unstrung hero?" David asked Brenda.

Brenda looked to Gil for help, but he only hunched his shoulders, leaving her to explain.

"You know what a hero is? Right?"

"Uh-huh."

"An unsung hero is a hero who does good things, for good reason, but doesn't brag about them."

"My daddy is a good guy then?"

Brenda gazed lovingly at Gil. "He sure is."

Gil flashed her a grateful look along with a devastatingly tender smile.

Carol's boys commentated non-stop about the scenery, the snowdrifts, how the lake had frozen over, and the people ice-skating on it.

"You ice-skate, Brenda?" Gil asked.

"When I was about seven and went to visit my Aunt Bertha, the neighborhood kids taught me. Those were some of the happiest times in my life."

"David has recently learned a few basic moves along with Carol's boys. Maybe we'll get to take them skating before they leave."

"Like a real family, huh, Daddy?" David asked.

Brenda could see how happy the thought of a family was to her son. She'd missed this with him. If she'd only kept him. Tears trickled down her cheeks, and she turned toward the window and wiped them away.

"Did I make you cry, Brenda?" David wanted to know.

"No, baby, you didn't. Us grown-up girls do that sometimes. It's no one's fault."

Gil knew she was thinking about her own son, what she'd given up, what she would always miss. He vowed that he and David would make sure she realized that she belonged with them and she could be happy. He handed her his handkerchief.

Brenda looked at Gil and David and saw a glimpse of the future she could have.

—≍≪◇≫≍—

Brenda had never seen real Llamas before and said so. David proudly showed her how to pet them. She thoroughly enjoyed the afternoon, watching her son roughhouse with his cousins.

"The longing in your eyes nearly breaks my heart, baby," Gil said gently. "He can be your son, our son. I know he can't make up for the one you—"

"Gave away." She blinked rapidly to stave off more tears.

"I didn't mean to hurt you."

She placed a gloved finger across his lips. "You didn't, it's only the truth. I have something I have to tell—"

"Come on, Daddy, and play with me," David shouted as he ran toward his father.

"It'll have to wait, baby," Gil said, letting David drag him away.

Carol walked up. "The three of you look like the perfect little family."

"I want that so much, but—"

"But you're afraid to take a chance. I feel troubled vibes coming from you. You need to find peace within yourself, Brenda. If you don't, very soon, I foresee a lot of pain in store for you, my friend."

"You practicing psychiatry without a license again?" Wayne interjected. "Or should I say practicing your witch doctoring hocus-pocus?"

Brenda looked from Wayne to Carol.

"Oh, I'm used to this." Carol's expression turned serious. "Heed my warning, Brenda." She shifted her gaze to her husband. "If you don't watch it, I'll put a curse on you."

"I thought you already did," he said, backing away from her.

"Why—I'm going to get you for that, Wayne Baxter." She

gave chase, picking up a handful of snow and shaping it into a ball to throw at him.

Gil returned with a snow-covered David. "I think we'd better take this little guy home and get him into some dry clothes."

"I think we all need to do that," said Carol.

During the ride to Gil's house, Brenda thought about what Carol had said. It was almost as if Carol knew everything about her, but that was crazy. Whether she did or was only guessing, Brenda couldn't help feeling uneasy.

"You seem to be the only one in the group who didn't get wet." Gil looked at Brenda. "You want to help me find some dry clothes for David?"

"May I?"

"You may as well get used to it."

"Gil—"

"All right, but I know you won't be able to resist me for very much longer because I know you're crazy about my son. He'll be the secret weapon I'll use to win you over."

He didn't know how close he was to having that happen, Brenda thought as she followed him up to David's room. They found him madly tossing clothes out of the drawers.

"Hey, my man," Gil called to him. "What are you doing?"

"I can't find my Mickey Mouse sweatshirt," he whined.

Brenda saw it on a shelf in his closet and brought it over to him.

"Are you gonna be my new mother, Brenda?" he asked.

Brenda got down on her knees to help him into the shirt. When she didn't answer he said, "If you are, can I call you Mama now?"

"One question at a time, son," Gil said with a smile.

Brenda looked into her son's eyes. "I—do you really want me to be? Your mother, I mean?"

"Yeah, I do, Brenda." David threw his arms around her neck.

Brenda drew her son into her arms and held him close, too moved by his spontaneous act to do or say anything else. She had longed for this day forever it seemed.

Gil hunkered down beside them and put his arms around them both. This was his family, his life.

Wayne dished up a delicious pot of chili he'd left cooking in the Crock-Pot that morning.

"You should open up a restaurant, Wayne," Brenda complimented him.

"We can't afford that yet, but I've written a cookbook and sent it to a publisher. The editor seemed pleased with it." Wayne laughed. "Now, if they'll only shell out the cash."

"They will, believe me," Brenda answered. "If they don't, I know a friend who's in the publishing business."

"Oh, really? Who?"

Brenda wrote down the name and the publishing house on a piece of paper and handed it to him.

It was just another thing about Brenda that made Gil curious to know more about her background, her friends, her parents. Did he really know the real Brenda Davis?

David asked Brenda to help tuck him in. Her heart turned over when she heard his prayer.

"Please, God, bless Mama up in heaven, bless my daddy and please let Brenda be my new mama real soon. Amen."

David kissed Gil and then Brenda before saying good night.

"He's such a darling child, Gil," she said to him as they descended the stairs. "You've done a wonderful job of raising him."

"Thank you. I couldn't love him any more if he were my own flesh and blood child."

"Does he talk about his mother much?"

"Sometimes, but he was only two when she died."

"He needs a mother's love."

"Are you going to be the mother he wants and needs?"

Brenda didn't answer immediately. The urge to tell him the

160

truth prodded her. "Gil, I don't know. I want to say yes."

"And I want you to, but only when you're ready." He drew her into his arms and held her close. "You have to come to terms with the loss of your son so you can love mine. I understand that. Look, I'd better take you home. You don't know how much I miss making love to you. I hope you're feeling as needy as I am at this moment."

"Believe me, I am. You're addictive, MaGil Jackson."

"I hope I always will be. I'm addicted to you and, right, now I need a fix. If I didn't have a house full of people, I'd lay you down before the fireplace and make sweet love to you all night."

"You certainly know how to get a girl all worked up."

"It's all a part of my master plan to convince you to marry me."

"You know what they say about the best laid plans."

"I don't think mine will fail. I'm going to make you my wife, Brenda Davis, so you may as well give in gracefully."

Tormenting images of Hudson Caldwell and her parents haunted Brenda's sleep. Gil's angry face after she'd told him the truth flashed before her mind's eye. Her son's dear face then another face: Monique Jackson.

Brenda woke up with another throbbing headache. She stumbled into the bathroom to get her tablets. She lay back down, and closing her eyes, waited for the medication to take effect. She didn't know how long she could stand it. The guilt she carried was becoming too heavy to bear.

Her son wanted her to become his new mother. She wanted that as much as she wanted Gil. She wanted them both.

She couldn't survive if she lost them.

Chapter Nineteen

"Are Dylan and your other brother Richard going to be there?" Brenda asked Gil when he came to take her to his parents' house for Thankgiving dinner.

"Unfortunately Richard couldn't make it, but Dylan promised to get away from the hospital when he could. There are always so many accidents on the road during the holidays. He couldn't say what time he would arrive. I'm beginning to wonder if I shouldn't be on the alert where my younger brother is concerned."

"Jealous?"

"You'd better believe it."

"You have nothing to worry about, Mr. Jackson. Haven't I told you lately that I love you?"

He grinned. "Yes, you have, but I never get tired of hearing it. Are you ready?"

"Almost. All I need to do is get my coat and pull on my boots."

"You'd better add a scarf and gloves. It's cold enough to freeze the fur off a bear's butt."

"Another one of Turner Jackson's sayings, no doubt." She laughed, reaching for her coat.

"Let me help you with that." Gil encircled her in his embrace once she had her coat on. "How did I get so lucky?"

"As I said before, I'm the lucky one."

⊷≍◈≍⊷

Gil guided Brenda up the stairs to the deck level of his parents' house.

"Careful," he said gripping Brenda's elbow to steady her when her feet nearly slid out from under her. "It can get pretty treacherous sometimes."

She smiled up at him. "I'm not worried about falling. I know you'll be there to catch me."

"Always."

When they reached the front door he stopped, turned her toward him, and lifting her face with his gloved hand, gazed into her eyes before lowering his mouth to hers.

The gentle massage of his lips on hers sent shivers through her, and it had nothing to do with the frigid chill in the air. All her problems seemed to slip away for the space of that one precious moment.

"Oh, Brenda."

"Gil, we shouldn't—"

The door opened.

"I had begun to wonder what was keeping you two out here so long," Dylan kidded. "I should have guessed what you were up to. You'd better get in here before you both freeze into popsicles."

"One of these days, Dylan." Gil gazed into Brenda's eyes. "Maybe being frozen with you wouldn't be such a bad idea."

"None of that," Dylan teased.

Gil glared at his brother.

"I think we'd better go inside," Brenda said, "I see your mother coming."

"I'm so glad to see you, Brenda. We've all been waiting for you and Gil to get here. Don't stand in the way, Dylan. Let Gil and Brenda come inside and warm themselves."

"Yes, ma'am."

Gil cast his brother a wry smile. "There's justice in the world after all."

Dylan smiled good-naturedly and closed the door. In the hall, he took his brother's and Brenda's coats and hung them in the coat closet.

The heat from the fire reached out to welcome them.

Durant and Turner rose from their chairs.

"I'm glad to see you, young lady." Turner smiled. "Come over here and give an old man a kiss."

She bent to place an affectionate kiss on his wrinkled brown cheek.

"And you're worried about competition from me!" Dylan teased Gil. "I think you'd better keep your eye on our grand-daddy, big brother."

Gil looked to his father. "At least I don't have to worry about you, Dad."

"No, you don't. Your mother might beat me up."

"Durant Jackson!" Sara exclaimed.

"Yes, dear."

Brenda smiled. "You all make me feel so welcomed."

"Where is my son and Carol and her brood?" Gil asked.

"Oh, they're in the kitchen helping Wayne," Sara explained. "He's baking cookies. It's hard to drag any of them away from the stove."

Brenda's smile brightened when she saw David come running into the living room followed by his cousins. A lump formed in her throat. A lifetime of watching him would never be enough for her.

"Uncle Wayne and Aunt Carol ran us out of the kitchen. We told them we wanted to stay and help, but they said we was eatin' cookies faster than Uncle Wayne could bake them," he grumbled, licking his fingers.

Gil aimed a fond grin at his son. "A man after my own heart." He opened his arms.

David ran into them. Noticing Brenda, he left Gil and went over to her and took her hand.

"David, you forgot to wash your hands!" Sara exclaimed, shaking her head.

"It's all right, Sara. We can all go wash our hands togeth-er," Brenda said to David and his cousins.

"Do you have any kids, Brenda?" David asked.

Brenda cleared her throat. "I—no."

Gil saw the momentary torment that flashed in her eyes before she went with the boys to the bathroom to wash their hands.

Turner laughed as he spoke to Gil. "I see you're as smart as I always thought you were, scamp."

"What do you mean, Granddaddy?"

"Getting David to help secure your prize catch. I'll help you all I can."

"Granddaddy, I—"

"No need to explain. I'd pull out all the stops too to have a woman like her."

Gil shook his head. There was no use trying to explain anything to his grandfather. In his own way, he was as one-trackminded as Aunt Shirley where Brenda was concerned.

Brenda and the boys came back into the living room. She was trying to recover from her reaction to David's innocent remark, but it was hard. She felt like such a fraud when she looked at Gil. She never wanted to lie to him. Pain started to hammer at the back of her head, and she tried to will it away.

"Are you all right, Brenda?" Dylan asked upon reaching her side soon after entering the room.

"I have a headache, that's all."

Dylan tilted her chin and looked into her eyes, then lifted her wrist to take her pulse.

Gil frowned. "Is anything wrong?"

"No, Gil," Brenda started to explain, when another wave of pain pounded through her head, and she closed her eyes tightly.

"I think you should go upstairs and lie down for a while," Dylan suggested. "Do you have anything for the pain?"

"Yes, in my purse."

Gil got the purse and handed it to Brenda.

"I'll get a glass of water." Sara headed for the kitchen.

"No need to take her upstairs. My room is closer," volunteered Turner.

Dylan and Gil helped Brenda down the hall to Turner's bedroom. Her senses seemed to swirl in a tide of misery.

165

"I'll stay with her until the pills start working," Gil said, his voice rough with concern.

"If you don't feel any better after a while, let me know, Brenda," Dylan insisted. "And I'll give you something, or we can take you to the hospital."

"All right. But I'm sure I'll be fine once the pills start to work."

After his brother had left the room, Gil took Brenda's hand in his. "Are you really all right, baby?"

"Yes," she said squeezing his hand, offering him a weak smile.

When he saw Brenda's eyes close, Gil quietly tiptoed out of the room.

Brenda opened her eyes and stared at the ceiling. Her fear of losing the two most important people in her life warred with the urge to tell Gil the truth. Then there was the torment of guilt over what she'd done, not only to her son but to Gil and his wife as well. No wonder these awful headaches had returned.

The doctor at the sanitarium had warned her about what stress could do if it wasn't controlled or alleviated. It was easy for him to say. His conscience didn't plague him night and day the way hers plagued her.

Of all the places on earth, why did she have to pick the one where her son lived. And she would have to fall in love with the one man who had every reason to despise her.

She recalled the adoption agreement. According to the arrangements, she was never to know the name of the adoptive parents although they would know hers. Bailey Johnson, her parents' attorney, had told her that they were a loving couple who would take good care of her baby. When she, her parents, Bailey Johnson, and the adoptive couple's lawyer appeared in court the judge confirmed this.

It nearly tore her heart out to sign those adoption papers. Her parents had convinced her that she was doing the right thing for her child, their grandchild. She'd wanted so badly to know who the adoptive parents were, but she never found out.

The judge said the records would be sealed. He gave her a chance to change her mind. She glanced at her parents and Bailey Johnson. She saw no weakening of resolve there. The looks they cast her were ones she took for sympathy and approval of what she was doing.

It wasn't until later that the doubts began to plague her. She had to have professional help to cope with her loss. She would go for long walks without telling anyone where she was going or she would forget to keep important appointments. She turned into a nervous wreck, and her attacks of guilt became so fierce they brought on the violent headaches, forcing her to take pills for the pain.

The pain became too much, and she took more and more pills until she collapsed and had to be taken to the hospital. It was then that she knew she couldn't live with her decision. She had to have her son back.

Her parents made sure that she couldn't get him when they presented proof to the judge that she was mentally unstable. She'd hired a lawyer to appeal the decision, but he betrayed her. She was convinced that her parents had bought him off, but she couldn't prove it. After she lost the appeal, she broke down completely and had to be admitted to Riverview, a private sanitarium.

The sound of the door opening brought Brenda out of her reverie.

"It's me, Carol. Are you feeling any better, Brenda?"

"Yes."

Carol pulled up a chair beside the bed and took Brenda's hand. "There is such pain in you. I feel it vibrating through you. It is not the physical kind of pain. Only you can put an end to it. Your spirit longs to be set free. Won't you free it, Brenda?"

"I want to, Carol, but—"

"You are troubled over the past, aren't you? It only has the power to hurt you if you let it. You hold the key to controlling your own destiny."

Brenda pulled her hand away.

"Free yourself of this pain, Brenda. Share the pain as well as your joy with MaGil."

"You don't understand."

"You don't think Gil can understand, do you? That's it, isn't it? You're afraid he won't understand or forgive."

"Carol, I can't talk about this."

"He loves you, Brenda, and so does David. My nephew wants you to be his new mother."

"He said that to you?"

Carol smiled. "Yes, he did. He and Gil are waiting for you to make their family complete. I know you love Gil, so why are you reluctant to accept his proposal? You care for David. I've seen it in your eyes."

"Yes, I do very much."

Carol stood up. "Now that you're feeling better, I'll leave so you can freshen up and join us."

Brenda left the bed, and picking up her purse, went into the bathroom to splash water on her face. She had just started to reapply her makeup when she heard the bedroom door open.

"Brenda," Gil called to her.

"I'm in the bathroom."

He strode to the doorway and peered inside. "Are you feeling better?"

"Much," she answered, easing her lips into a smile.

He came into the bathroom and slipped his arms around her waist, drawing her back against his body.

"I'm glad."

Brenda nestled her head against his shoulder reveling in his warmth.

"We'd better go back. Dinner is ready. The family is waiting."

When they walked into the living room, all eyes seemed to rivet on her. Brenda saw the looks of concern on their faces. These wonderful people cared about her. They were her family now.

"You and Carol seem to have hit it off," Gil said later when he took her home. "I saw her leave the bedroom before I came in. So what did you two talk about?"

"You and David mostly. She's a lot like you."

"You really think so? In what ways do you think we're alike?"

"You're both intense, caring, thoughtful."

"Twins often share the same personality traits. I thought you should know that twins run in the Jackson family. If you marry me, we may have a set or two."

"A set or *two*!"

Gil laughed. "Does the idea scare you?"

"You're teasing me, aren't you?"

"A little."

"I enjoyed the evening with your family."

"I want you to consider them your family too. You'll get another invitation to spend Christmas Day with them. I guarantee it. My mother has already sounded me out about it. You don't have any other plans, do you?"

"I don't know."

"When will you know?"

"Soon. Will Carol and Wayne and the boys be staying until then?"

"I doubt it. She's high on individual family celebrations of Christmas. They'll be back to ring in the New Year, though. Even Richard wouldn't dare miss that. According to Aunt Shirley, families are supposed to be under the same roof when the New Year comes. It means that the family will be united for another year.

"I like that idea. I've learned how important a strong sense of family is."

Her expression made him wonder again about the relationship between her and her parents. They had failed to instill the joy of family into their only child.

Gil drove up in front of Brenda's apartment building.

"You don't need to get out, Gil."

"You're really wiped out, aren't you, baby? You don't

169

have to answer. I can see it in your face. I'll just go in with you and start a fire—in the fireplace this time, because you're not in any shape to stoke the other kind I have in mind."

"Next time."

"Is that a promise?"

"Yes. One I intend to make sure you keep."

"I know you will."

Chapter Twenty

"Quilt Lodge, Brenda speaking. How may I help you?"

"Pretty lady, how about having dinner with two lonely, handsome bachelors?"

"Two?"

"David and me. Carol and Wayne and the kids have gone back to Omaha."

"I suppose I should take pity on you. Where will we eat?"

"My house. Unless you want to go out to eat."

"I like the idea of going to your house better."

"It's my CD collection that's the real draw, isn't it?"

"You've found me out."

Gil laughed. "David made me promise to bring you over."

"And we wouldn't want to disappoint him."

Gil noticed the glimmer of tears in Brenda's eyes when she listened to David's prayers asking for a new mother and naming her his favorite candidate.

"Is it too much for you, Brenda?" he said to her as they descended the stairs.

She glanced up at him. "Too much?"

"Being around my son when yours is lost to you. I want you in my life so much, baby. Am I being selfish? Insensitive to your feelings?"

She smiled. "You could never be that. I have to learn to

live with my decision to give up my son." God, this was hard. She wanted to confide in Gil about this so much, but—

Gil led her over to the bank of pillows before the fire.

"You mean everything to me, Brenda."

"As you do to me."

"Marry me, baby. I know I'm beginning to sound like a broken record."

"No, you're not. Give me more time, give us more time."

"Time won't make any difference to me. I won't change my mind."

Brenda wondered if that would still hold true once he knew the truth.

Mistaking her silence, he asked, "You doubt me?"

"No, never."

"The look in your eyes just now—"

"You and Carol are truly twins."

He laughed. "I make no claims to being psychic."

"I'm glad. I'd hate to think my every thought was revealed to you." She snuggled against him.

"I don't need to be psychic to read your thoughts at this moment, though, do I?"

"No, you don't." She reached up to caress his cheek.

Their eyes met and held.

He moved his lips over hers, melding them together in a mind-burning kiss. He twined his fingers in her hair, enjoying its silky rich texture. This woman, his woman, was something special. He splayed his fingers over her shoulders, then eased them down her back to caress her soft yet firm buttocks. He lay back against the pillows, bringing her hips against his erect manhood.

"I want you so much, Brenda."

Her desire for this man temporarily suspended all thought, except for him. "Gil, you don't think David will wake up and come down here, do you?"

"You could drop a bomb, and he'd sleep through it."

"I want and need you to make love to me right this minute, my darling."

172

Gil didn't need any further prompting. He helped her out of her clothes, then swiftly shed his own. He gazed at her body for a moment, savoring the thrust of her full breasts, the indentation of her small waist, her curvy hips and slender thighs and legs.

"You have a beautiful body, baby."

"I'm glad you think so."

He drew her into his embrace, his breath catching in his throat when her naked softness came into contact with his hard aroused male body. He never appreciated the differences between a man and a woman more than at this moment.

Gil lowered Brenda to the carpet. The look in her hazel eyes was like smoldering pieces of jade. The brown and green flecks darkened, glittering hot with desire. There was something about her eyes that struck him as oddly familiar.

When Brenda squirmed beneath him, she obliterated his thought processes. Acting on instinct, he flicked a nipple with the tip of his tongue and circled the hardening peak again and again until a moan escaped her lips.

"Do you like that, Brenda?"

"You know I do."

"You want me to continue?"

"Umm."

He did, with more intensity this time. Her stomach quivered when she felt his fingers move down her belly to the dark curls covering her womanhood. He parted the soft thicket and delved a finger inside her.

Brenda gasped and bucked against it as delicious sensations skittered through her body. When he circled her pearl of desire with his thumb, she groaned softly. The groan grew louder when he insert a second finger and moved both in and out, in and out, causing her excited feminine wetness to cream over his fingers.

"Gil," she cried out. "Oh, Gil, darling now, now!"

"Not yet, baby." He quickened his movements until he had her writhing upward in euphoric bliss.

Brenda grasped his male member and moved her fingers up

and down its hard, smooth length.

"Brenda!"

As she continued to caress him, he seemed to grow larger and harder with each stroke.

Unable to endure anymore, he removed her hand and plunged his throbbing hardness into her welcoming heat. Her sheath felt like hot, wet silk enveloping him in its soft caressing folds. His heart rate speeded up and his breathing grew ragged with the force of his passion.

Gil twirled his hips against hers again and again, working his flesh in hers. His movements grew frenzied and so did hers faster and faster they moved, the intensity building and building, until suddenly they were racing toward rapturous ecstasy. In one quick burst of glory they jetted across the finish line to claim love's wondrous victory.

Brenda lay on the carpet minutes later, Gil's head resting on her breast. She never dreamed that love could be as all-consuming as this. She softly ran her fingers over his hair and down his neck. He was what love was all about. He personified the word.

Gil reached up and caressed her nipple. "What are you thinking?"

"That we never seem to make it to the bedroom."

"If you can think at a time like this, I haven't been doing my job properly, but I intend to rectify that." He lifted his head and took her nipple into his mouth and sucked. She cried out. That little desire-filled cry was all he wanted and needed to hear. He drew her down beneath him and parting her thighs, guided his throbbing sex deep inside her, rediscovering paradise.

"I'll never get enough of you, sweet woman," he uttered moments after their climax.

"And I'll never get enough of you, my darling man."

For the next week Brenda spent as much time as she could

with Gil and David, their relationship growing stronger with each passing day. On the following Saturday, Gil and David came to pick her up so they could go shopping for a Christmas tree at Miller's Fir Tree Farm.

"There's so many of 'em, Daddy!" David exclaimed, his voice filled with wonder as he ran through the snow, playing a game of tag with the trees.

"We'll be lucky to go home with only one." Gil laughed. His breath caught at the look in Brenda's eyes. "You look as excited as David."

"Oh, I am. My parents never got a real tree. It was always the silver aluminum kind you could put away until the next year. There was never the fresh scent of pine in our house."

"Well this year you're going to be a part of the special celebration of the Jackson clan. What would make the season even brighter is if you let me announce our engagement."

"I—"

"Come on, Daddy and Brenda, I found the bestest tree on the farm!"

David grabbed Gil's and Brenda's hands, urging them forward.

Gil shrugged and smiled.

David brought them to a six and a half foot pine tree. Brenda had to admit that it was perfectly formed.

"It was meant to be ours," Gil said softly, obviously as moved as Brenda and David by its perfection.

While Gil talked to Mr. Miller and purchased the tree, Brenda and David walked back to the borrowed pickup truck to wait.

"Me and Daddy didn't get a tree last year. We stayed at Granddaddy Durant and Gramma Sara's. This time, we'll have a tree of our own and you, Brenda. Can I call you Mama when you marry my daddy?"

"David, I don't know—"

"Mama up in heaven won't mind."

"Oh, David," she said, hugging him tight. Her heart swelled with love for her child. Just to be able to hold him like this was joy pure and simple.

"You don't think Daddy'll mind if I call you that?"

"Mind what?" Gil asked, climbing into the truck and taking in the closeness between the two people he loved most in the world.

"I wanna call Brenda Mama when you'n her get married."

"If she doesn't mind, neither do I." Gil looked at Brenda trying to gauge her reaction. What he saw was a tender smile trembling on her lips. He knew that smile wasn't exactly an acceptance of his proposal, but it brought them closer to the ultimate outcome. Soon Brenda would agree to marry him.

After the tree was loaded onto the bed of the truck and they were on their way, they sang Christmas carols on the way home.

Home. That was how Brenda felt about Gil's house. The three of them managed to get the tree into the living room. Gil had brought the tree stand and ornaments from the basement earlier. He'd also stopped by Aunt Shirley's for the special ones she'd made for them, as she did for everyone in the family.

"Brenda, David and I want you to open Aunt Shirley's box," Gil said softly.

She gazed into her son's smiling face, then opened the box. She gasped at the contents. There was a roll of strung popcorn and candy canes. In the center of the box were three ornaments with their names painted on them.

Brenda lifted out the one with her name on it. Tears swam in eyes. The ornament was in the shape of a house similar to Gil's. She touched the tiny door and it opened. There were three tiny painted, cardboard figures of a man, a woman, and a little boy gathered around a Christmas tree.

The perfect family scene.

Shirley knew what family meant to Brenda. The older woman knew how much Brenda wanted Gil and David to belong to her.

Tell him the truth now, the voice of her conscience exhorted.

"Gil, I—"

"You don't have to say anything, sweetheart. It's there in your hands, gleaming in your eyes, warming your heart." He leaned over and kissed her lips. "It's called love."

David smiled at them, then reached for his ornament. His was in the shape of an airplane with the name *David* painted on the side. He squealed with delight.

Gil picked up his ornament. One side of the red ball showed his name, the other side a man's and a woman's gold, entwined wedding rings. He showed it to Brenda and gently touched her cheek.

"Can we put these on the tree now, Daddy?" David asked.

"Yes, we sure can."

"I don't have to ask how your weekend went," Laura said when Brenda virtually floated into the Lodge Monday morning.

"No, you sure don't. I'm so happy, Laura."

"Are you going to marry Gil?"

"Yes, I am."

"You've told him who you are?"

Brenda's smile faded. "Not yet."

"Brenda—"

"I know what you're going to say. Do I really have to tell him?"

"For your own peace of mind, yes, I think you do."

"I have peace of mind knowing Gil loves me and that I'll be a mother to my son."

"It's up to you, Brenda. Your fears and insecurities will hover over your head like a boulder perched on the edge of a cliff. Can you live like that?"

"I don't want anything to spoil what I have, Laura."

"Gil is a fair and compassionate man. He'll—"

"Forgive and forget? What I've done is a lot to ask a man to forgive."

"But is it too much if he loves you? Tell him, Brenda, trust him."

"I do trust him, but—"

"You're afraid?"

Brenda didn't say anything else, there was no need. She had to conquer her own fears and slay the dragons of her insecurity.

Chapter Twenty-one

Brenda smiled when she saw Shirley Edwards walk through the door of the Lodge with David in tow.

"We came to take you Christmas shopping with us. You'll be getting off in fifteen minutes."

David looked to Brenda. "Is that a long time?" he asked.

"Not long." She laughed. "Not long at all. You want to go upstairs and play with your cousin for a while?"

"Okay, but he's just a baby."

It wasn't so many years ago that he was just a baby, Brenda thought, watching him climb the stairs. And she'd missed that part of his development.

"You love him very much, don't you?" Shirley asked.

"As if he were my own son."

"He *will* become your son once you and Gil are married."

"What was Monique like, Shirley?"

"Why do you want to know that? Surely you don't feel threatened by her memory."

"It's not so much a question of feeling threatened. I know that Gil loved her, and David—"

"Barely remembers her. Monique was one of the sweetest persons you'd ever want to meet. She was strong, too, but I feel that what you and Gil share is different than what he had with her. There was an instant fiery attraction that sparked to life between you two the moment you met. What Gil had with Monique was comfortable and easy.

"There are all kinds of love, Brenda. There is no contest where Gillie's feelings for you are concerned. Monique is not a ghost you have to exorcise. Gillie will always hold a special

179

place in his heart for her, but you've carved your own place there as well. And you're alive and ready to share his love."

"I'm glad you came by, Shirley."

—◦≫◊≪◦—

Brenda heard a knock at her door and glanced at the clock. It was nearly seven-thirty, and she wondered who it could be. She put down the book she was reading and went to answer the door.

"Gil!"

"Don't look so shocked to see me. Don't I rate a kiss?"

"Of course you do, but—what are you doing here and where is David?"

He came in and closed the door, then removed his coat, hat, and gloves.

"David and Aunt Shirley are up to something. He begged to spend the night at her house. I figured they didn't want me to see what they got me for Christmas, so I let him stay the night. I love the little guy, but I wanted to spend some quality time with a certain lady I know. And I was sure she would be starved for my loving."

"Conceited man." She laughed.

"Did I lie?" He wrapped his arms around her and kissed the side of her neck.

"No, you didn't," she said, sliding her arms around his neck. "I am a very hungry woman, hungrier for you than you could ever imagine, my darling man. Are you going to spend the night?"

"That was my intention, yes, that is if you want me to."

"I want you to all right."

He needed her so much. She was his lover, his woman, his soul mate. He wanted to bury himself so deep inside her that he'd become a part of her forever and beyond. Sweeping her up in his arms, he cradled her in his embrace and captured her mouth in a thoroughly mind-altering kiss. He parted her lips, and his tongue surged inside her hungrily waiting mouth.

She liked him wild and intense. From the beginning, they seemed to share that same need and desire. Loving him always excited her beyond reason, beyond any romantic fantasy. She missed him even though it had only been a day since she'd seen him and yet it seemed like months.

When Gil finally raised his head, they were both breathing hard. His eyes glittered with hot passion. She'd never seen him quite like this before.

"I had every intention of taking you into the bedroom, but I find that I want to make love to you here, right now."

"I want you to love me right here, right now, my love."

He kissed her deeply and quickly undressed her, then himself. He lowered them both onto the carpet in front of the fireplace.

Her body quivered when his naked skin made contact with hers. The caress of his hair-roughened body against hers set her on fire. She felt his fingers find the hardened peak of a breast. A moan of pleasure left her lips. He continued his winning ways and treated the other nipple to the exact same rapture.

His lips found hers and he melded their mouths in a wildly intense kiss. The taste of him was making her crazy. She knew it would always be that way for her. He owned every part of her, heart, mind, her very being, as she owned his.

She arched against him. The instrument of his desire for her moved against her stomach. When she heard him groan, she reveled in the power she had over him.

"Oh, Brenda, sweetheart, I burn for you."

"You want me to cool you down?"

He laughed. "In this weather you've got to be kidding."

"What do you want me to do? Make you hot?"

"I'm already hot, just let me love you. I want to see you respond with that glorious abandon I've come to treasure." He moved his mouth over hers and delved his tongue inside, caressing the sensitive walls and roof until she trembled with need. He too was shaking from the impact of his passion.

He breathed in the scent of her perfume and her unique

womanly fragrance. He raised himself on an elbow and trailed his fingers down her stomach to the center of her desire and aroused that ultra-responsive place, homing in as though programmed, delving deep inside her heated flesh. As she arched upward, delicious sensations began to build with each stroke of his seductive fingers. It was heaven, it was hell. Suddenly she couldn't wait, she didn't want to wait.

"Gil, please—"

"I will please you, baby. I'll please you out of this world."

She moved her thighs wider apart giving him better access. The movement of his fingers grew more frenzied. He did as he vowed, driving her to the edge of eternity.

He swiftly removed his fingers and guided his hard shaft into her throbbing wet center, sinking to the hilt, then remained still as the rapturous sensations of her inner muscles pulsing around him gave him a glimpse of heaven.

"Yes," he shouted.

Brenda wrapped her legs around his hips. He began to move in lightning-quick strokes, each thrust driving deeper, exciting every nerve ending within her. She was filled with him, she was a part of him, moving with him, demanding everything from him.

His body's own demands made themselves felt, becoming more insistent, craving more and still more. As he drove deeper, harder, he felt her pulsing sheath quicken with each thrust as Brenda twisted and strained against him.

"Can you feel how much I love you, baby?"

"Yes, yes, yes," she chanted in time to the driving motions of his body. "I love you—I love you.

He joined her litany of love and they reached love's highest pinnacle, exploding together in ecstasy.

He rolled to his side taking her with him.

"You've got to marry me, Brenda. It's torture lying alone in bed every night when I can have you in my arms. I want you in every aspect of my life as my lover, my wife, the mother to our children, everything. Do you understand what I'm saying?"

"I do want to share every part of myself with you."

"Then do it soon."

As she lay wrapped in the warmth of his love, Brenda shoved the decision to tell him the truth to the back of her mind.

---※◈※---

"Brenda, I have to go," Gil whispered in her ear the next morning.

"Do you have to?" she grumbled sleepily.

He smiled. "Yes, I do sleepyhead. Don't you have to go to work?"

The fog of sleep cleared, and she opened her eyes.

"You look so sexy in the morning, baby. I wish I could crawl back in there with you and make love to you all day, but I'm due in court in less than two hours."

"Oh, Gil."

"You could always agree to marry me."

Brenda held up her hand. "I know, I know. You don't play fair."

"All is fair in love and war. You know what they say."

"No, I don't. What do they say?"

"Love is like war: easy to start, but hard to stop. If I started making love to you, I wouldn't be able to stop." He cleared his throat. "There's a skate party Saturday. David and I want you to come with us. All the ponds are frozen over now. You can show me your skating skills and David can show off what he's learned. Will you come?"

"You don't have to ask. Of course I'll come."

"I didn't think you had the heart to refuse."

"All a part of your master plan, I take it?"

"But of course."

He ducked as she threw a pillow at his head, then wrestled her flat onto the bed.

He grinned. "You're magnificent when you're like this."

"Like what?" she said squirming her body beneath him.

"Oh, you know what." He kissed her thoroughly. "I hate to go," he groaned, brushing his thumbs across her nipples.

"I definitely don't want you to leave," she said in a sultry whisper.

Gil eased off the bed, his breathing ragged, and for a second he was unsteady on his feet.

"There should be a law against what you do to me, girl."

"How you do talk, counselor."

He backed away from the bed and headed for the door.

Brenda left the bed and ran over to the door ahead of him and stood in front of it.

"Oh, Brenda," he growled taking her in his arms.

Brenda smiled, remembering that last good-bye kiss and what it led to as she showered and dressed for work. Her life couldn't be more perfect than it was right now.

Not so perfect, her conscience reminded her.

The thought of how that perfection could so easily change sobered her. But Gil loved her. Surely he would understand and forgive her.

The day of the skate party dawned bright and crisp. But not as cold as the Weather Channel predicted, Brenda thought as she gazed out her bedroom window.

She would be spending the entire day with the man she loved and with her son, like a real family. That word never meant so much to her before. She'd learned the true meaning from Gil and his family. They accepted her and cared about her the way her mother and father never had. Only Aunt Bertha had shown her that kind of love.

When Brenda, Gil, and David arrived at the pond, Laura and Carl were helping Jon-Marc build a snowman in the specially fenced-in playground created for the very small children.

Shirley was one of the people in charge of that.

David pointed to the area in disgust. "It's for babies. I'm big," he said proudly, drawing himself up to his full height.

"Almost too big for your pants, I'd say." Gil laughed. "I think we'd better find the ice skate rental stand."

Brenda noticed peripheral areas on the outskirts of the pond that were cordoned off and asked Gil about them.

"That's for safety. The pond is thoroughly inspected before anyone is allowed on the ice. Sometimes there are weak spots that aren't as thick as they should be, making them potentially dangerous. You'll see the safety patrols stationed at those places."

"I'm impressed."

"Maybe later you'll let me impress you."

"You're wicked."

"What does *wicked* mean, Brenda?" David asked.

"It means your father is full of, ah, fun."

David grinned. "Am I wicked too?"

"Just like your father."

❄️

Brenda stood watching as Gil took David out onto the ice. For a four-year-old, her son had amazing agility. She smiled, awed that something so perfect could have evolved from her relationship with Hudson Caldwell.

"You look like the protective lioness watching over her cub," Dylan teased, skating up beside her.

"I didn't know you'd be here. Gil didn't mention it."

"He wouldn't. No more headaches?"

"Hardly any."

Dylan frowned. "I didn't say anything to Gil, but I know that was no ordinary headache you had. I saw the pills prescribed for your pain. They're for cluster headaches, one of the most violently painful kind there is."

"Dylan, please—"

"They can be very dangerous, Brenda," he admonished.

185

"Especially if they're emotion generated. Is there something stressing you out?"

Gil and David came, so she didn't have to answer Dylan's question.

"I see you made it, little brother. What have you been saying to my lady?"

"Nothing you have to worry about."

"Tell me anything."

"Gil Jackson," Brenda scolded.

"How about some hot chocolate and a pretzel, David?" Dylan asked his nephew.

"With mustard?"

"With mustard." Dylan took David by the hand and led him in the direction of the concession stand.

Brenda smiled. "You're not really jealous of Dylan, are you?"

"Around the edges." Gil quirked his mouth.

"We're just friends." She kissed him. "I love only you, you impossible man."

He took her hand and drew her out onto the ice. It was so wonderful being surrounded by his love. She felt as special as he often told her she was.

More people arrived, Gil noticed, more than was anticipated. People from neighboring towns must have decided to come. He wondered if the city council had enough safety patrol on watch to accommodate the growing crowd.

"You're frowning," Brenda commented.

He held her closer and changed his frown to a smile. "Is that better?"

They heard a hard thud that reverberated on the ice, then saw Dylan speak to David and urge him in the direction of the small children's playground. The next minute Dylan hurried over to the man who had taken a nasty spill. He called for an ambulance on his cell phone. There were some tense moments until the paramedics came and loaded the man into the ambulance.

Brenda and Gil watched as Dylan skated toward them.

"Mr. Tilman broke his ankle," Dylan explained. "I sent David to Aunt Shirley."

"I'm sure he didn't like that idea. He thinks the playground is for babies. He's so pleased with his budding talent on the ice." Gil turned to Brenda. "I think we should rescue him. What do you say?"

"I say let's go."

"Good." Dylan agreed. "Once you get him, you'd better keep an eye on him. There are so many people out on the ice today. I think I'll check with the safety patrol leader and make sure they have enough men patrolling the ice."

"Okay. We'll see you later," Gil said.

Brenda and Gil skated over to the small children's playground to get David.

"I don't see him, Gil," Brenda said when she didn't see her son.

Gil called to his aunt. She met them at the gate.

"Where's David, Aunt Shirley?"

She looked around. "He was here just a minute ago."

Brenda frowned, suddenly feeling uneasy. "I think we had better find him, Gil. I'll go that way." She indicated an area to the right of where they were standing.

"All right. And I'll skate by the concession stand."

A few minutes later when Brenda saw David, a wave of relief swept through her, but died a quick death when she noticed how close he was to the cordoned off area. And where was the safety patrolman who was supposed to be there? Just as she called out to David, he lost his balance and fell, sliding underneath the cord.

A streak of panic slammed into her heart, and she skated madly to reach her son. As he started to get up, she heard a cracking sound. Her heart shot up in her throat.

At that moment Gil and Dylan saw them and sped in their direction.

Brenda crawled across the ice to reach David. The cracking sound grew louder. She held out her hand to her son.

"David, honey, take my hand, I'll help you."

"I'm scared," he cried, tears streaming down his frightened face.

"I won't let anything happen to you, I promise. Do you trust me?"

He looked behind him at the widening crack, then back at Brenda. He was shaking with cold as he tried to reach Brenda's hand.

She inched closer. "Just a little farther, honey. Mama will save you," Brenda said, easing a little closer, stretching her arm to the limit, scooting along on her stomach to reach David's hand. "I can't lose you again."

Brenda grabbed David's hand and pulled, then shoved him to safety with a hard push. As she was about to follow him, the ice completely separated, plunging her into the freezing water.

Shirley grabbed David. They watched as Dylan and Gil made it to the edge of the crack. Gil reached into the frigid water and with superhuman strength pulled Brenda out. Dylan helped him get her to safety.

Dylan yelled to one of the safety patrol for help.

Not waiting for him, Gil swept Brenda's shivering body into his arms and headed to the nearest warming booth. Dylan took her inside and immediately removed her clothes, wrapped her in a thermo heat blanket and sat her in front of the heater as he dried her hair and body.

"We need to get her to the hospital," Dylan said, massaging Brenda's feet.

"No hospital," Brenda whispered when she saw little David's shocked expression.

"Your house is closer, Gil. We can take her there," Dylan suggested to his brother.

Wrapped in blankets, they took Brenda to Gil's house.

"She needs to be put into a warm shower. I don't think she was in the water long enough to suffer any lasting effects or hypothermia, but we can't be too cautious."

"I'll take her into the shower."

"And I'll keep David company," said Dylan. "It's been

quite a shock for him."

"Tell him I'll be down as soon as I can."

Any other time Gil would have enjoyed showering with Brenda. When he saw her fall into the icy water, his heart had stopped. She was a brave woman to do what she did. He admired her before, but now—his love for her knew no bounds.

"Are you all right, baby?" he asked, parking her in front of the bathroom heater after they stepped out of the shower. He immediately started drying her hair and body.

"I'm fine." She shivered. "I'm just cold."

Gil reached for his terry-cloth robe hanging behind the door and helped her into it. He quickly dried himself, hitched the towel around his hips, then lifted Brenda in his arms and carried her into the bedroom. He went out to the linen closet in the hall and brought back one of Aunt Shirley's quilts. He heated it on the heater and put it over her.

"Better?"

"I'd feel even better if you were in here with me sharing your body heat."

He grinned. "As soon as I put David to bed, I'll be back."

No sooner than Gil had left, Dylan came in to check on his patient. When he finished his examination, he sat on the edge of the bed.

"I heard what you said just before you pushed David to safety."

Brenda looked questioningly at him. "What I said?"

"You told David that Mama would save him and that you couldn't lose him again. You're his real mother, aren't you?"

She was quiet for a moment, then answered. "Yes."

"Does Gil know?"

"No," she said, lowering her head.

"That's what's stressing you out, isn't it?" Dylan took her hand in his. "You've got to tell him the truth, Brenda."

"I know that. But how? He's told me how much he hates the woman who gave birth to David."

"True enough, but he doesn't know that woman is you. In

189

any case, he loves you."

"Maybe now he does, but after I've told him—"

"He'll get over it."

"Can you be sure of that?"

Dylan mulled it over. "It may be hard for him at first, but his love for you is strong. He's let me know in any number of ways how strong."

Her shoulders slumped, then she jerked in pain.

"Is it another headache?" Dylan asked with a concerned frown.

"Yes." She balled her hands into fists in the folds of the quilt.

Dylan reached inside his bag and brought out a syringe and a small bottle. "I'm going to give you a sedative for the pain. It'll calm you. What you don't need is more stress."

After giving her the shot, he rose to his feet.

"Tell him the truth, Brenda, for your health's sake."

―――

"How is she?" Gil asked when he saw Dylan descend the stairs.

"I've given her something to make her comfortable."

"Are you sure everything is all right? If you think we should take to her to the hospital—"

"She's fine where she is. How is David?"

"He was a frightened little boy, but I managed to calm him."

"I can imagine. He kept asking me earlier if Brenda was going to die"

"He did?" Gil's eyes widened in concern.

"Don't forget that he was in the backseat of the car when Monique was killed."

"He was so young, I didn't think he remembered."

"He was young, but he remembers that she wasn't moving when the fire department pulled her out of the car and that he never saw her again. He begged me not to take Brenda to the hospital because he associates it with his mother never coming home."

"I had no idea he felt that way."

"Brenda has come to mean a lot to him. He thinks of her as his new mother."

"As I think of her as my wife." Gil grinned. "I'll convince her to marry me, and we'll be the perfect happy family."

"That's quite a pedestal you've put her on."

"What do you mean?" Gil demanded.

"I mean that no one is perfect. We all make mistakes."

"I know that."

"I wonder if you really do."

"Dylan—"

"I'd better go. If Brenda experiences any pain, nausea, or severe chills, call me at the hospital. I'll be on duty tonight."

"All right."

Gil sat staring into the flames wondering what his brother meant by his words. He knew no one was perfect. His love for Brenda was, though. He never felt so connected to another person, aside from Carol. Not even with Monique, and he had loved her dearly.

He smiled, remembering what Brenda had said when she was reaching out to save his son. It had to mean that she felt as though she was his mother to have said something like that. Then he recalled the rest of what she said. She probably equated almost losing David with losing her son. Whatever. Her words seemed to calm David. If he had anything to say about it, Brenda Davis would become his wife and David's new mother.

Gil went to check on his son and found him fast asleep with his toy airplane nearby.

He tiptoed out of the room and headed for his own. He eased the door open. The bedside lamp was set on low. He stood studying the woman he loved, snuggled deep inside the covers. She was peacefully asleep. He sat down on the edge of the bed and reached out to touch her cheek.

Brenda opened her eyes. "Is David all right?"

"He's fine."

"Are you going to get into bed with me?" she asked, yawning sleepily.

He removed his robe and climbed into bed next to her and drew her into his arms.

"Is that better?"

"Much," she whispered drowsily.

"I want you to know how much you mean to me, Brenda. And after what you did today—"

"I love David," she said simply.

"And I love you." He tightened the embrace. "If anything were to have happened to you—"

She snuggled closer. "Nothing did. Make love to me."

"Brenda, I don't know if we should."

"I need you to love me, right now, this minute."

"I never knew you were such a demanding woman." His breath caught in his throat when she slid her hand over his sex. "Are you sure?"

She moved her lips over his, silencing any protests he might have offered.

Their loving was slow and tender, all-encompassing, fiery and passionate, a celebration of love, commitment, and the joy of being alive.

Gil covered them and held Brenda in his arms as she drifted back to sleep. How he loved this woman. They would have a perfect life together, he'd settle for nothing less.

Chapter Twenty-two

Brenda awoke, momentarily disoriented. This was not her bed or her bedroom. She pushed up the sleeves of the overly large pajama top that definitely didn't belong to her. She heard a door open and eased herself to a sitting position. Then she saw Gil and remembered how she came to be there.

"You don't have to worry, I've fixed breakfast," Gil said, settling a tray across her lap.

"Gil, I—where's David?"

The door opened. "Daddy forgot the orange juice." Holding the glass in his two hands, David slowly made his way across the room and set the glass down on the tray without spilling it.

"I got my Christmas wish before Christmas," he said with a wide grin. "The star on the tree is magic."

Brenda glanced at Gil. He shrugged.

"Christmas wish?" she asked David. "What do you mean?"

"I been prayin' real hard on the star for you to be my new mama. I thought 'cause I was bad God was punishin' me when you fell in the pond. But He didn't, He answered my prayers. You didn't die and go to heaven like my mama. You're here in my daddy's bed. Mike said that's where mamas sleep with the daddies."

"I'll have to have a talk with that nephew of mine," Gil said, smiling.

"Mike said that's where his brothers got made." David looked at the bed and then at Brenda. "You and my daddy gonna make me a brother in this bed?"

Brenda only smiled and left it to Gil to get them out of this one.

"I'll make you a brother someday. Now let's get out of here so Brenda can eat her breakfast. I'll fix you some Eggos."

"Okay." David leaned over and hugged Brenda. "Please be my new mama. I love you, Brenda, and so does Daddy. He told me so."

Brenda blinked away tears as she watched the two men in her life leave the room. She remembered what Dylan said and also something that Carol had said. "My brother is a compassionate man, but don't cross him."

Would he feel crossed when she told him the truth? Would he forgive her? Would he still love her?

—⚬❖⚬—

Gil insisted that Brenda spend most of the day in bed. He and David went over to her apartment and brought back a change of clothes. Later that evening the three of them sat before the fire, drinking hot cider and admiring the tree they so lovingly decorated.

Brenda had never seen such a beautiful tree. She adored the ornament Shirley had made for her and wished upon the star at the top of the tree as her son had done. Maybe her dreams of being a mother to her son would become a reality. And maybe her wish to have Gil as her husband would also come true.

After putting David to bed, Gil led Brenda back into his bedroom and quickly undressed her, then himself.

"Marry me, Brenda." He kissed her lips and splayed his hands over her body, brushing his palms against her nipples.

She gasped. "Oh, I—"

"But?"

"No buts this time. The answer is yes. But there is one last thing I have to do. Then if you still want me—"

"Still want you? I'll always want you, girl." He took a nipple into his mouth and sucked strongly.

194

She whimpered. "I want you to remember those words."

"Let's forget about everything else except us. The night belongs to us."

He rolled onto his back, bringing Brenda atop him and thrust deeply into her welcoming heat, quickly initiating the rhythm of love. He soon had her moving in unison with him.

For these precious moments, Brenda's problems ceased to exist as she lost herself in Gil's exquisite lovemaking.

"Are you sure it's all right for you to come to work today, Brenda?" Laura asked.

"I'm fine."

"I must say you look like it. You have a special glow about you this morning, girlfriend."

"I'm going to be Mrs. MaGil Jackson very soon."

"I couldn't be happier for you. When's the big day?"

"We haven't discussed a wedding date yet."

"Did you—"

"No, I haven't told him, Laura, but I will soon."

"I won't throw snowballs on your parade. You know best what to do."

"I hope I do. I love Gil and David so much. And to be able to watch my son grow—there are no words to describe how I feel at this moment."

"I want you to stay as happy as you are right now."

Gil came into the Lodge at closing time with a wide grin on his face.

"What brings you here, counselor?" Laura smiled. "As if I didn't know."

"I came to get my lady."

"But I drove my car to work, Gil."

"That's all right. I'll bring you back later to get it."

"Sounds mysterious. Is that all you're going to tell me?"

"Just get your coat, woman."

"I don't know if I like your me-Tarzan-you-Jane attitude."

"I'll close up, Brenda. I can see this man means business."

"You're a smart woman, Laura."

"Gil Jackson, where are you taking me?" Brenda demanded once they were in his car.

"Can't you wait a little while longer, my impatient love?"

"No," she pouted, crossing her arms over her chest.

Gil grinned. "You'll love this place, I promise you."

Brenda's eyes widened when they drove up in front of a jewelry store.

"Gil, what—"

"Keep quiet, woman, and follow me." He got out of the car, walked around to her door and opened it, offering her his arm.

Happy tears crowded against her lashes as Gil escorted her to the door of the jewelry store.

"It says they close at five. It's five-thirty."

"Mr. Dorsey agreed to stay open later this evening." Gil opened the door. "After you, baby."

"Gil," the man greeted him warmly. "This must be the lovely lady you spoke about."

"Yes. This is my fiancée, Brenda Davis. Do you have what I asked for, John?"

"I believe so." John Dorsey locked the front door, then turned and said with a smile, "If you would follow me."

He led them to a private viewing room beyond the display counter. As they seated themselves, he stepped over to the vault and took out a tray of rings.

Brenda gasped when her eyes caught on a jade and diamond engagement ring.

Gil noticed and lifted it from its bed of black velvet and pushed it onto her finger.

"It's a perfect fit," she cried in an awed voice.

"That proves that it was meant for you."

Brenda held her hand up and examined the flawless two-karat diamond set between two S-shaped pieces of jade.

"I don't know what to say."

Gil whispered in her ear. "The jade is the color of your eyes when we make love."

Brenda blushed and looked to see if Mr. Dorsey had heard.

Gil laughed, then cleared his throat. "Do you like the ring?"

"It's got to cost the earth."

He gazed into her eyes. "You're worth it, Brenda."

"I hope you'll always think so."

"I will," he vowed.

Mr. Dorsey cast them a knowing look and quietly left them alone.

Gil took Brenda's hand and brought it to his lips. "I'm taking you to St. Paul Saturday to celebrate. I've already had André reserve the private dining room for us."

"I love you so much," she said softly, gazing at the wedding ring and the man's matching wedding band. A sharp-hot pain stabbed through her head, but was gone as quickly as it had struck.

"Are you all right, Brenda?" Gil asked when he saw her blink and close her eyes.

"I'm fine." She smiled reassuringly. "It's just a headache."

"I'm not surprised after the soaking you got at the pond. I don't want you getting sick."

"Neither do I."

You have to tell him. Tell him this evening.

Brenda wet her lips and swallowing hard, began, "Gil, there's something you have the right to know about me."

"You told me that you love me, that's all I need to know. If what you have to say is about your past, I don't want to hear it. The past is past."

"But, I—

He put a finger across her lips. "We should be going. John was kind enough to keep the store open for us. I'm sure he wants to get home to his family."

"Gil."

"I love you, Brenda Davis." He drew her into his arms and moved his mouth gently over hers.

Brenda slid her arms around his neck and gazed at her engagement ring and knew she had to tell him tonight, whether he wanted to hear it or not. She couldn't put it off any longer. Another pain sliced through her head. She closed her eyes and waited for it to go away. The anxiety and the pangs of guilt her conscience meted out were now more than she could bear. She hoped fervently that everything would turn out right. It just had to.

⚬⚬⚬⚬

Gil drove Brenda back to the Lodge to pick up her car, then followed her home. After she parked, Gil got out of his car and walked over to hers.

"I'm not going to come in. I have some packing to do."

"Packing?"

"I have to go to Duluth on business. I agreed to help Carl with a timber-harvesting problem. There is a dispute with the government over timber rights on the reservation, and he needs my help in the negotiations."

"How long will you be gone?"

"Two days, three at the most. Don't worry. I'll be back in time to take you to St. Paul to celebrate our engagement. David will be staying with Aunt Shirley until I get back. You can spend as much time as you want with him. I know he'll love every moment of it. We'll tell him about the engagement when I get back. Don't look at me like that. You don't know how much I want to stay."

"I think I have some idea."

"I'll call you tomorrow." He gave her a slow kiss good night, then headed back to his car.

Brenda was relieved, but at the same time frustrated. Before they discussed a wedding date, she still had to tell Gil the truth. The inevitable had only been postponed.

Chapter Twenty-three

"Quilt Lodge, Brenda speaking. How may I help you?"

"How does an officially engaged woman feel?"

"Gil!"

"That's how I like my woman to sound when she hears my voice. You all right, baby?"

"I'm perfect now," she said happily.

"The highway is treacherous between here and Duluth because of the snow and ice, but I'll be careful. I've been thinking about a wedding date. How does Christmas Eve sound?"

"That's only three weeks away."

"Too soon?"

"No. It's perfect."

"You going to invite your parents?"

She was silent.

"Brenda, I know how you feel about them, but—"

"I don't think you do. I don't know if I can ever forgive them for what they did."

"Family is precious, baby. I can't imagine not ever speaking to my parents."

"Your parents would never do what mine did, and you know it. I'm satisfied to adopt your family as my own."

"We'll talk about it when I get back. Remember how much I love you."

"I love you more."

"That's impossible."

—❊❖❊—

Brenda decided to call the only person she considered family, her Aunt Bertha, when she got home from the Lodge.

"I've been worried about you, child. Your father keeps calling and asking me if I know where you are."

"I'm not ready to talk to either him or my mother. I don't know if I ever will be."

"I'm sure they have regrets, Sheila. After all, that baby is their only grandchild."

It felt strange hearing someone call her Sheila. She'd almost forgotten it was her real name.

"That didn't seem to matter to them when I had him," Brenda answered shortly. "I can't see that it would bother them now."

"You sound so bitter, child. I was hoping that time away from them would help heal your hurts. I see that is not the case."

"I called to tell you that I've met a wonderful man. His name is MaGil Jackson, and he has a child."

"Tell me about him. I hope he deserves you."

"He wants to get married on Christmas Eve. I'm so happy, Aunt Bertha."

"I'm happy for you, Sheila. You mentioned that he has a child."

"He's a beautiful boy and so smart."

"How old is this child?"

"Four years old."

"He's the same age as—doesn't that—I mean—"

"It's all right, Aunt Bertha. I'm ready to be a mother to little David. I'm learning to live with the past."

"I'm happy to hear that. For a while I wasn't sure you'd survive the adoption. I guess I have this MaGil Jackson to thank."

"Yes, he's very special."

"I'm looking forward to seeing my girl happy."

After hanging up with her aunt, Brenda began to wonder if

maybe she should have waited to call her. She had yet to tell her aunt about her name change and the truth about her situation. She knew she would have to do it soon, but first she had to talk to Gil.

───❖───

Brenda picked David up on Wednesday to take him to see a Christmas movie he'd been dying to go to. She loved watching her son's animated face as he watched the characters in the movie. He was such a good boy. And he was hers. She helped create this miracle. God willing, she'd dedicate her life to making him a happy, well-adjusted young man.

By Thursday, Brenda was anxious to see Gil and get the telling over with. She'd had several headaches, but they weren't serious ones. As soon as she told Gil the truth, she was sure they would stop. She didn't like keeping things from him. She'd never wanted to do that, but her fears and insecurities had driven her to do it anyway.

She thought about what her aunt had said about healing the breach between herself and her parents, but right now telling Gil the truth was her main focus. Maybe after that, she'd consider it.

By Friday, the waiting had taken its toll on Brenda, and she was a nervous wreck. At two o'clock, Laura sent her home. A pain at the base of her head had begun to throb.

At five, she nearly jumped out of her skin when she heard a knock at the door. She ran sweaty palms down the sides of her green velvet dress and went to answer it. Brenda was sure that facing a firing squad felt like this. She opened the door to a pair of smiling faces.

Gil gazed at her for a few moments before wrapping his arms around her.

"I've missed you, baby." He glanced down at his son. "And this little guy can hardly wait to help us celebrate our engagement."

As if on cue, David wrapped his small arms around

Brenda's legs and squeezed her tight.

"I'll have a mama just like my cousins." His child's voice rang with happiness.

"Yes, you will, son," Gil said, drawing his family close.

As glad as Brenda was to see her son, disappointment that she wouldn't be able to tell Gil the truth tonight took the edge off her happiness.

Gil's eyes narrowed as he noticed her expression. "Is anything wrong, Brenda?"

"No. Being with you and David like this feels so right. I guess I'm just overwhelmed. Just think, we'll be married in less than three weeks."

"Yeah. We'd better get going. I don't want to keep David out too late."

"Aw, Daddy."

Brenda smiled. "Your father is right."

They went to Heritage House. Brenda and Gil toasted their engagement with a glass of champagne while David had sparkling apple cider in a small wineglass Gil had the waiter get for him.

David smiled, clinking his glass with theirs.

Brenda and Gil let him believe he was drinking champagne.

Gil took Brenda's hand in his and gazed at her ring.

"In a matter of weeks you'll be Mrs. MaGil Jackson, and I'll be taking you home for good, to love and cherish for always."

Brenda sighed. "It sounds so wonderful, doesn't it?"

"You and Daddy can tuck me in every night," David inserted.

"I'm looking forward to it," Brenda said softly, putting her arm around David's shoulder.

Gil grinned, thinking that his life couldn't get any better than this. He would have a piece of heaven right here on earth.

David yawned, trying valiantly to keep his eyes from closing.

"We'd better get this young man home, Gil."

"I'm not sleepy," David said, yawning again.

Minutes later, Gil drove up in front of Brenda's apartment. She gazed at her son asleep on the backseat.

"I'll come by at about five," Gil said, "so we can get an early start for St. Paul. David is going to spend the weekend with his favorite great-granddaddy."

"Do you think he'll complain about not being included?"

"Probably."

"Gil, maybe—"

"This is a special time for us. I've arranged a special celebration. We'll let him be a part of the wedding ceremony."

They got out of the car and headed for her door.

She sighed excitedly. "I don't think I'll be able to sleep tonight."

"Don't think you'll be the only one." He gave her a quick kiss. "Did I tell you we'd be spending the night in St. Paul?"

"No, but I'd hoped that we would."

"I'll be so high on you that there's no way I'll be able to drive back to Long Rapids."

"Are you saying I go to your head?"

"Yes, you have from the first moment I saw you. I already don't want to leave, but I've got to get David home." He kissed her again, savoring the feel of her soft mouth beneath his.

"Christmas Eve can't come soon enough to suit me."

"Or me," he said tenderly. "I'll call you in the morning."

Brenda watched Gil drive away with a feeling of trepidation, hating that she would have to wait another day before she knew her fate.

Tomorrow.

So much hinged on how Gil took what she had to say. She hoped that Laura and Dylan were right and Gil loved her enough to forgive her.

—⋇⟡⋇—

Working on sheer nervous energy all day, Brenda cleaned

her apartment from top to bottom. When she had finally finished, she stopped long enough to run out and get a new dress for her special evening. She decided on a simple, form-fitting long white velvet dress with three-quarter length sleeves. She styled her hair in a classic chignon, with whispy side curls framing her face.

She had just added the finishing touches to her makeup when she heard a knock at the door. Her heart was tapping out an anxious tattoo when she opened it.

"You look unbelievebly beautiful," Gil said appreciatively as his eyes hungrily roved the curves of her body. "That dress definitely does you justice, baby."

Brenda opened his coat. "You're looking exceptionally handsome yourself." And he did, too, in his black tux.

He tossed his coat on a chair and drew her into his arms, closing the door with his foot. "Now that we've got the preliminaries out of the way." He slipped his fingers inside the back of her dress. When he felt her shiver with desire, his breath caught in his throat.

The heat from his fiery touch made Brenda burn for him. It took every ounce of strength she possessed to resist his passionate onslaught, but she pulled away.

He reeled her back into his embrace. "Baby, we have time before we have to leave." He slid the zipper of her dress down.

"I have to—I need to—" She trembled when he slid his hands around her body, brushing his fingers across the filmy silk of her bra, abrading the sensitive nipples inside.

"Need to what?" he murmured in her ear, moving his lips against her naked back.

"Gil, please, I must—" She felt as if she was floating on wave after wave of the delicious sensations he sent washing over her with his touch.

A knock at the door brought back a semblance of reality to Brenda, and she eased the zipper back up, wondering who it could be. It was probably the landlord. He had mentioned the other day that he wanted to check her pipes since the sudden drop in temperature.

She cleared her throat and straightened her dress. "I'd better answer it. It's probably my landlord, Mr. Sloan."

"The man sure has a damned bad sense of timing," Gil grumbled.

Brenda smiled. "This shouldn't take long. I'll tell him we're on our way out."

Gil grinned. "He won't believe it if he sees the flush on your face."

"You're wicked, MaGil Jackson," she said over her shoulder as she moved to answer the door.

"Sheila."

"Daddy!" she gasped.

"We finally found you," her mother cried, hugging her tight.

"Aren't you going to invite us in, girl?" her father said.

"Brenda?" Gil arched his brows questioningly at her and the couple standing in the doorway.

A feeling of dread clamped around her heart like a vice. Shards of pain stabbed into her brain. Her legs threatened to buckle, but by sheer force of will she remained upright and conscious. She opened her mouth to speak, but no words came out.

"We're Sheila's parents, Charles and Isabella Walker," Brenda's father volunteered.

"Sheila Walker," Gil said in a strangled voice when the reality of the name and what it meant hit home.

"Gil," Brenda finally managed to utter. "I can explain."

His face harshened. "I don't think I need one."

"But you do, my darling. You have to give me a chance."

"Do I?" he answered coldly.

"Who is this, Sheila?" her father demanded.

"I'm her fiancé," Gil said grimly.

"Sheila, why didn't you get in touch with us and tell us you were getting married?" her mother cried. "We've been so worried. If not for the call from Bertha, we still wouldn't know where you were or anything else about you."

"I know the last time we saw you, it wasn't a pleasant

visit—" her father began.

"No, it wasn't," Brenda said, never taking her eyes off Gil's face.

Tension held them all tautly in place for long moments.

Gil recovered first. His words pelted Brenda like stones. "We were just going out, but I guess we'll have to cancel our evening for obvious reasons.

"Gil, no, please let me—"

"What? Explain? Explain what? How thoroughly you've deceived me all this time?"

"I never meant to."

The raw pain she saw in his eyes broke her heart. Regret that she hadn't been honest with him when she first realized who he was stormed through her.

Gil grabbed his coat and headed for the door.

"Gil, wait, we have to talk," Brenda cried grasping his arm.

He jerked away from her touch. "Not now," he spat, ice coating his voice. Shooting her one last contemptuous look, he stalked from the apartment, slamming the door behind him.

Brenda closed her eyes as sharp talons of pain clawed at her brain. The intensity of the pain made her sway.

Her father reached out to steady her. "Sheila, what's wrong? Are you all right?"

"I was until you—" She wanted to free herself from his hold, but the pain sharpened, becoming razor-edged as it slashed unmercifully.

"You're trembling," her father said. "Isabella, help me get her over to the couch."

"Why did you come here?" Brenda gritted out as they helped her over to the couch.

"You're our daughter. Despite what you think, we love you, Sheila," Charles answered.

Brenda closed her eyes trying to stave off the agony. It was no use. The pain continued to spiral as the moments passed. What could she say now to the man she loved? Another pain hit, faster, harder, a cruel instrument of torture cutting into her right temple, while a vice-like pressure sought to crush her skull.

"You say you love me and yet you—"

"We did what we thought best," her mother said defensively.

"What you thought?"

Brenda's groan turned into a raw shriek of pain as a sudden smashing sensation struck her brain with the impact of a wrecking ball slamming into a building. And with each succeeding blow she moaned in agony.

"Sheila," her father said urgently. "What's wrong. What can we do to help? Who's your doctor?"

Brenda reached for the phone but found her fingers were numb. Her sight began to blur and her eyes to sting as a whirling, white-hot squiggly circle of pain blocked out the center of her vision. Nausea bubbled in her stomach and rose up her throat, making her feel the violent urge to vomit.

This was no ordinary migraine attack. The pains started coming at her in merciless intermittent tidal waves, warning her that excruciating headaches like the ones she'd suffered right after losing her son, were back and threatening to close in. She tried to will the pain away by playing mind games, telling herself it was mind over matter and she could control it, but it wasn't working.

"Charles, we'd better get her to a hospital," Isabella said desperately.

He grabbed the phone book and quickly flipped through it for the listing for hospitals.

"Take me to Long Rapids Memorial—my doctor—Dylan Jackson," Brenda managed to say before blessed darkness descended, sucking her into its pain-free, bottomless depths.

Chapter Twenty-four

Through the fuzzy haze of pain Brenda heard voices.

"What's wrong with our daughter, Doctor?" Brenda heard her father ask.

"Apparently, she's suffering from a severe migraine attack," Dylan answered.

Charles said, "My grandfather used to suffer from some pretty severe headaches, and so did my father. They must be hereditary. We knew Sheila had them in the past, though she tried to hide them from us."

"Sheila?"

"Yes, Sheila Walker. Though we learned from her driver's license that she's going under the name of Brenda Davis.

Dylan cleared his throat. "I think her headache goes beyond a simple migraine. What we're dealing with is an off-shoot known as cluster headaches. They aren't of themselves serious, but the combined effect of the recurring torment over an extended period can prove too much for some patients to endure, and their brain shuts down to temporarily escape from the pain—therefore blackouts, unconsciousness, or coma."

"What can set off headaches of that magnitude?" Isabella asked.

"Any number of factors such as injuries, severe emotional trauma, physical weakness, or genetic predisposition. In Brenda—Sheila's case, I'd say she experienced some kind of heavy emotional trauma coupled with hereditary factors."

Brenda opened her eyes and tried to sit up. A groan of pain escaped her, and immediately Dylan was there, gently easing her back against the pillow.

"You need to relax and allow the medication to work. I've decided to keep you in the hospital overnight."

"But, Dylan, I—"

"Your doctor is right, Sheila," her father chided. "We'll be back to take you home in the morning."

She felt her father's dominating will closing around her—as it had in the past—and she turned her back on him.

"I think you'd better go now. Brenda needs to rest."

"We're staying at the Long Rapids Inn if you need to get in touch with us, Doctor."

"I don't think we'll have to, but if it becomes necessary we'll call you there."

There was a short silence.

"You can open your eyes, Brenda, they're gone. You told Gil the truth, didn't you?"

"Not exactly."

"You want to tell me what happened?"

Brenda explained and waited for him to answer.

"He doesn't know you're here, does he?" Dylan frowned. "That's a stupid question. Of course he doesn't. And you don't want me to tell him, do you?"

She didn't answer.

"I think you're wrong. He's in part responsible for your being here."

"I don't want him to know. He's had a lot to handle all at once."

"So have you, Brenda. I must tell you that if you can't bring the stress level down, you're headed for more pain, worse than this. You and Gil were meant for each other, he'll see that."

"I hope he will, Dylan. You didn't see the look on his face when he found out who I really am. He was so hurt and angry and bitter."

"He'll get over it, you'll see."

Brenda's eyes began to droop.

"The medication is beginning to kick in. I'm going to

leave you now to get some healing sleep."

—⋙⟨⟩⋘—

Gil was in a haze, barraged by questions he didn't have answers to. Why hadn't Brenda told him who she was? Had she been using him to get to David? Could it be guilt? If it was she should feel guilty, he thought angrily. When she had changed her mind about the adoption it had nearly driven his wife to a nervous breakdown. He had sworn to hate the bitch forever. Instead he'd fallen headlong, heart deep, soul connectingly in love with her.

He needed answers to his questions. But they would have to wait until he calmed down. He headed to the only place he could find peace: the reservation.

—⋙⟨⟩⋘—

Carl was shoveling snow off the sidewalk in front of the reservation office when Gil drove up.

"I need to talk to you, Carl."

Carl knew if his cousin called him by name in that tone of voice, he was upset about something. He leaned the shovel against the porch railing and motioned Gil into his office.

"What is it, Gil?"

Standing by the window and looking out over the snow-covered moonlit reservation grounds, Gil explained.

"That's quite a story. Have you talked it out with Brenda?"

"No, I don't trust myself to be in her company. The way I feel right now, I might break her neck."

"You need to hear her side of it. Don't you think she's suffered too?"

"I'm sure she has, but—I love Brenda, damn it!"

"Life can be a real bitch, can't it?"

"That's putting it mildly. I need to be alone to think. I'm going to take a walk."

"Don't stay out there too long. It's freezing cold and

you're definitely not dressed for it."

As Gil walked down the path to the new school, he thought about David. He was glad his son was spending the weekend with his grandparents. He couldn't handle seeing him right now or any other member of his family.

He felt so betrayed, used, and deceived by the woman he loved, and at this moment, also hated. No. He didn't hate her, he could never truly hate her. Could he ever really trust her?

Gil blew on his hands and sat down on the front steps of the school. Only an hour ago, his life was perfect. Only an hour ago, he'd burned with desire to possess her. And now—

And now what, Jackson?

I'm numb. I don't know how to feel, how to react.

You love the woman. Face that fact and go from there.

It wasn't that easy. And there was David to consider. Brenda couldn't have known who he was when she first came to Long Rapids. He thought for a while. It had to be at his parents' house when she suddenly got sick after—after looking at the photos on the mantle.

That picture of David. That had to be when she found out.

He remembered the expression on her face when she asked if David looked like Monique. He had inadvertently given her the answer she was seeking. She could have told him the truth then. Why hadn't she?

Did she love him as she'd said many times? The question of whether or not she saw him as a way to get her son came back to taunt him. He didn't want to believe that.

Gil rose from the steps and headed back to his car. He said good-bye to Carl and drove to his house. The peace he sought was not to be found in Long Rapids. He had to get away for a while. He'd call his parents and tell them something had come up and if they would keep David for a few days.

As he packed, he remembered to call André. That done, he called his secretary to tell her to cancel his appointments for the week. He went back to the reservation to borrow his cousin's Land Cruiser.

"I always wondered what it was like to drive your Jag,"

said Carl. "How long are you going to be away?"

"I don't know. Until I can figure something out, I guess."

"You should call Brenda."

"I can't talk to her yet. I don't know if I'll—" His voice trailed off.

"Don't lock any doors and throw away the keys, or burn any bridges, Gil."

"I won't, cuz. I have to go now."

"I understand. When I was going through hell with Laura over custody of Jon-Marc, I needed isolation to gather my thoughts." He threw Gil the keys to a farmhouse seventy miles from Long Rapids that had belonged to his late wife.

Gil smiled. "Thanks, cuz."

Brenda woke up at around midnight and stared into the darkened hospital room.

"You should be sleeping," Dylan said from the doorway. "It's not good for you to brood, Brenda. It only adds to your distress."

"I can't seem to help it, Dylan. My life is in limbo, completely out of my control. My son's happiness hangs in the balance. I love him. What if Gil can't forgive me?"

"He will. You have to think positive."

She sighed. "If he would only let me—" She suddenly gasped in pain.

Dylan rushed to her side and turned on the light, took out his optical light, examined her eyes, then took her pulse. He picked up the phone by the bed and instructed the nurse to bring a sedative.

"You can't take much more, Brenda. I should call Gil and—"

"No! Don't do that, Dylan."

"But—"

"I'll come to terms with this. I don't want you laying any guilt trips on him. I have to give Gil time."

Chapter Twenty-five

"I'm glad to see that you're looking better this morning," Dylan said, writing on Brenda's chart.

"My parents should be here any minute to take me home."

Dylan looked up, brows arched. "How do things stand between you and your parents?"

"They don't, but I know we'll have to talk. There are too many issues left unresolved between us."

"They care. I could feel it when they brought you in. Maybe there's a chance that you all can—"

"I don't want to talk about it right now, Dylan."

"I've prescribed some pain medication," he said, returning his attention to her chart. "The nurse should be here soon with it and your discharge papers. I can't stress strongly enough what you need to do to stop the headaches. Starting with your feelings toward your parents is a step in the right direction."

"Dylan—" Brenda warned.

"End of lecture." He smiled.

Brenda's parents arrived minutes later. There was an awkward silence at first, then Dylan said, "I want you to make an appointment to see me in three days, Brenda."

"We'll see that she makes one, Dr. Jackson," Charles confirmed.

Brenda sliced an annoyed glance at her father.

"Is there anything I can get you, Sheila?" her mother asked anxiously, once they arrived at Brenda's apartment.

"No, Mama."

"Sheila—" her father began.

"Brenda," she corrected.

He frowned. "Why did you change your name? Just to spite us and so we couldn't find you?"

"Actually, you didn't have anything to do with it. After I left the sanitarium, I wanted a new life, a different life, one I could feel comfortable in."

"You've never felt that way about our lifestyle, have you?"

"No, never," she said flatly. She glanced at her mother. "You were always pushing me to be like you. All I wanted was to be normal, not a society debutante."

Isabella exchanged looks with her husband.

"How did you happen to move here, Shei—Brenda?" Charles cleared his throat. "Bailey told us this was where the adopted parents and your son live. But how did you find out?"

"I didn't. My moving to Long Rapids was purely coincidental, a quirk of fate, whatever."

"Bertha said, and your Mr. Jackson confirmed, that you two were getting married." Her father shook his gray head. "I don't understand."

Brenda closed her eyes, kneading her bottom lip with her teeth. "I did what I thought I'd never do after—I fell in love."

"We know that Hudson Caldwell is the father of your son," her father said.

Brenda's eyes flew open. "What?"

"He came to see us to ensure that you didn't go to his wife."

"I never would have done that. I didn't know that he was married when I started seeing him. He conveniently kept that from me. It wasn't until I told him I was pregnant that I found out the truth."

"He told us you had purposely gotten pregnant to force him to marry you."

"He lied to you, Daddy. After I told him about the baby

214

and he revealed that he was married, all I wanted to do was go away and have my baby and forget he ever existed."

"But we wouldn't let you," her mother finished. "We were only doing what we thought was right."

"Oh, Mama, please. All you cared about was how it would look to people you knew."

"That's not true, Sheila," Charles countered. "It would have been uncomfortable, but we knew the gossip would die down. We were more worried about your mental state. You seemed so depressed and withdrawn. We thought the burden of carrying a child and raising it alone would be too much for you. The reason we didn't seek custody is that I didn't want one mistake to destroy you. You had your whole future ahead of you."

"But I told you how much I wanted to keep my baby, Daddy. All I wanted from you was your support, but you wouldn't give it. Instead you made sure I would never see my son again," she said bitterly. "Your only grandchild."

"And to your way of thinking, we let you down. I'm sorry, but we truly did think it was best that you give up the child. When you broke down after you were denied the appeal, we realized how deeply you felt about the child, but it was too late."

"We vowed to see that you got the best help available."

"I survived, Mama. I was determined to exclude you and your lifestyle from my plans for the future. I wanted to start fresh. Then I found out my son was here, but I'd already fallen in love with Gil Jackson. Now that he knows who I am—" her voice faded.

"If he loves you—"

"I know he loves me, Mama, but I'm also sure he feels betrayed and doesn't trust me."

"Once he's had time to think about it—"

"There is more to it than that, Daddy. I caused his late wife a lot of heartache. He worshipped the ground she walked on. I don't know if he'll ever forgive me for that."

"Our coming here—"

"I was planning to tell him the truth myself yesterday, but—"

"We spoiled everything." Her mother started to cry.

"No, you didn't. He probably would have reacted the same way if I'd been the one to tell him. You see he can't get past the fact that I deceived him. I didn't mean to hurt him, but I have."

"What about your son?" her father asked anxiously.

Brenda smiled. "He's such a wonderful child, Daddy. He has our eyes. I love him so much, and I know he loves me. It was as though my moving here was providential, that I was meant to be reunited with my son, meant to be his mother in the truest sense of the word."

"Can you ever forgive us for interfering in your life, Sheila?" her mother asked with a sad, pleading look.

"I realize that I may have been wrong about your motives. I told Gil that I thought you loved me in your own way. It seems that I was right." Brenda sighed. "Gil said he could never go through life not speaking to his parents. I didn't want to take his advice when he said I should make it up with you. He really believes in families sticking together.

"He's right. I can't hold on to my resentment and bitterness forever. I have to let it go. I'm now convinced that you only did what you did because you cared. It wasn't what I wanted, but I can't keep punishing you for doing what you felt was right."

Charles sat down next to his daughter. "I can't make up for all those unhappy years. You see, by the time you came along, your mother and I were already set in our ways. We didn't think we'd ever have a child. Then we were blessed with you. We wanted the best for you. We just didn't realize how unhappy we were making you. Maybe we can start over."

"I don't know, Daddy," Brenda sighed tiredly.

"We could try, couldn't we?"

Brenda saw the hope in her father's eyes and the uncertainty in her mother's, and her heart melted. Tears slid down her cheeks.

Charles drew his daughter into his arms. Isabella moved closer to them. Moments later, all three were crying and embracing. For the first time they had expressed their true feelings.

"How long are you going to be in town?" Brenda asked.

"We don't know. We didn't know if you would even want to see us," Isabella answered.

"We can stay as long as you want us to," her father added in an eager voice. "Do you think we'll be able to see our grandson?"

"It depends on Gil. He's really a wonderful man, Daddy. I know I've hurt him, but he's also fair. We'll just have to wait and see."

"We can't ask any more than that," her mother said. "You're looking tired. I think you'd better lie down. Dr. Jackson said rest is important."

Brenda studied her parents for a moment. She was seeing a side of them that she'd never known existed. She began to see their past life in a different light. Maybe it wasn't as she had perceived it, maybe they were caring parents all along, and she had just refused to see it. She should have made it clear how unhappy she was when she was growing up instead of just going along with the program.

She realized now that getting involved with Hudson Caldwell had been her way of defying her parents. Well, that was all water under the bridge. She had a chance to forge a new relationship with them. She was sorry that it had taken all these years of pain and suffering to reach this point.

Brenda felt that a burden had been lifted from her soul, and that some of her pain had diminished. There was still her relationship with Gil facing her. She wished that it could be as easily smoothed out.

If only Gil would only let her explain, give her another chance, let her show him how much she loves him and their child. David truly was *their* child.

—◆◆◆—

Brenda gazed at the phone willing it to ring, willing it to be Gil. When it didn't ring, she picked up the receiver, then cradled it. No. Gil needed to come to terms with everything. She decided that she would give it to him. Then they would talk.

—❖—

Brenda felt eyes on her back. She didn't need to turn around to know that Laura and Shirley were watching her. Laura had expressed her concern and remarked on Brenda's lackluster expression when Brenda had come in to work on Monday.

Shirley had been excited about the Christmas Eve wedding date when she came into the Lodge on Wednesday, until she had talked to Laura. Then both Laura and Shirley gave her concerned looks.

Brenda didn't have the heart to tell them that there might not be a wedding. It was a prospect she herself didn't want to think about.

Friday dawned and Brenda still hadn't heard anything from Gil. What did it mean? she wondered. The stress of not hearing from him was getting to her. She had little appetite and she'd lost weight.

"Brenda what's wrong?" Laura asked when Brenda came to work. "You should be over the moon. You told Gil the truth, didn't you? How did he take it?"

Brenda explained what happened.

"You haven't heard from him?"

"No."

"No wonder you're looking so fragile. You're worried sick that he won't call, aren't you?"

"I'm all right, Laura. I know I have to give him time to absorb everything."

"The other day Shirley said that something was wrong, that you didn't act like a happy bride-to-be. Are your parents still in town?"

"They said they were going to see me through this. That's

the one up side in this whole thing. We've gotten closer, we're communicating with one another, something I never thought would happen."

"I'm happy for you."

At three o'clock, Shirley brought David to the Lodge to visit with Brenda. Brenda had purposely avoided going to see her son. She didn't want Gil to think that she was going behind his back. His trust in her was already at an all-time low. She'd made up her mind to wait until the end of the week. If she hadn't heard from Gil then she'd call him.

David ran to Brenda and grabbed her around the legs and looked up at her. "I'm so happy to see you, Brenda," he chirped happily. "Aunt Shirley said you was busy, but I told her you wouldn't mind if I came to see you. You don't mind, do you, Brenda?"

"No, I don't mind. I'm always glad to see you."

"I'm stayin' at Granddaddy Durant's house until my daddy comes to get me. Do you know when he's gonna get back?"

She forced a reassuring smile to her lips. "No, I'm afraid I don't."

"Since you're gonna be my mama on Christmas Eve, can I call you that now?"

Brenda blinked back her tears. "I think maybe we'd better wait on that."

When she glanced over at Shirley, she saw the concerned look in the older woman's eyes. She wanted to reassure her that everything would turn out right, but there was nothing she could say until she spoke with Gil.

So he had left town. Was the possibility of running into her so unbearable? When he got back she'd make him listen to her.

The sound of the shop bell scattered Brenda's momentary reverie. Her eyes widened when she saw who had walked in. It was her parents.

219

"We hope you don't mind us coming to see where you work," her father said, striding toward his daughter, her mother following.

"No, I don't mind." Brenda cleared her throat. "Daddy and Mama, I'd like you to meet Gil's Aunt Shirley and his son, David. Shirley, my parents, Charles and Isabella Walker."

Her father's eyes softened and her mother's misted with tears when they looked at their grandson.

"I'm pleased to meet you," Shirley said shaking their hands.

"You're really Brenda's mama and daddy?" David asked.

"Yes, we're really her parents, young man," her father answered.

Brenda saw the sadness and regret in his eyes and knew he was suffering. Her heart went out to both her parents. She now realized how hard their decision had been on them.

"You musta came to see Brenda and my daddy get married," David innocently stated.

"Yes, we did," Isabella said softly. "You'll be our grand— son." The words caught in her throat.

Brenda saw Shirley shift her gaze from David to Charles, then to her. Prickles of pain jabbed into Brenda's brain. She was sure that Shirley had guessed the truth. With her father standing next to David, it was plain to see the truth of her mother's words.

Brenda couldn't help wondering about Shirley's opinion of her now. When the older woman signaled her over to the windows, her nerves vibrated in uncertain anticipation.

"You're David's real mother, aren't you? And Gil knows it."

"Yes, I am. And yes, he knows."

"It's the reason he took off on this sudden trip. You don't have to answer, my dear. You're worried that he'll call off the wedding and put you from his and David's life, aren't you?" She affectionately squeezed Brenda's arm. "I know Gillie. He won't do that. I've seen him happy for the first time in years, and you're responsible for it. I don't care what you've done in the past."

"I'm so glad you aren't—"

"Angry? I remember what he and Monique went through, and I can't say that I appreciate the pain you caused them. But I've come to think of you as the daughter I never had. I'm not going to change my opinion. You and Gillie belong together. You deserve another chance to be a mother to your son."

Brenda hugged Shirley. "Thank you for your understanding and support. I hope you're right about Gil."

For the first time since Saturday, Brenda felt hopeful.

That evening she took her parents to the Jacksons' at Sara's invitation. Shirley had called her sister to tell her that Brenda's parents were in town.

Brenda felt apprehensive when Sara opened the door. But Sara immediately put her and her parents at ease. Durant was his usual charming self.

David ran to Brenda and practically dragged her over to his great-granddaddy's chair.

"Brenda said you was one of her favorite people, Great-granddaddy."

Turner Jackson smiled. "I'd better be or I'd want to know the reason why."

"Now, Dad," Durant chided.

"Oh, be quiet," Turner groused.

Brenda laughed, letting the warm family atmosphere bolster her spirits. Her parents got along well with Sara and Durant. Turner, she was sure, was holding back his opinion as he studied her parents.

When Brenda and her parents sat down on the couch, Turner plopped down in the easy chair across from them.

"I hope you appreciate this girl. She seemed a little lonely when I first met her. I think you're responsible for that, and I want to make sure you do something about it."

"Turner always speaks his mind," Brenda explained to her parents.

"Don't need no help expressing myself, girl." He focused his gaze back on Charles and Isabella. "You'd best be at that wedding."

"We wouldn't miss it, Mr. Jackson," Charles replied.

"Call me Turner. I think we're going to get along just fine."

When Turner left them alone, Charles smiled. "He's quite a character, isn't he?"

"He's how I imagined grandfathers should be like," Brenda said.

"He reminds me of my father," Isabella remarked. "I'm sorry you never got to know him. He died a few years after your father and I were married."

"I've found one in Turner."

Dylan arrived after managing to get away from the hospital to join the get-together. And just as they all gathered around the tree, Gil came.

David ran to greet his father.

"I'm so glad you're back, Daddy."

"So am I, son," Gil said to David, but he fixed his gaze on Brenda.

"I'd say it was about time you got back where you belong, Scamp," Turner grumbled.

Gil smiled. "It's always refreshing to know that you'll never change, Granddaddy."

Brenda swallowed uncomfortably, trying to digest the subtle dig she tasted in his words.

"It's wonderful that Brenda's parents are here, don't you think, Gil?" Sara interjected.

"Yes, isn't it," Gil said keeping his attention focused on Brenda. "I'd like to speak to my fiancée alone. We can go in Dad's study. We'll only be a minute." He held out his hand to Brenda.

Heart in throat, she followed him. When she heard the study door click shut, she tensed.

"I've decided that the wedding will go on as planned for Christmas Eve, Brenda, Sheila—whatever your name is."

"Gil, please don't—"

"Don't what, my love?"

The chill in his voice made her shiver.

"You do well to be wary, Bren—Sheila," he said watching her reaction.

"Gil, we—"

"Sit down," he demanded tersely.

Brenda didn't miss the steel backing his words. She watched him shove his hands in his pockets as if to keep himself from wrapping them around her throat.

"I won't try to deny my attraction to you, Brenda. I let you work it to your advantage on me. Now it's my turn to enjoy playing the game."

"It was no game and you know it."

"So you say."

"Gil, I love you"

"And your way of showing it is by deceiving me. So much for love."

She bit her lip. "It wasn't like that."

"How was it then? I'm sure you have an answer ready by now."

"Don't be like this, Gil."

"How else do you expect me to be?" He walked over to her and stopped in front of her. "I should hate you, but damn it, I still want you so much, I—"

He hauled Brenda into his arms and brought his mouth down on hers in a punishing kiss that changed the moment he tasted her. His hands roved her body in a hungry exploration. Then he ground his hardened manhood against the cradle of her femininity.

"Oh, God, Gil, I've missed you so much."

"You're like an addiction, Brenda. I can't help myself, I keep coming back for more. I just can't let you go."

"You don't ever have to."

At her words, she felt him retreat back into the disturbingly controlled reserve he had adopted.

"We need to get a few things straight. David is the important person in all of this. He loves you and expects to get you for his new mother. I intend to see that he gets you."

"At the cost of marrying someone you hate?"

"I don't hate you—I wish I could. David wants a real family, and I need you to help me make it happen."

"Gil, why won't you let me explain?"

His laugh was brittle. "What is there to explain? You regretted giving David away and you didn't care whom you hurt when you decided that you wanted him back."

Brenda's heart sank. He would never understand. A steady, penetrating pain drilled into her skull. She turned away from Gil and closed her eyes, willing it to cease.

"It's not going to work, Gil."

He whirled her around to face him. "It damn sure will work. I'm not going to let you hurt my son. Do you understand me? You claim to love him so much. His love should be worth any price you have to pay. There's no reason why we should deny ourselves the pleasure of each other's bodies."

"Don't you dare reduce our relationship to just gratification of the body."

"Why not? You'll finally have what you say you want: me and my son."

"I do want you. But without trust, our marriage will be doomed. If you can't bring yourself to trust me—"

"I can't, but whether I trust you or not, we're going to marry and give that little boy the security and love he deserves."

"What about us? Our love? Doesn't that matter? Can't you forgive me, Gil?"

"I love you, damn it, but I don't trust you, and I don't know if I ever will."

"Won't you even try to believe that I never meant to deceive you? I tried to tell you, but you said that you didn't want to hear it. You said the past was the past and that you loved me."

"How obliging of me. Convenient for you."

"No. I still wanted to tell you the truth. But one thing after another kept getting in the way. Then when you came to take me to St. Paul, I tried to tell you—"

"But I couldn't keep my hands off you," he bit out. "Damn it, I still can't. I thought that if I went away, I could put things in their proper perspective, but it was a waste of time." He paced back and forth. "David is the only reality I have to hold on to. After we're married, don't even think about trying to take him from me."

"You can't believe that I'd do that!"

"You tried it once before and for all I know you still might."

Brenda gasped. Her heart shattered into a million jagged pieces of misery, and she was bleeding to death. How could he think that of her?

She stared at the man she loved. Was this a glimpse of what her life was going to be like? Full of suspicion and distrust? Was this the price she would have to pay to be near her son? To be near the love of her life?

She tilted her chin confidently. "All right, Gil. We'll be married. Since you feel that you can't trust me, I'll sign an agreement stating that if the marriage doesn't work out, I won't try to take David away from you."

Brenda started toward the door, then stopped when she got there. "I think we'd better go back to the party."

She opened the door and walked out .

—⋙⟡⋘—

After hearing her words, Gil expected to feel relieved, but he wasn't. He felt more uncertain than ever. He didn't like the feeling of not being in control. When he had Brenda follow him into the study, he felt justified in speaking to her the way he did. But after seeing the hurt look in her eyes, he began to feel like a villain.

But he wasn't. Maybe he'd consider doing as Brenda said and drawing up those papers. He was after all an experienced attorney.

Chapter Twenty-six

Brenda observed the strained look on Gil's face at the engagement party Sara and Durant gave for them a week later. To everyone they appeared to be the perfect engaged couple.

"Are you two really working things out?" Dylan asked.

So intent on watching Gil, Brenda hadn't noticed when he walked up. "We're trying, Dylan."

"And not succeeding from what I can see," Dylan said with a worried frown. "I think I need to have a serious talk with that brother of mine. You're as tense as a tightened bowstring, Brenda."

"I'm all right."

"No, you're not. How are the headaches?"

"I'm still having them, if that's what you want to know. But I'm managing, Dylan."

"From what I can tell, just barely. You've done an excellent job of hiding that you haven't been sleeping, but you can't hide the fact that you've lost weight. I'm worried about you, Brenda."

"There's no need for you to be," Gil injected harshly. "Brenda is my fiancée, and I don't want you to forget it."

"Gil, what's wrong with you, man?"

"Nothing is wrong. I think you pay too much attention to your brother's woman. Maybe it's time you got one of your own."

"Gil!" Brenda gasped.

"It's all right, Brenda." Dylan glared at his brother. "If you hurt her, you'll have to answer to me," he said and walked away.

"You have a legion of Jackson men ready to come to your aid at the drop of a hat, don't you? If Richard were here, he'd probably join their ranks."

"What's happening to you, Gil?"

"You are what's happening to me, Brenda."

"Saint MaGil. You've never made a mistake, never done anything you regretted. You're so perfect and you expect everyone and everything around you to be that way."

"Brenda!" he warned.

"I'm sorry that I'm not the perfect woman your wife obviously was."

"Don't even go there," he gritted out.

Brenda sighed. "I love you, Gil, and I love my son. Why won't you accept that? When you do, then, maybe, we can go on from there."

"It's not that simple to forget all that has passed between us. Don't you think I want to?"

"You want to trust me, but you can't. Right? I made a mistake by not telling you the truth when I knew it, I admit that and—"

"You're sorry now? It's easy for you to say that *now*."

"No, it isn't. You're so fair with everyone else, why can't you be that way with me?"

"Were you fair to me and my wife? Tell me, were you being fair when you kept your identity a secret? Deceiving me all this time?"

She didn't answer.

"I came to get my girl," Turner said, holding out his hand.

Gil said, "It seems I have a never-ending line of Jackson men vying for my woman's attention."

"A little jealousy builds character, Scamp," Turner said, winking at Brenda.

Gil frowned as he watched Brenda walk away with his grandfather.

"When are you going to stop punishing her, Gillie? Hasn't she suffered enough?"

"Aunt Shirley—"

227

"Don't you 'Aunt Shirley' me. I've seen how you've been treating Brenda. I never thought I'd be ashamed of you, but I am. I know you're upset about what she did, but that's no excuse. People make mistakes, Gillie, even you." With that, Shirley stalked away.

"Shirley looked a little pissed just now," Carl said as he walked over to Gil.

"She's that all right."

"Things not working out between you and Brenda?"

"Don't you start."

Carl threw his hands up. "I have no weapon. Honest Injun."

Gil laughed. "I'm sorry, cuz, it's just that—I don't know. I want things to be the way they were before, but it's just not happening. I want to trust her, but—"

"Getting away didn't help then, did it?"

"I know in my head I should be more understanding, more forgiving, but for some reason, I just can't."

"There's a certain realization that you'll have to come to. I hope for all your sakes that you come to it before it's too late."

"What do mean?"

"It's nothing I can explain. You'll know when it happens."

❖

Brenda stood at the window and looked out over the snow-covered garden.

"I saw Carl talking to Gil a little while ago," Laura said.

Brenda turned to face her friend. "I wonder if it did any good."

"Gil was so sensitive and supportive when Carl and I were going through that bad time. I can't believe that he isn't that way with you. I know he cares about you. He's told Carl that he loves you. I don't understand."

"I guess he can be more objective when he's not so personally involved."

"Carl is looking for you, Laura," Gil said, walking toward

them.

"I'll talk to you later, Brenda."

"All right." Brenda watched Laura walk away.

"There's something I have to talk to you about."

"What is it, Gil?"

"I'll tell you after the party is over and I take you home."

The rest of the evening dragged for Brenda as she waited for the party to end. Her parents had had to make a quick trip to Chicago, and she wondered if she'd have to call and tell them that there was no need to return because there would not be a wedding.

Or had Gil come to terms with his feelings and was now ready to listen to her?

She noticed how quiet he was during the drive to her apartment. And when they arrived, she was sure he was going to tell her that he forgave her for deceiving him.

Brenda took Gil's coat and hung it in the closet, then joined him in the living room.

"Do you want some coffee?" she offered.

"No. What I want is to believe that you won't try to take David once we're married."

"I've already told you that I wouldn't do that. I know how much he loves you and how much you love him."

"Who's to say you won't change your mind the way you did before."

Brenda walked over to the fireplace and stared into the banked embers. She remembered thinking that Carl might take Jon-Marc from Laura if they married. It was shades of déjà vu. She glanced at Gil. Could she really blame him completely for the way he was feeling about her? She had tried to take David from him once.

It looked as though he would never come to trust her. Pain streaked through her head. She shifted her gaze back to the fireplace and closed her eyes seeking to ward off the aura of an oncoming headache.

"What can I do to make you believe me, Gil?" She heard the unfolding of paper and turned to face him.

He held up the paper. "This is an agreement similar to the one you suggested."

"What?" Pain radiated over her eyes, and she tried to blink it away. Surely this wasn't the man she loved doing this to her? Suddenly whole portions of her vision were blotted out by blistering eruptions of pain behind her eyes.

"Brenda, I—"

"You're never going to trust me, are you? Even if I sign a basketful of agreements in blood." She grabbed the paper out of his hand. Bitter disappointment filled Brenda. She felt a tingly sensation in her fingertips and rubbed them down the sides of her dress.

"I can't forget what you did to my wife and me. I refuse to go through that kind of pain again. I can't forget how you deceived me."

"Oh, Gil." She brought her hand up to her temple when she felt sharp-hot splinters of agony jab into her skull from the inside. "I would never—"

"I'm just not willing to risk it. Are you going to sign the agreement? Well, are you, Brenda? You can't change your mind again."

She took a step away from him and the floor beneath her feet began to waver and the room took on a phosphorescent glow.

"I love you and my son." She swayed. "You don't need a piece of paper to ensure that I won't take David from you. I never would. But if you want me to, I'll sign the agreement. I'll—just give me a minute." Flashes of blinding red light colored her vision, dizziness and overwhelming explosions of pain burst in her brain, then a horrible darkness descended. And she sought sanctuary in its promise of painless escape.

Gil reached for Brenda as she started to slide to the floor.

"Brenda! My God, what is it?" He lifted her in his arms and carried her over to the couch. He tried to rouse her, but she lay still and unresponsive as death. He reached for the phone and punched in his brother's number.

"Dylan, it's Gil. Brenda just fainted, and I can't bring her around."

"Was she in pain?"

"I don't know. We were talking, then all of a sudden she moaned and then—what is it?"

"I'll explain later. Get her to the hospital right away. I'll meet you there."

"Dylan—"

"No time to explain. Hurry, Gil."

Gil drew Brenda into his arms. He noticed that the agreement was clinched tightly in her hand. "Oh, God, what have I done?"

⊷⊱◈⊰⊶

Gil paced back and forth in the waiting room. He was out of his mind with worry. It seemed like days instead of hours since he'd brought Brenda to the hospital and seen Dylan rush her into the emergency room.

The grim look on his brother's face had unnerved him. He kept playing back in his mind the way Brenda looked when he handed her that asinine agreement.

What had he been thinking to do something like that? Sure, it was her suggestion. But he didn't have to follow through.

You weren't thinking, you were reacting to your own feelings of pain and betrayal not taking into consideration how much she might be suffering.

And I call myself a fair man.

You let your pride get in the way, Jackson, and now you'll have to pay the price.

Would the price be losing the woman he loved? No, he wouldn't believe that. He couldn't believe that.

He'd worked so hard to make her see that not all lawyers were like the men she'd had to deal with in the past. But when it came right down to it, he was worse than any of them. He'd gone after her and conquered her apprehension only to bring it crashing down on her. He felt like such a bastard right now.

"What a stupid fool I've been."

"You definitely won't get an argument out of me about that."

"Dylan!" Gil clutched his brother's arm. "How is she?"

"She's in a coma."

"What?"

"The emotional trauma was more than she could handle."

"What are you telling me? That she might—" His mouth was dry like desert sand.

"I can't tell you anything specific right now. But I need to know exactly what went on between you two to put her in this state."

"I wanted her to sign a prenuptial agreement."

Dylan frowned in confusion. "Why would you want her to do that?"

"It's a long story. But I did it to ensure that she wouldn't try to take David away from me if things didn't work out between us."

"Gil, how could you—don't you know her better than that?"

"I do, but—"

"But you wanted to punish her."

"No, I didn't."

"I think you did."

"Wait a minute. You're not even surprised by what I just revealed, are you? How long have you known who she is?"

"Since the day she saved David from falling through the ice."

He recalled that day and what Brenda had said. His brother had caught on right away. Why didn't he? He was supposed to be the smart one in the family.

"She loves her son, Gil, and she would never do anything to hurt him, including, especially including, taking him from his father. I know she tried to do that after she'd given him up, but that was the past. She's matured since then. She knows the price of love and she was willing to pay with her life, if need be, when she saved David."

In light of everything his brother said, what he had done was all the more reprehensible, Gil realized.

"You just don't realize the damage you've done, Gil. She and I have been working on getting the stress level in her life under control and you've blown whatever progress we've made."

"We? Progress? Stress level? What are you talking about? You mean this isn't the only attack she's had? I knew she's had several bad headaches over the last couple of months, but—"

"Her parents brought her in to emergency the night you found out who she was."

"How bad was it? And why wasn't I told?"

"No one knew where you were. And besides, she didn't want me to tell you."

Gil closed his eyes. He'd brought such misery to the woman he claimed to love.

"Not really knowing where she stood with you raised her stress level to an unbearable degree. I've sent for Mark Stevens, the best neurologist around."

"A neurologist?"

"We've done a CAT scan and there is abnormal brain activity, which indicates seizures brought on by constricting blood vessels in the brain. There is swelling in the tissue surrounding these vessels. I'm hoping that we can reduce the swelling with medication and the body's own healing process, but if we can't, Brenda may need surgery."

"You're not confident that the medication will do it though?" Gil asked dully. "What you're really saying is that we'll have to wait."

"I'm sorry, but yes. We're doing everything we can. I've already contacted her parents. They should get here soon."

"God, this is all my fault. Can I see her?"

"She won't know you're there, Gil."

"It doesn't matter. I have to see her, touch her, know she's alive."

"All right. She's been moved to ICU."

233

Chapter Twenty-seven

When Dylan and Gil walked into the room, a nurse was checking Brenda's vital signs. Dylan signaled her over to a corner. While they were talking, Gil stood beside Brenda's bed. She was so still, her light-brown-sugar skin had darkened.

Gil barely took notice when his brother and the nurse left the room but sat down in the chair beside the bed and took Brenda's small cold hand in his.

"You've got to get better, baby. I love you. I'm sorry for hurting you. I know this is coming a little too late, but it's true."

Brenda didn't move nor did her eyes open. Only the beeping of the machines she was hooked up to filled the room.

"I feel so damned guilty. All I could think of was that you deceived me, not the possible reason why. I never let you explain. I was so caught up in my own misery. Despite that, I knew you loved me.

"I don't know what drove me to do what I did. Aunt Shirley said she was ashamed of me. I'm ashamed of me too. I knew in my heart I was wrong, but I couldn't seem to keep myself from hurting you. You have every reason not to want to have anything to do with me."

He leaned over and kissed her lips. They were cold to the touch.

"Brenda, you've got to be all right. You're my whole life, girl. My heart belongs to you. You've completely wrapped yourself around my very soul. Come back to me, my love."

He heard the door open. It was his brother with a tall, distinguished-looking man.

"This is Dr. Mark Stevens, Gil. You'll have to step out into the hall while he examines her. Brenda's parents are out there and they want to talk to you."

"You'll let me know if there's any change?"

"You know I will."

Gil didn't want to leave, but he knew he had to. He wondered what he was going to say to Brenda's parents. When he walked out into the hall and saw them in the waiting room across the corridor, he joined them.

Charles rose from his chair. "Dr. Jackson told us what happened. How is our daughter?"

"The same as when I brought her in. It's my fault. I wasn't a big enough person to understand and forgive. She's the one who should forgive me. I let my pride and my rigid sense of right and wrong blind me to the fact that we all make mistakes. And I'm certainly no different."

"What about David?" Isabella asked.

"He doesn't know yet. I don't know what to tell him. He loves Brenda. If anything—"

"We know you love our daughter. We haven't had much chance to talk, but we do know that," Charles said.

"Yes, I do, Mr. Walker. Very much. I'm hoping that after this is over she'll still love and want to marry me."

"I'm sure she will," Isabella said confidently. "All we want is to see our daughter happy. Being married to you and having her son with her is what she wants, what she needs."

Dylan and Dr. Stevens came out of Brenda's room. Gil and the Walkers rushed to meet them.

"There's no change," Dylan told them.

Gil looked to Dr. Stevens. "My brother mentioned the possibility that you might have to operate."

"I don't think it's indicated at the moment. We want to wait and see if the medication will work. Sometimes when emotions cause a disruption in the brain's normal functions, the relief of the anxiety can reverse the effect."

"Talking to her may bring her out of the coma," Dylan

added.

"I'll talk to her twenty-four hours a day if you think it will help."

Dylan smiled. "I know you will. We don't know how much she'll comprehend, but you can give it your best shot."

"Is there something you're not telling us?" Charles asked.

Dylan looked uncomfortable.

"We want to know the truth, Dylan," Gil's voice was unsteady.

Dr. Stevens cleared his throat. "If we do have to operate, there's considerable danger of brain damage or disability."

Gil groaned, closing his eyes.

Charles drew his wife into his arms.

"None of that may happen," Dylan said. "There's still the possibility that the swelling will go down on its own."

"In the meantime, we wait," Gil said quietly.

Brenda heard voices, but it was as though they were coming from far away. Her brain felt fuzzy and she was disoriented. Where was she? She had been talking with Gil. The prenuptial agreement.

Pain flashed, intensifying until it blanked out all thought and she drifted beyond consciousness to where pain could no longer reach her.

"It's been forty-eight hours, Dylan."

"She's no worse, Gil."

"But she's not any better either. When will you know?" Frustration laced Gil's voice.

"There's still a chance we can get her through this."

"Do you think if I bring David to see her, it'll help?"

"It's worth a try. There's a risk in bringing him to the hospital. He's so young, it could be very traumatic seeing her like this, considering his feelings about hospitals. After all, he saw Monique in a similar condition."

"I know, but he loves Brenda."

—⋙◈⋘—

Gil returned to the hospital with his son. He'd told him on the way there that Brenda was sick, but not any of the details. He took him into the waiting room first.

"Daddy, will she get better so you'n her can get married?"

"I'm hoping she will, David. We may have to keep telling her how much we love and need her, until she hears us."

"We can do that easy, Daddy."

"Yes, we can do anything, son."

Then with Dylan, they went in to see the woman they both loved.

Gil watched his son's reaction to Brenda and all the equipment in the room. The boy's eyes filled with wonder, not horror. David's eyes were so like Brenda's it brought the sting of moisture to Gil's own.

David asked Dylan about the machines and what they were doing to help Brenda. Dylan tried to be as honest as possible without scaring his nephew, Gil realized.

They walked over to the bed. Gil smoothed back a stray lock of hair from Brenda's face. David put his hand in hers.

"Brenda, you've got to get better so you can hurry up and be my mama. Daddy's sad 'cause you're sick and me too." He looked up at Gil. "Do you think she heard me?"

"I'm sure she did. It may take her a long time to open her eyes though. It's hard when you're so sick."

David brushed his cheek against the back of Brenda's hand. "Please wake up," he pleaded. "I love you."

Gil sat down in the chair beside the bed, lifted David onto his lap, and put his hand over his son's and Brenda's.

"I love you so much, Brenda. Come back to us, baby."

"Daddy! She squeezed my hand," David said excitedly, his eyes lighting up like a neon sign.

237

Tears brimmed in Gil's eyes.

Brenda opened her eyes and smiled briefly before closing them again.

"Dylan!"

Dylan checked the monitoring equipment. "There's definitely a change. I think she's going to be all right."

"When is she gonna wake up, Uncle Dylan?"

"It's hard to say. It could be a few minutes or a few hours."

"Hours! That's too long," David grumbled.

"I agree." Gil took his son in his arms. "We'll wait together."

Brenda woke up to a room filled with flowers, and two happy pairs of eyes watching her.

"David," she called in a low, tired voice.

"I'm so glad you're better. Can I call you Mama now?"

Brenda gave Gil a wary look.

"Yes, you sure can," Gil answered with a tender smile.

Dylan walked in.

"How's my patient this morning?"

"I'm fine, Dylan."

"I can call her Mama now," David said proudly.

"That's great, my man. Want to go have lunch with your uncle?"

"Yeah."

"It'll give your mama and daddy a chance to talk."

The door had not quite closed behind Dylan and David, when Gil said, "I know you love David, Brenda. I want to understand why you could ever give him up?"

"I'm not sure if I can explain it to you. As I told you before, I found out my child's father was married. I was devastated."

"But David was your own flesh and blood, how—"

"I was hurt and confused when I gave him up. My parents had convinced me that I would be hurting my child if I kept him, considering how I felt about his father."

"After you'd done it, you realized that you couldn't live with your decision and wanted him back."

"Yes."

"When you knew the truth, why didn't you tell me?"

"I knew how you felt about the woman who caused you and your wife so much pain."

Gil groaned. "How it must have hurt you to hear me say that."

"Yes, it did. But I understood what you were feeling—and are probably still feeling."

"No! I don't feel—considering all I've done to hurt you, how can you be that generous to me?"

"You wanted guarantees, and with love there are none."

Gil sat on the edge of the bed and pulled her into his arms. "Can you ever forgive me, baby?"

"I can because I love you, Gil."

His lips worshipped hers, renewing his promise to always love her. He said tenderly, "I love you, Brenda. You won't regret giving me another chance."

"I know I won't."